Penshurst Publishing / Penshurst Books   **First Edition—June 2018**

ISBN 978-0-9959906-1-6

Cover Photo—A reproduction of a portion of an image placed in the public domain by NASA—The National Aeronautics and Space Administration.

Past Immortal As We

By F. Bradley Reaume

To the conundrum of utopia

where there are

many truths

Chapter One

The darkness was almost absolute.

Only headlights illuminated the highway. Beyond its margins was blackness. This late at night there were few cars.

The stars were visible, the bright streak of the Milky Way obvious to anyone who looked. Some people did take the time to pull over, shut off their car lights and look in wonder at the wide sky. Inevitably the sounds of the desert, the breeze and the incredible sense of emptiness pushed them back into their vehicles where the catch of the engine provided a sigh of relief.

As they made their way east in the dark, the eyes of a curious passenger might be drawn to the light of a low smallish building halfway up the horizon, floating in the middle of a stark desert, in a distance difficult to determine. Lit by a few spotlights, painted bright white, the cinder block building was starkly visible despite the darkness. It seemed to hover above the broad valley floor.

It was built hugging the ridge line near the top of a low range of mountains, remote from population centers but visible from both sides of the ridge at about 7,400 feet. At night the building could be seen for miles, seeming to hang in the air on moonless nights, when there was no light to catch the crags and lines of the mountains. And yet, there were very few travellers in this remote part of northern Arizona who would chance to glance up to see it as they concentrated on the limitless road before them. Though fewer still had not seen it before, a known and ignored quantity.

At night the array of giant satellite dishes that also rode the mountain crest were invisible to human eyes, save for the blink of lights at the top of each dish to warn low flying aircraft of their existence.

Conspiracy theorists, UFO lovers and the curious, would race by on the valley highway and wonder why the odd formation of UFOs seemed to hang there. As the blinking lights were not co-ordinated, so it looked as if the spots were moving, especially if a viewer was moving rapidly, Flagstaff bound.

Despite the sometime view from the highway, the nights of routine and monotony which accompanied telescope work all seemed to run into each other with a dull sameness. But this night was destined to be unlike all the others.

John Overholt, an associate professor of astronomy at Louisiana State University, was just past the half way mark in his year-long research sabbatical, looking at light and radio pulses from nearby stars. His research was focussed on the elemental make-up of distant suns, but his work was piggybacked with SETI research, essentially as a way to help pay for his project.

The government stretched SETI funding this way and the Search for Extra-Terrestrial Intelligence unit was able to operate more efficiently, according to the government's way of thinking, by having those at this array and other telescopes across the country working double duty. Monitoring vast streams of data to catch the occasional anomaly was not terribly time consuming. A nuisance perhaps but the astronomers and physicists understood their research projects relied on the dollars it provided. The SETI project offered some extra cash to astronomers at several installations asking only that SETI scans be monitored while the academics conducted their own mainstream scientific research.

It was all boring work, mostly scanning print outs and making calculations based on the variations of light and radio waves that emitted from certain directions in space. On rare occasions they received a bit of time with the space based telescopes in orbit around the Earth to peek in on their research subjects. It was an opportunity to confirm with some detail what their other research had shown. Normally they would record the scans and look at them in detail when time permitted. Individually they only received a few minutes of telescope time but they poured over the results for hours. Correlating it with other data took days, even with computers doing most of the sorting.

Professor Overholt was a math and space geek. He had loved the vast unknown of the sky for as long as he could remember. He still loved it once he had realized the utter vastness of the universe. For a short time as a young teen the unreachable distances had set him back, but he recovered his wonder and allowed himself to hope that somehow those distances could be breached.

He thought of the peacefulness of space and the contrast between it and the unknowable violence of star collisions and the crushing appetite of black holes. His youthful desire to explore morphed into a more adult interest in time travel, the kind you experience by peeking at light that had travelled through space for millions of years.

He was much disappointed the day in his youth when the utter size of the universe was explained to him and he realized he would never ever physically get past the inner planets of our own solar system. He tried to get interested in the gas giants of Jupiter and Saturn but they barely raised his curiosity even considering the possibility that they were failed stars.

Even the further planets in our own solar system didn't capture his imagination. If the failed stars of Jupiter and Saturn couldn't stir his imagination the remote hunks of rock further out, without purpose, had no chance. His head was in the real stars even if his feet were now firmly planted on the ground.

Very tall, with light brown hair cut short but with a wave left on top, he looked younger than his 28 years. He was slight of build, and when combined with his height, almost comically thin. He walked hunched over, head down as if lost in thought, which he often was. The posture was really the result of hunching over computer monitors built for smaller people, but it gave him an air of gravitas.

His sojourn at the array was a forced absence from the rest of his life, and he thought, the opportunity to decide what path he should continue on, once his current project was completed.

Overholt had a team of graduate students on various projects of their own, who he could tag with various small duties but who he also had to watch over. The distances of the stars brought their mysteries no closer to him and he struggled with what appeared to be a lifetime of no answers, no chance to be thunderstruck by knowledge or discovery. Pure research, and research on things and places that were so remote to our own experience that they were almost mythical, gnawed at him, as if he would accomplish nothing important because it was all so remote.

Outside the bright lights of the station were a complete contrast to the darkness of early morning. The outside lights on the building illuminated a few dozen yards of parking lot, showed the start of the gravel road down the mountain and a bit of rough topography. Beyond that were dragons, except of course in the daylight, when the dragons turned into hillsides and mountaintops.

"It's a night job," he thought ruefully for the thousandth time as he contemplated his sandwich. He hadn't really realized when he got into astronomy that it was basically a graveyard shift interspersed with months of 9-5 classroom work, assuming you were so fortunate to get a professor's job with a tenure track. So many of the jobs these days were associate or adjunct professorships which paid poorly, were completely dependent upon enrollments and the whims of the school. Some of his old grad student friends had complained that some of their junior colleges had been pushing for a study of astronomy from an astrological perspective. They called it astro-history or something but essentially took the science right out of it. Overholt shuddered just thinking about it.

Not that he was unhappy, he had managed to land a spot at a good university even if it was known more for football and baseball. At least they produced stars, one of his tenured colleges had said when pressed. And at least people had heard of the school. Better that for moving on when a more prestigious job came up, than running the astronomy program at Podunk U, he thought.

He looked at his lunch. When you look forward to lunch knowing it's only a pathetic sandwich on slightly stale white bread, saved from the elements by a snap on plastic container; and it's the only variation from the routine, and it's 3 AM, then you know there is nobody else around.

He slid the sandwich container down and placed a can of soda on the desk. He always ate lunch at his desk, not because he was so wound up in his work that he couldn't bear to be away, but rather because he could use his terminal for more leisurely pursuits as well as some of the necessary things one did to live, like paying the rent, trolling for the weekly grocery store coupons to see what he would be eating for the next few days, and managing his bank balance.

Always hovering in the back of his mind was his chance to become an astronaut. At LSU one of his colleagues had been recruited. Okay he was an engineer but his specialty was Building Materials science. He was older and told Overholt that they looked for astronauts who were in their late 30s or early 40s because they wanted maturity, and because it appeared that everyone who had spent any time in space suffered significant physiological damage from the experience. Witness that no astronaut had fathered a child after returning from space. Radiation, gamma rays or god knows what else were not deflected away by the Earth's protections once you reached beyond a low orbit. And prolonged weightlessness took a heavy toll on health. Even a few weeks of zero gravity required time for recovery. Lengthier stays required special measures, like tension suits to improve blood flow and forced exercise to maintain muscle mass. And that was difficult in the confines of a space craft.

Overholt put those thoughts in the back of his mind and started to investigate the astronaut selection process. He figured he had about a decade to advance his career and his life to be in a good position to be chosen. His colleague told him his height may be a detriment to his selection, but his wiry body type might compensate.

Back in the present, Overholt started reading his emails and checking his personal social media contacts. His girlfriend of a year had recently been to Arizona to spend some time with him and he had arranged a week mostly off to spend with her. She had left the week before, acting as if she did not want to go, but packing for the trip two days before she left, in the wake of several comments about the heat, the dust and the loneliness.

She was a graduate student in biology who was toying with medical school or a more academic career. She really did seem to sense his longing for a more regular life and his desire to continue his studies. He was preparing to write a book about the starlight he was studying, and he had hoped that the research he was conducting would make his career. Of course a large number of things needed to happen for that to occur.

As a scientist he was acutely aware that even disproving a theory was an advancement in scientific knowledge, but one that did not really advance his career. What he needed was a proof of something that previous data had rendered possible and was a bigger eye-opener for his career, and finding something completely unexpected might open many important doors.

He noticed that many of the top scientists and people who rose to the top of other professions often did it on the back of one significant achievement. It was that achievement that they rode for their entire career. The lucky ones managed to find that notoriety early on.

In the end he still felt he was just a kid, okay, maybe a young adult, who loved the vastness of space and the idea that it was essentially unexplored and unknown. Maturity had not quite jarred that thrill even if he knew that there wasn't much to discover looking around vast amounts of empty space that had already been scanned multiple times. The great distances did not stop him from dreaming, though his practical self had to pause at the impossibility of it all. And he was nearing 30 without much to hang his hat on, personally or professionally.

That special line in his personal sands of time also reflected his pain at watching the universe unfold millions of years in the past. Reaching out to the vastness of space was like trying to touch the sky, it's right there and yet so far away as to be essentially unknowable. Even if something tremendous occurred to a distant star under his watch, that thing would likely be so remote and ancient as to be similarly unknowable.

A spot as an astronaut was a bit more tangible and the potential mission perhaps more pedestrian but infinitely more real. Collecting rocks had a certain charm that views of supernova couldn't quite manage to overturn. He dreamed of looking around Mars, or maybe a near Earth asteroid or something unusual in the Asteroid Belt. Knowing many astronauts were geologists he had made a special effort to get more than a basic background in that field, just in case.

And while he battled within himself to chase the chance to close his grasp to the sky or keep his eyes on the heavens and maybe see a wondrous thing, a star collision, a new planet or study an unexpected comet; he also wondered about Arizona, Louisiana and Allie.

The inside of the cinder block building was pretty sparse. There were a few cabinets of technical equipment and things marked with electrical hazard signs. Not surprisingly the place was wired up with electrical power, enough for a small town.

One of the graduate students had called the style Post Modern Science Guy, because everything was a bit threadbare and worn but it all had maximum utility. If they needed it they had it. If they needed it for the project it was top of the line. If it was to sustain them it was old but functional. If it was for creature comfort it was bare minimum, enough to push it into their need for sustenance.

Overholt knew enough about the electrical requirements of the array to look inside the electrical cabinets with insider's knowledge of the connections and how they worked. Having to fix something or make a repair was not his area of expertise - though he figured he could wing it in an emergency. At least he knew how to kill the power feed.

There was a small kitchen area, a sink, a small bar fridge that sat on top of a file cabinet, and a hot plate rather than a microwave. It was much like a standard dorm room. Microwaves were out because they would interfere significantly with all the electronic gadgets. There were the obligatory bathrooms, an unnaturally large storage room for this type of facility and the main work area outfitted with three desks, one against each wall except for the fourth wall, the one with the door to the real world.

In his spare time Overholt was a bit of a news junkie, it came from the need to keep his mind occupied. So he trolled various news and current affairs sites to stay informed on a wide variety of topics. It hadn't made him rabidly engaged on one side, rather it had pro-vided him with a perspective on both sides. And that bothered him as he also understood that seeing both sides of the great debates meant that he was unable to chose one as the correct course, which he thought made him weak. So he had little voice in current affairs as he couldn't find a side to support with any enthusiasm. To him it was more like a period drama than a sporting event.

There was little that he cared to know, where he had not gathered in enough information to have a passing understanding or at least satisfy his immediate curiosity. On some things he became obses-sive, and thought nothing of two days of searching out background info on something he was curious about.

On most nights he liked the work of astronomy. It came down to scanning data sheets and plot points looking for something that had never been there, or correlating information to prove what appeared to be there. Each hour or day seemed invariable, but the data collected over the course of months provided the depth and detail he was looking for. There was enough variety in the light signatures that he found it illuminating for his research thesis.

On other nights the vastness of space and the 'needle-in-a-haystack' approach to discovery seemed a bit pointless and got him thinking in circles about the value of his life and the choices he had made. In the end he realized that this work would likely be automated in the future with the results going to an even smaller number of scientists to make sense of it. His life was pointing him to be one of those scientists.

Days he slept, conducted his personal business and looked about for full professorships. He even started his publishing effort, before having the data points, but writing the general bits of the book his completed research would let him write. To this point the data fit his expectations with just enough juicy stuff to make it worth the additional PhD. He needed six more months of data points to validate his research.

He was acutely conscious of writing his research with a conclusion in mind, but he couldn't help but use the free time to get started. He reasoned that astronomy was really pretty predictable so having a likely conclusion was not a stretch. And deep down he wasn't married to his expectations, and knew he would adjust his conclusions if by happy chance the research indicated something unexpected.

So, here he was at the half way point in his midnight to 8 am shift, with his glorious lunch spread out before him. A sandwich cut in half. But cut in half on the angle, down from the top left to the bottom right, making it a Tuesday. Two apples, both pre-cored and cut in half, two halves for now and the other two halves saved to snack on later, and two cans of soda.

In the middle of a crossword puzzle, he answered a few messages, work and personal, before moving back to the puzzle.

"Acronym for First Contact? Four letters," he spoke the clue aloud. "Well, I'm right in the middle of it . . . SETI - he pencilled the letters into the puzzle. "And that means 42 Down must be 'starless'. He checked the clue . . . 'Start of Bible Black in Crimson." He nodded and looked at the puzzle again to see if the new letters revealed any other likely words.

"And 45 across 'Touch' is 'contact'," he pencilled in the word, not even conscious of talking to himself. "And 53 Down's clue is 'view finder' and the answer is 'telescope'. This puzzle is made for me." He looked around the empty room expecting to see someone jumping out from behind a file cabinet, sporting a big grin, outing a prank.

For another hour he puzzled back and forth, moving to his messages during dry spells in working out the clues. Then he started to clean up his lunch remains, which consisted of him sweeping everything into a plastic bag to be sorted later. There was no garbage collection in the remote area. He switched the computer back over to the data program from the array.

While pouring over the data bits his phone beeped, it was a message from his girlfriend. It was approaching 8 a.m. in the east.

"Got an acceptance to medical school, going to start next semester," the text read.

"Thought you wanted bio research?" he typed back.

"I do and did, but the opportunities are few. Medicine pays and gives me an immediate path. Having my life on hold isn't a good feeling."

"Well, I understand that," he said out loud. "So that's that I guess."

' Where?' he texted back, his chest beginning to pressurize. The answer came back a little slower than he would have liked.

"Got two options. North Carolina." He waited for more.

And waited some more before typing, "So you are you going to North Carolina?"

The wait was interminable. "Or Arizona."

Then immediately following, "I'm coming to Arizona. Three years basic then residency."

"I am done here in six months. Are we just going to trade locations?"

"Didn't you say you could get an extension?"

"Yeah, I think I can, but only another year at most. I'd have to switch universities."

"Then do it. Gotta run to my TA class. Talk later."

A small smile crossed his lips. His chest lightened and he felt a bit more awake. He put the phone down.

"Well that's news," he said aloud. "A seismic shift."

Staring at his monitor, thinking about the near future in some detail but knowing it was time to put his domestic thoughts aside, he touched the key that brought his work display to the screen.

Expecting the usual readouts, he was still contemplating his girl-friend's choice as the command brought up the main readout screen.

The new image popped up. It was so bizarre he blinked. It looked like a mistake, like he had touched the wrong key and had called up another set of data. Or the computers were malfunctioning. He immediately wondered if he'd read the texts wrong and Allie was going to do biology in North Carolina. He turned away, jarred by what he saw.

The display glowed out at him, the numbers still there. Now he took a deep breath and systematically switched programs. No change. Expecting a mistake or computer error, he switched off the entire system and let it settle a few minutes, using the time to finish his lunch clean up. He was jittery, very jittery. He reviewed Allie's messages and smiled again, but he couldn't get the computer screen display out of his mind. He started to shake a bit. Then he turned it back on, all the electronics popping back into operation in sequence. When the display settled back on-line, it was still there.

The data points had a pattern. The readout, which moved slowly across the screen refreshing as they were processed from the mirror scanning the cosmos, was thick with crooked numbers. The entire page, usually covered in ones and zeros, had none.

This was the starlight mirror display, he checked. Then he ran his own results from the array, the radio telescope results. There was nothing new there, so he adjusted the array to focus in on a small area of space suggested by the strongest signal being caught by the mirror.

He looked at the result. There were at least three previously identified exo-planets indicated on the display that were in the Goldilock's zone of their stars. Two of them strongly suggested liquid water was present. The other appeared to have oxygen in a gaseous form.

Overholt looked back to the mirror display, which recorded light, looking for variations in intensity. There had never been more than a few higher numbers in a row before, and when there were it indicated a light source and its intensity, which did not vary, save a tiny bit, which was attributed to atmospheric conditions. They never had a pattern. The computer processor compensated somewhat for atmospheric conditions which could cause the starlight to flicker - though sometimes the electronics couldn't compensate enough. The lack of a pattern in these anomalies was the indication they were natural weather phenomenon.

In fact the readouts rarely varied from the ones or zeros as the array was focussed on apparently empty spaces. Occasionally there was an anomaly, a singular two or three indicating a stronger signal from the cosmos, and even more rarely that number was repeated but rescanning the area had never led to a repeat or suggestion of a pattern.

This time it was different. From the midst of the page came a 5-5-5 -5-5-5-5-5 repeated pattern which after about 30 seconds was a pattern of 9-9-9-9-9-9 interspersed with the fives. The pattern remained as the telescope moved on through the sky. And then it was gone.

"Shit, shit, shit, what the crap is that?"

He moved quickly to relocate the signal direction and set the array to track this singular spot across the sky. It took a few seconds for the commands from his terminal to translate into the mirror section of the telescope's array.

The data display returned and did not change, running through a pattern of data results.

3-3-3-9-3-3-3-9-3-3-3-9-0-9-9-9-9-9-9-9-9-9-9-3-9-9-9-9-9-9-9-9-
3-9-9-9-9-9-9-9-9-9-3-9-9-9-9-9-9-9-9-9-3-9-9-9-9-9-9-9-9-9-3-9-9-
9-9-9-9-9-9-9-3-9-9-9-9-9-9-9-9-9-3-9-9-9-9-9-9-9-9-9-3-9-9-9-9-9-
9-9-9-9-3-0-3-3-3-9-3-3-3-9-3-3-3-9-0-9-9-9-9-9-9-9-9-9-3-9-9-9-9-
9-9-9-9-9-3-9-9-9-9-9-9-9-9-9-3-9-9-9...

It printed out the pattern of three threes, each set of three ending with a nine and the set of three ending with a 0 and then nine nines, with each set of nine ending with a three and the entire set of nine nines ending with a 0. The pattern was caused by a tightly focussed blinking light source, a laser which the mirror was capturing like a Morse Code. The blinking lights also ramped up in intensity with each iteration, the zeroes being the lowest brightness and the nines displaying nine times luminosity, the highest level.

He stared at it. The telescope was detecting a light signal flashing three times and then nine times like an interstellar Morse Code coming from a particular spot in space. The array was set up to collect radio waves, which move in a widening field, like the ripples of a stone thrown into a pond. The mirror telescope was there to analyse starlight, which is more narrowly focussed. This transmission was behaving like starlight, emanating from a particular point in space.

He pinched himself. This was more than just unusual. He straightened up in his chair then rose. He looked out the window of the low flat building. Nothing seemed amiss. His car was right where he had parked it, still with the Louisiana license plates. He checked his messages. There was nothing unusual and nothing more from Allie.

In the past he had simply printed out pages with anomalies and then drawn circles on the pages to highlight unusual sections. They were correlated and packed off to the SETI research center to be analysed. This was not the usual small signal change, a stray number or three, this was either a major malfunction of the telescope or a monumental discovery. On this day he had to think a bit to decide what to do, stopping himself from calling his department head until he was sure it wasn't a mistake.

He thought for a minute and then recalibrated the telescope to resume its systematic scan of the sky. It returned to its standard stream of ones and zeros. Everything was back to normal, and the digital stream was gone.

He breathed a heavy sigh and let it run for 15 minutes. He then returned to the anomaly's co-ordinates. Immediately he began to pick up the pattern again. He let it run for a couple of minutes, until the pattern had repeated three times, and then switched back again to the standard scan.

Back and forth he moved at 15 minute intervals for the next two hours. The threes and nines pattern remained. It was not there in radio waves, which surprised him, as they would have been easier to detect as they had a wider field. Then he set the telescope to remain on the spot with the signal and to continue its regular scans. The pattern never let up.

The area being scanned on this night was unusual. The mirror was usually aimed away from the moon, largely because of its luminosity and because it caused problems as it moved through the sky. Given the thin crescent moon was at its lowest luminosity except during an eclipse they had decided to scan in the wake of the moon's track across the sky. They had undertaken the effort only since last night, to scan areas along the moon's orbital path, despite the difficulties, in a effort to collect some data on a forgotten segment of the sky.

Satisfied he had covered his bases he typed all the detail into his report and prepared to leave at the end of his shift. He made his report and notes available for the next person to handle the data sets and copied his messages to his supervising department head at the university.

The door outside opened. He hadn't heard any crunching gravel or slamming car door.

"Hey John. Give me a minute I forgot my lunch in the car." The door closed behind him. Overholt tried to figure out how he was going to drop his bombshell. The door opened again a minute later and Ethan Harendez, a physics student on the next shift, entered as he always did, just a little bit unready.

"Okay, sorry about that, I have too much to think on. I have an exam in particle physics tomorrow and I brought my notes to review while I'm here."

"Ethan?"

"These exams are murder. First thing in the morning, I'm a mess, can't think straight until at least noon. At least it all makes sense, even if the details sometimes elude . . ."

"Ethan?"

"Yes John, what is it?"

"Take a look for yourself," John Overholt was standing in front of the desk and gestured down to the terminal in front of him. John's height lent him an air of being a bit laconic most times. He would never have interrupted even a waitress reciting the daily specials, and his interruption caught Ethan.

With a quizzical look on his face, which consisted mostly of a wry smile and severely crinkled eyes, Ethan moved to the desk. He was shorter than John, though pretty much everyone was shorter than John. He had dark hair which he wore a bit longer than most and combed back with only the slightest touch of gel. Jeans and a button up, collared shirt completed the graduate student ensemble.

"Don't tell me a gremlin got into the data sets. Have you gone and physically looked at the dish to see if it is working alright?"

"A gremlin, that's it. A gremlin that can multiply prime numbers."

Ethan's gaze narrowed. He moved his shorter body to the chair and slid in. He focussed on the screen. He was silent for a long while.

His voice was quiet, "I take it you've checked for anomalies? Checked for computer function, the electronics and checked the array? Overholt nodded.

Ethan hadn't taken his eyes from the screen.

"That pretty much settles it. First Contact. Now they'll pull our SETI money."

Overholt couldn't help but laugh. "I doubt that. But I do like the fact that you have made First Contact, the most momentous moment in human history, all about you."

Harendez smiled. "No matter what happens, it's always all about me. The world laps its waves on my shore; I got that from a poem somewhere."

"It's nice to know that the liberal arts have had their impact on even the most cynical science student."

"Let's not take too much of a leap. I think I read it in middle school."

"Apparently your most productive education. And what else have you retained from those halcyon days?"

"I can multiply. So, thinking on it again, now I think they'll double our SETI money. First Contact leads to two way communications and then eventually a face to face visit. Right?"

"First Contact Ethan. Let's just take our time on this one. Unless I miss my guess, these signals seem to be coming from an Earth-like planet about 5.5 light years away. Close cosmologically but still a bit far for us to travel to easily."

"Who are they? What do they want? What does this number sequence mean?"

"I'm glad you asked," said Overholt. "So I will tell you. I have had several hours to puzzle it out."

Ethan's eyes went wide. Overholt stared at Ethan, preparing to speak, but didn't. Ethan looked at Overholt's forced bovine calm and they both began to laugh. They laughed loud long and nervously, realizing as they did, that they were at the center of a maelstrom of publicity and science which would wash over them, consume them and spit them out very much changed, as the astonishing news spread.

For now, they alone knew the future. It wouldn't stay that way for long. Knowing the report would generate a call from the Head of the Department, a nano-second after he read it, John waited at the array, enjoying the effect his news would have on his supervisor, the President of the University and everyone as it rippled out across the whole world. He texted Allie, wanting her to know but swearing her to secrecy.

And Ethan couldn't stop talking about the inevitable media inter-views, and practicing his responses. And they laughed and laughed, giddy at the sudden ridiculousness of it all.

In the beginning

Huddled in a little ravine, protected by a copse of trees, or a cave or some other natural shelter; since time immemorial human beings have grouped together, for protection, warmth, a place for their few possessions - a place called home.

The fire at the center with clean water nearby, humans built shelters in defensible places, high up to see any approaching terror, or low down to hide from anything that might be seeking them out.

Life was simple many thousands of years ago, with food and shelter at the center of their lives. But with that simplicity came fear, the brutish understanding that life was short and cheap. Injury often meant death. Illness the same. Living past 40 was rare, past 70 legendary. Always a dangerous predator, man had lived for many generations without being at the top of the food chain, in an uneasy balance with what he hunted and what hunted him.

Generations of hunters honed the art, they became more practical, smarter about their prey and more efficient. And when they learned to sow and reap those humans banded together and found a way to live and grow. They had time to consider their existence and created language, traditions, laws and worship among their own tribes - those accepted as part of the same group, those who could be trusted to uphold the tribe's wants and needs. They created culture, an agreed upon set of values and beliefs that everyone subscribed to, or was banished from the tribe for failure to adhere.

And for lifetime upon lifetime upon lifetime they survived with their primary goal to extend their lives, make them easier and guarantee the continuance of the clan and the tribe.

Among the tribes there were certain necessary traditions which had to be upheld, what to eat, how to hunt, what to plant and harvest, how to raise children, what was right and what was wrong and how to punish transgressors.

Eventually to secure the loyalty of the entire tribe and to explain why some laws were laws, the tribe's elders ascribed their traditions and laws to a divine origin. It gave them weight and majesty and ensured the power of adherence rooted in fear.

"It was the gods themselves who provided us these rules so we may live in holy peace," they would say. "Stay true to the will of the gods and the laws of men are also followed."

It is a wonder that God's Law was also the work of thousands of generations of trial and error, of learning what was good and fair and what was to be marked as evil. Those who followed were accepted and those who did not were banished or worse. Peace among men was highly prized as men did not have the luxury of time to consider all his doings, he had to hunt to eat and eat to survive. Peace was necessary among the tribe.

These tribes grew and joined other tribes, and those tribes started to agree on certain cultural touchstones which transferred to their religions. They forgot the origins of their laws and traditions that were lost in time and began to believe the stories of gods who sewed the tapestry of their lives. They fought with other tribes who did not share their gods. They forced their gods on others through violence and bloodshed.

Culture was religion.

Chapter Two

"Flash - News Bulletin - Telescopes around the world have picked up and confirmed an intelligent transmission from well beyond our solar system, according to a joint press release from the United Nations Secretary General Xavier Armando, the Presidents of Arizona State University and Louisiana State University and Cameron Whitehead, the Director of the Search for Extra-Terrestrial Intelligence program.

"The transmission was first uncovered three weeks ago, picked up by researchers in the SETI program stationed in Arizona, and has been confirmed by several telescopes around the world.

"Mathematical in nature, there is no known information associated with the transmission, which is a patterned set of numbers, which astronomers and mathematicians confirm are not random or accidental. Astronomers have

pinpointed the source of the transmission as a small body, likely a comet or asteroid orbiting a star 4.3 light years from Earth.

"The United Nations will convene a session to discuss the transmission and options in the next few weeks. END"

The news quickly passed around the globe. Media outlets relayed the release, talking heads interviewed local university astronomers, government officials and scientists. There was no confirmation of extra-terrestrial life but neither was there any denial. Most observers agreed that the transmission was tacit proof that there were intelligent beings outside our solar system. After the initial shock, religious leaders began to issue statements. Debate became heated as people worldwide grappled with the new reality.

Everybody had a take on the news. Religious leaders defended their sects' beliefs and briefly there was a backlash against millennia old teachings, as everything religious appeared to go up in smoke. However, almost as fast, religions rebounded as people flocked to safe havens of philosophy and moral teachings. It didn't take much for religions to embrace the new normal and extend their creation myths outside of the small blue marble of Earth. In fact, some of the debate centered around why mainstream religions had not accepted the inevitable of extra-terrestrial contact and moved in advance of the discovery to expand their creation stories and widen their claims of moral high ground. Surely if God created the stars, the thinking went, then he created whatever else may live out there.

"We are not alone," was the neutral theme of t-shirts and personal expression.

"Aliens must think we are crazy" was the position of most comedians who tried to cash in.

"God created the universe and so is likely known to extra-terrestrials, perhaps in the same way he revealed himself to us," was the grinding motif of most updated religious views, playing catch-up.

There was much speculation on the method of counting that the transmission revealed. Mathematicians and civilizationalists vied back and forth to decipher the meaning and method of the number stream.

Perhaps by design, by the time the UN convened its panel much of the discussion had already been had in coffee shops, at kitchen tables and in the media. The UN simply formalized every nation's position on what should be done. Left unsaid was that while every nation had an opinion, not every nation was capable of taking action. That was pushed to the UN Security Council, whose members were generally those capable of action.

To be sure, many nations suggested that no action be taken. They suggested that many other messages might be found in other parts of the universe and that some systematic approach to sampling the sky be undertaken and completed before any course of action was contemplated. The SETI teams loudly reminded them that this was being done, though slowly, so perhaps more money was needed for research. No nation committed to additional funding.

Many people wondered if humanity should be rushing off willy-nilly at the first sound from space. Others said it was better that we meet this civilization on their turf rather than our own. Some wondered if they hadn't already revealed themselves to us on Earth. Governments issued denials.

Other nations wanted to send a mirror broadcast of the transmissions back and await an answer. The eight and a half year round trip on an answer was too much for those who wanted immediate feedback. Several more aggressive nations wanted to investigate immediately, deciding that a manned presence was necessary.

There was a small contingent who wondered why the signal was so close to the Moon, and had managed to elude searchers for so long. The explanation lay in the Moon's orbit around the Earth, the band of sky in which it traversed was where the signal came from, because that same region and orbit had forced searchers to ignore this area with mirror telescopes due to the interference of reflected light. Essentially they got a bigger bang for their research by choosing darker portions of the sky to scan. Doubly it was assumed that SETI would find its signal indicating intelligent life through radio waves, and that's where it put most of its research dollars.

The debate on what to do broadened and then contracted. Essentially three choices were considered. They were: Do nothing. Send off a like-minded response. Go as fast as possible and find the source.

The Do Nothing contingent spoke of the expense, the time frame, the uselessness of what we might find or the inherent danger of poking the hornet's nest of an alien culture. They suggested the money spent on reaching the source of the signals be used to strengthen Earth's defenses.

Those in favor of taking action reminded those who were less adventurous that the nature of the signal suggested it was a beacon to anyone in space to pinpoint this civilization. If they weren't afraid then perhaps we shouldn't be either. And if they were so strong and determined to assimilate us they probably would already be here and would either have made their intensions plain, or they would not have announced their presence but worked to whatever nefarious end they had in mind.

These same people said that man's inherent curiosity to see over the next hill and explore the great unknown had led to many expeditions of years in duration. The money involved was inconsequential given the benefits that such exploration might bring. That touched off a storm of protest in revisionist history, the apparent lack of benefits of European exploration had on native populations in North and South America, Africa and Australia. There was an historical free-for-all for a while which then settled down to the usual historical societies, published books and the occasional documentary.

Russia and China both backed a wait-and-see approach. Behind their official diplomatic facades they were furiously considering the needs of an intercept vehicle, as they wanted to be the first to the scene of the transmission. Potential technological advancements were too big a lure. The Americans were determined to go on their own if they had to, and did not hide that fact.

The like-minded responders were curious but in no hurry to upset the current world order, precarious as it was and always has been.

The Go-getters like the Americans wanted to find out yesterday about tomorrow. They could not wait to move ahead. Though they played the sober second thought game in public, and scratched their chins, their astronomers and science communities started preparing for a long trip.

In the end, the Do Nothing contingent was overwhelmed by human curiosity and the desire for advanced technology. So transmissions were prepared and sent acknowledging the discovery, asking for a meeting with whoever was out there, inviting a visit and announcing our intention to visit them as we were preparing to send envoys.

One ambassador to the United Nations insisted that we make an effort to meet halfway to give each of us the chance to meet and exchange greetings before continuing the rest of the way. That

33

way some protocols could be arranged before we arrived and those on Earth would be in a position to better understand the visitors. Of course the length of time such messages would take and the potential negotiating time necessary to hammer out these protocols, if they were even received, precluded this approach. Diplomacy at this distance was impractical.

While these debates took place in private and in public, splinter groups of almost all major religions on Earth became the norm - with each taking the major tenants of their faith and gloaming on some extra-terrestrial mumbo-jumbo to universalize it. As the debates raged, and the mindset of every Earthling was being altered to take in the new reality, nothing happened. The build up of discovery and the expectation of something more, such as a change in the message, a visit, or some other sign acknowledging the presence of another civilization did not occur. The original transmission was monitored and continued over and over again. After several hours broadcasting its pattern, it began again, ran through its counting and then ran again.

It was complicated enough not to be random and yet short enough to catch attention but no more. People speculated on its meaning but in the end it was seen as a collection of numbers with enough of a pattern to be obviously not accidental or natural.

It didn't take long for the press and media to find John Overholt and Ethan Harendez. And it didn't take long before they zeroed in on Overholt as the discoverer and first contact of the First Contact.

He was accosted during a night shift. He was hounded as he left the observatory and later as he tried to go grocery shopping. For the briefest of moments the notoriety was exhilarating. Soon however, he was talking to the University administration on how he should proceed.

They decided upon a press conference and a series of sit down interviews. None of these touched upon the actual research he was doing in any detail, but he made an effort for the University and for himself to speak on his research. His actual research project was largely brushed aside, or at best given a half a sentence in the press reports. He was able to pump it up in sit down interviews to a minute or two, as most media wanted to zero in on his expertise and background.

Ethan Harendez too, was accosted and often included in the formal interviews once it was understood that he was the second to know, and the interaction between the two men when faced with their revelation is what appeared to fascinate the press. Without an alien staring them in the face, the fact that two of them shared the moment of First Contact appeared to be as good as it was going to get, at least until Second Level contact was made.

"So what did you feel when you saw the number stream?"

"As I said, I first thought it was a technical error, or even a practical joke," said Overholt, perched on a tall stool, in a studio backed by tall photo tapestries of spacey views. "I double checked the computers, the array, and the electrical grid to assure they were in working order."

"So you didn't immediately know what it was?"

Overholt was hunched over due to the stool's height and his own. He straightened up perceptibly, his head almost poking out of the top of the camera shot, giving the control room director an apparent heart attack, followed by a lot of cussing and complaining in the control room about 'makeshift studios in the middle of a god-damned desert'.

"Oh, I knew exactly what it was, I just had to eliminate any chance of an outside reason, as that would be the first question I would be asked when I reported it. This is not something you want to get wrong."

"Were you shocked or excited?"

Overholt remained starkly upright, "Shocked? No, surprised yes. But then such a thing isn't going to announce itself a couple of days ahead so you can be ready for it. I was surprised I suppose by the randomness of it. From a relatively quiet night to the revelation of all time, not an unexpected revelation, but still a confirmation that we here on Earth are not alone in the universe."

"Relatively quiet? Were there other incidents of note that evening."

"Yes, I had just received some good news from my girlfriend."

The smile from the interviewer tipped Overholt off to the blunder he had made. He made a mental note to use that question in the future as a way to highlight his own research.

"Well, that must have put you in a good mood?" The interviewer paused to let Overholt bite at the soft questioning tone of the leading question. Overholt nodded.

"Yes, she had received an acceptance to medical school in Arizona, so yes I was happy for her." Overholt smiled at his recovery.

"How did you tell Mr. Harendez of your discovery?"

"No. He doesn't know Allie, so it would not have been interesting to him. . . . Oh, you mean . . . When he came in for his morning shift I told him to scan the logs of the array. He knew in an instant what it meant, and in fact, questioned me on the operations of the computers, the array and the electrical grid before acknowledging the truth of what he was seeing.

"Truth is, we had a laugh, made a few First Contact jokes and anticipated the news coverage. At that point in time I figured it wasn't a practical joke. I guess it's the times we live in - our first thoughts go to media."

The interviewer smiled. "People want to know John. This is perhaps the most momentous event in human history - and it happened to you. Would you like to be on the mission that goes to investigate the source of the broadcast stream?"

"A good question. Part of me, like all people on Earth, is very curious, and as the person who first saw the evidence, I would love to follow up. I think that's likely the scientist in me, and maybe the kid who looked up at the sky and wondered what was up there. Ever since I was little I have desired to go into space and explore. However, it is going to be a grind of maybe 10 years of confined travel. Such a thing is best left to the trained astronauts. I can only imagine that the trip itself is the most difficult thing - with what I know of the effects of weightlessness on the human body, and the effects of loneliness on the human soul, it will be a harrowing journey. Given my age and place in life, I think it best if I stay behind."

"Have you been approached? There have been reports that you had considered applying to the space program, prior to this discovery."

"No, I haven't been. Nor do I expect to be. The expectation is to leave within a year, which requires a massive effort in engineering, building and training for such a long flight. Those who are chosen will likely be already on a short list and are likely already in the program. Such a list is exceedingly short as the chosen astronauts have to be many things to qualify and they also have to be willing."
"So your part in this is at an end?"

"I hope not. I hope to include a number of observations and experiments on my own star research as part of the mission. Remember, the astronauts who go will need something to do for a decade, on their way to and from whatever awaits them. They will have the opportunity to do some serious star gazing and get measurements of light effects which could help us identify planetary systems and planets with the potential for harboring life. Being able to do this for so long, and outside of the interference of Earth's atmosphere is a huge boost for my own research. I am excited in trying to maximize the gain through a small part of the mission that will feed my own research.

"This flight presents some unique opportunities to deep space researchers in a wide variety of fields. Just the length of the mission itself is enough to have botanists and particle physics experts drooling with the possibilities of experiments. The opportunities that this mission provides are huge for the scientific community. It may turn out to be the most important part of the whole effort. What experiments and observations will be carried out will be as much an issue as the design of the craft and who goes."

"What exactly might be happening and how might that affect us here on Earth?" asked the interviewer.

"Well the payoff is difficult to ascertain. Space flight forces us to improve technology. It is the engine of necessity. Just remember that the original push into near space in the 1960s and 1970s provided us with a huge boost in technology, from miniaturization due to the limits of payload on the moon shots, to medical discoveries and advances in materials science. Myself, along with identifying planetary systems, I am still trying to determine the elements of the Big Bang, specifically where we fit in a universe where everything seems to be moving rapidly away from us. All of this is a study of light. One would presume that we should have been flung out of the Big Bang at the point of the initial explosion and that we would be moving in the same direction as some galaxies and therefore be moving at relatively the same speed as those flung in the same direction as we were."

"I have grappled with the idea that the Big Bang was actually a series of smaller Bangs, but if that is the case, what precipitated the sequence? It also appears that Earth-like exo-planets, those habitable planets attached to other solar systems, have a light signature which mimics a certain kind of star, making their discovery a bit more of a crap shoot."

The interviewer looked a bit stunned. He had endeavored to keep Overholt talking as he struggled to reign in a conversation that was moving out of the realm of must-see TV.

"John, there appears to be many, many threads attached to this project. What is it that people on Earth can expect when the mission returns?"

"If they return, you mean. This is a very dangerous thing. We have never attempted anything remotely close to this. It's not unlike Columbus deciding to sail to the end of the Earth. Even Magellan knew with some certainty that the Earth was round and that given enough time and relative safety, they would return to Spain. Some research suggests he left Spain with a fairly useful map.

"In this expedition there is no guarantee of success. However, should we be successful, we will have achieved an additionally closer contact with an alien culture. At the very least we hope to get some back and forth dialogue and at best an actual meeting between them and us, a Third Level of Contact, if you will. Technological gains just from the attempt alone should be huge even if our contact with an alien culture doesn't result in anything new to us that they willingly give us. Understand that alien life is very possibly hugely different from life on Earth and could take almost any form, forms that are so alien to us that we cannot understand them.

"Though, if we are able to communicate with them, look out, there could be many advances that will change the way we live on Earth, though that will likely not occur for several decades or more from right now, given the travel time and the implementation of advanced technology. Think about the improvements to our own technology in the last several decades. We have improved reliability, efficiency and materials to a huge degree. But due to economics and materials science and other factors, it happens quite slowly even though it feels rapid, as everything you know is in flux."

"So the rapid changes happen slowly that we almost don't notice them, but they feel fast because nothing remains stable during the change period?"

"Yeah, that's about it. The span of human life being what it is, one generation gets the benefits of the improvements without having any experience with the previous way things were, or the process it takes to achieve the advance. For example today's young people don't understand how advanced and reliable automobiles have become in only a few decades. To them, current standards have always existed. Previously they needed direct maintenance frequently and still there was always a chance of an unexpected breakdown. It is likely that soon, motive transportation will change so dramatically that the concern for maintenance will evaporate and be accomplished in the back office. Much as people don't think of the preparation of meat but only acknowledge the shrink wrapped product they buy at the grocery store. In some ways, if there are huge improvements to human life upon the return of the mission, the knowing that those changes will occur is about 15 years away even though we will not see them entirely for perhaps 25-30 years. And that's a long time in terms of a human life span."

Overholt had any number of these types of interviews in the first few weeks after the discovery of the signals. Eventually the focus switched from him to the United Nations debates and eventually to the construction of the space ship that would host the mission. The choice of astronauts was kept a closely guarded secret. And even though the press was able to ferret out many of the potential choices, those potential astronauts were told to keep quiet or their chances were zero.

That approach loosened some tongues as astronauts who did not want to participate or who had been ruled out began to speak privately, allowing lists of those still in the running to be compiled. A few new astronauts were taken on and most of those being considered were members of the military precisely so their public face could be controlled.

While nobody would officially admit it, many of the astronauts had been identified early in the process and had been informed they were on a very short list, as the numbers and skill sets of the actual travellers had yet to be determined. In addition the major nations of Earth negotiated for one of their nationals to be on the team. China, Russia and the United States were automatic but other nations had to fight for a spot. Early in the design phase it was determined that six astronauts was the best number, given the necessary skills and potential replacement over the long mission.

Overholt had been approached to help identify the necessary skill sets of those on the mission in terms of star light research and science background. He was one of many, many scientists who were consulted. However, he asked for and was granted a title of Mission Payload Engineer for his contributions which did wonders for his saleability to various university research programs. As the end of his sabbatical approached he was about to apply to have it extended when he received a letter from LSU granting him a full professorship in physics and astronomy. After a talk with the Dean he was essentially given carte blanche in his research as long as he was able to do a series of lectures at various universities while advertising his position with LSU and continuing to teach a single annual course in a subject of his choosing. He'd gone from a cog in the physics and astronomy department to a star academic in only a few months. It wasn't the single accomplishment he had hoped for to launch his career, but it was particularly advantageous given the public notoriety.

In the meantime he was also approached by Arizona State University to take a research chair there which opened some doors to getting additional time with the array and considerable kudos on his academic profile.

For John Overholt his experience with First Contact had been a blessing. Ethan Harendez was taken on by Overholt in his LSU position and upon receipt of his PhD, Harendez was sought by several universities to enhance their program profile. He eventually landed with the University of Hawaii as the main researcher on their telescope observatory on Mauna Loa. His tenure track would put him in charge of the entire program within a few years. For now he was free to widen his research using several post graduate students to pursue leads as long as he flouted his attachment to the University, its telescope and academic programs.

Allie made plans to move to Arizona and start med school. Overholt was particularly busy when he decided to fly to Louisiana and drive back to Arizona with Allie and a U-Haul. The quiet, below the radar approach they took was a measure of quiet in a very busy world; a lengthy, touristy drive through Houston, San Antonio, Dallas, Oklahoma City to see some relatives, to Albuquerque and Las Vegas and the Grand Canyon. After they set up their new home they decided to take a week's trip into southern California as they had a lot to think on given the new realities of their lives. Medical school was no picnic and setting up courses and lectures and figuring out a lecture circuit and doing the background work to make those events memorable and worthwhile for students was going to put a lot of strain on their private lives. They agreed without speaking that investing some time now was a wise investment in their future.

Overholt planned his course and figured he would teach it partly remotely and partly by being on campus at LSU for several in-person lectures in addition to his required public lectures which the university insisted upon to increase their public profile.

He decided that a 10 lecture tour, done in two circuits of five over a 10 day period in the fall and winter semesters was best. He was sought after for the public lectures, deciding on Harvard, Yale, North Carolina, LSU and Florida in the east, and Stanford, UCLA, Arizona, Colorado and Washington State in the west.

God created

Man invented. He invented things to improve his lot. He invented to address his needs. He invented to address his economic requirement to assign value. He invented to provide necessities like running water and better lives for his people. He invented to make his life easier and solve the wants of people. He invented to extend his life.

He invented agriculture to regulate the harvest. Why range far and wide for growing edibles when you can plant them and harvest them together? Organization of farms and domesticating animals for use as food solved the nomad's problems - and ended the constant need to build and create new safe places to live.

And he built civilizations, widespread areas under one rule. In the Nile Valley a civilization flourished that was at once cohesive and powerful. Unwilling to expand past its natural limits the people there were able to keep a hold on Egypt without natural enemies. The Egyptians of the Old Kingdom built the pyramids which were ancient structures millennia old during the latter centuries when the New Kingdom rose and flourished. And older still once decline set in and outside civilizations began to eat at the remains of the glory of the Nile.

A chief rival was the rise of civilization in the fertile crescent of Mesopotamia where two rivers created a land of plenty. Groups of men fought over these lands. The Sumerians and Assyrians of the early Bronze Age gave way to the Babylonians then to the Iron Age Hittites and reincarnations of what had occurred before as small kingdoms rose and fell over hundreds of years. But this grinding of tribes, of traditions and of culture produced civilizations of vast potential and achievement.

And far away in China much the same rise and fall was taking place where Yellow River tribes battled and forged through many hundreds of years of dynastic rule. While the power of Greece and Persia fought out their determinations the Chinese were equally engaged in power struggles of their own. Traditions were absorbed and knowledge shared over a wide area unconfined by natural boundaries. Various tribes controlled parts of China, warring on their borders for hundreds of years while the central power of the Zhou Dynasty gave way to the Han Dynasty interspersed with periodic power struggles and waxing and waning smaller powers.

In the Americas civilizations also rose and fell. Much of their glory is now consigned to the jungle lying undiscovered. Stone temples and marvelous engineering feats only hint at the vast cities and developed cultures of Central and South America. And strange artifacts and locales dot the countryside as all that remains of another culture in the North that did not value construction or edifices but rather spirit and harmony with their natural world, while fearing their neighbours.

And through all this, perhaps fuelled by it, in an effort to gain an advantage over their neighbours civilization slowly improved its technology, from bronze implements to iron, from gathering food stuffs to planting and harvesting them. Once agriculture fed him, man improved his place, by building sewers, water courses and other handy, clean and safe ways to live. Populations exploded and so did the desire for control, to safeguard what they had built and the people they counted on to maintain it.

Once the improvements of civilization took hold and men no longer looked solely for protection, he demanded his freedom to control his own destiny and he invented profit to insure it. He sold his labour, his production or his knowledge to others for something of value. He invented specialization of labour and the production of things was increased many fold.

Once he invented profit he invented ease, and invented a way to ease want. And with his profits he searched for underlying truth, and created artwork and expressions to celebrate longer lives and to enjoy the fruits of his labours while giving them to the future.

And then he reached for immortality.

Chapter Three

Astronauts were chosen, the vehicle designed and built, the mission parameters studied and planned meticulously. A bit more than a year after the transmission was discovered, the mission was launched. Record time in the aerospace industry requiring a hugely concerted effort between several space agencies worldwide.

After much back and forth negotiation, and battles both scientific and political, the spaceship that launched carried six astronauts - two from the European Space Agency, including a Russian and a Frenchman, two from NASA in the United States and two from Asia, a Japanese and a Chinese.

The mission was expected to last a bit longer than the 12 years of travel time, with an expectation of several weeks or more of exploration at the destination. The ship, the largest ever to leave Earth, was designed to include necessities for several modes of exploration depending on what the astronauts encountered.

It was launched in several sections with the main ship launched into orbit without the full crew or most of the supplies. The run up to the launch of the rocket and its payload of people, machines, experiments and a whole host of other necessities, was momentous with the mission's astronauts becoming celebrities. Though celebrities at an arms length. They were announced with great fanfare and briefly feted, but kept sequestered until just prior to the launch to keep publicity and support for the mission high while maintaining a strict quarantine and mission focus.

The world held its breath on the launch and its immediate aftermath. This craft was the largest ever to reach space and its payload was pushed as was the technology required to put it together and get it off the ground.

Communication was frequent as the craft travelled into low orbit where it docked with the International Space Station, taking on additional supplies. It was necessary to gain supplies this way as it meant a smaller initial launch weight. The interstellar ship took a module of the ISS with it when it undocked two days later, vastly increasing the size of the ship and giving the astronauts significant additional space.

A top of mind topic on Earth in the days after the discovery, the length of time required to explore the beacon signal meant that the public discussion lost its focus and immediacy.

Still there were many people convinced that at any moment they would see a flying saucer land in Central Park or Red Square or the Forbidden City. Others said no, any landings would take place at remote airbases, secret locations and unknown government installations. It spawned a cottage industry catering to the curious and the conspiracy minded. Daily life went on but the mission and its issues bubbled away under the everyday concerns at the front of the public mind.

They flew toward the Moon, where they did a triple orbit while accelerating, gaining speed for a slingshot maneuver prior to gearing up to maximum velocity, just under the speed of light. Once the slingshot acceleration occurred, engines were fired to accelerate as much as possible, and the astronauts settled in for a nearly six year journey, including time required to speed up to maximum velocity and slow down as they neared their destination. As they accelerated away from Earth communications became more difficult and less interesting as a natural back and forth became impossible with distance. As they got further and further away questions posed about health, boredom and relations on board the craft were dished to the press as they had been anticipated and answers thought out in advance. However, the speed of the craft eventually ruled out anything like normal communication and the lengthy journey soon fell back from a top of mind topic in the news as the world moved on.

When the Russian and the Japanese became engaged during the flight nobody on Earth knew there was even a mutual interest until they neared their return and had been 'married' for seven years.

When the Frenchman and the Chinese had a fistfight over historical differences in national policy in Indochina, nobody on Earth ever knew about it, the spat was cleared up long before Mission Control found out, and the two astronauts became friends. Tensions were thick onboard for several months as both the French and the Chinese expected the Americans to blunder in on one side or the other, but it never happened.

The Americans were under strict orders to maintain their professionalism and neutrality for the entire trip. All astronauts brought with them segments of their own work so they could continue their projects during the lengthy trip. All of the astronauts were accomplished pilots and had trained to fly the ship if necessary. Although they all sneered openly about the application of their terrestrial flying skills to flying a spaceship in the weightless void of space, they all knew their trip presented the possibility of difficulties they had never experienced or perhaps even thought of.

Two of the six astronauts were mathematicians, Jenn Fielding in ciphers, and Japanese Mika Oh in physics and statistics. Mika was a communications expert and had been assigned the duties necessary to run the starlight research that Professor Overholt managed to get on-board the craft.

The other four were engineers. American Mike Donohue and Russian Ivan Bolrenko were civil engineers specialising in materials, Jimmy Ho Yang from China was a chemical engineer, and Frenchman Renaud Martin an electrical engineer. They brought small laboratories with them so they could conduct experiments to pass the time. These small labs had been meticulously engineered to allow the greatest latitude in experimentation while using up the smallest amount of space and weight possible. Among all the aspects of the mission that had to be put into place in just over a year, the research experiments were perhaps the greatest feat of ingenuity on board. It had occurred to Ho Yang that the materials and construction engineering involved in building the experiment package might be the greatest accomplishment of the mission. That he had a direct hand in this did not influence his judgement, he strongly believed, only his familiarity with the project suggested that conclusion.

Much of the experimental direction was given to things that could be, or needed to be repeated, or required lengthy gestation and were particular to a weightless environment. Most of their early experiments were prescribed once outside of their communities, with only a light contact with mainstream scientists during the initial stages of the mission. They did find themselves moving in different experimental directions from their terrestrial peers, though they only realized it upon their return to Earth.

Overholt's desire for a small telescope to be mounted on the outside of the craft had been honoured. Oh was in charge of the research uses of it but all the astronauts monitored its operation and used it for their own interest and pleasure. It's primary findings, regular photos of hundreds of places and objects in space, were simply recorded to be analysed once they returned home. One of the most important tasks they had was to study Earth's sun once they were far enough away from it to permit lengthy observations.

In most cases the weightlessness of space suggested the direction their experiments took, as nobody else had the opportunity to conduct lengthy experiments in that environment. Even the astronauts themselves were experimental subjects, as their health, digestion and physical stamina were monitored in detail.

Several of the astronauts had another significant specialty or deeply engrained hobby that also contributed to the mission, future science and helped to keep them sharp. Keeping active and mentally engaged was important and difficult in the extremely limited environment in which they lived. Three were botanists, two were interested in propulsion for small drones and one was a sports nut interested in physics of motion and human kinetics.

And so ultra-slow motion video was taken of various sporting equipment in limited use. A baseball's flight, a football's spiral, a soccer ball's compression and spin were all filmed and studied in the weightlessness of space. It was quickly realized that the element of gravity and the effect of air and pressure were integral to studies of motion, so the torque and flex of human joints under the duress of sport and motion was perhaps the real crux of the study.

Plant growth in a weightless environment, including hydroponic approaches produced some interesting results once the plants were shorn of gravity.

A small drone was flown through the crew cabin and photo-graphed to see the effects of standard aeronautics in a light atmos-phere environment, which they thought might be the case at their destination. the drone had been modified prior to leaving Earth so that it could be flown in a low, or no gravity environment. They were able to take measurements of the operational aspects of flight that existed solely to combat gravity. Propulsion experiments with small drones inside the confines of the craft showed the diffi-culties of manoeuvring in weightless environments where hyper-specific positioning was almost impossible but nestling and coupling landings were fairly easy.

They also released a metal ball into space, carefully aligned with their flight direction to study the motion of that projectile as it flew alongside them at virtually the speed of light. It was near impossible to get the trajectory of the launch exact, but merely extending a mechanical arm from the ship and releasing the ball and withdrawing the arm was the best hope for an identical forward motion of the ball.

They fixed a laser monitor on it from inside the cabin and found that it actually had the slightest variation in motion from the ship, moving away from the ship but at a rate undetectable except over several Earth days of time. Eventually the ball slipped further and further from their course and was unseen by the astronauts but still tracked. Given the speed and distance that they travelled the ball was remote to the ship after only a few weeks of flight.

They did extend this effort to a rocket propelled drone outside the ship. Without air to use to steady the craft or to push against for propulsion, rocket manoeuvres were tricky, requiring an adept use of countervailing forces to keep the craft steady especially in tightly controlled flight. When Ho Yang bumped it against the outer skin of the main ship, there was a collective gasp of fear, but even at the speed of light, the extremely minor difference in their relative velocities produced no ill effects. Though Ho Yang couldn't stop from monitoring the spot where the collision had occurred in case there were micro-cracks that might develop into a problem over time.

About eight months into the journey, once the ship reached its terminal velocity just under the speed of light, all communication with Earth had ceased as transmissions could not catch up to them until they dropped down to begin their braking procedure. They were truly alone.

Five years was a long time to maintain a regular daily routine, getting exercise to maintain muscle mass and strength, getting enough sleep and breaking up the day with social activities and work related responsibilities. The ship was divided into several cabins so astronauts could get time alone or in smaller groups to break up the social aspect of their journey.

All the astronauts settled into their personal length of day and sleep patterns. Ho Yang moved to a very regular 28 hour day with a predictable need for just over eight hours of sleep. He was so regular at this that his mates used him as their unofficial clock.

Mike Donohue maintained an Earth normal 24 hour routine, though he did vary depending on the vigor of his daily efforts and sometimes slept in for more than his standard seven and a half hours of shuteye.

Mika Oh and Ivan Bolrenko similarly maintained standard Earth times, feeling that since the mission was using Earth standard time they should comply. Jenn Fielding was unpredictable in her patterns, with strong intellectual stimulation demanding of her a lengthy sleep compared to more routine activities. Her situation became apparent several months into the flight when she and Rene Martin became embroiled in a multilayered chess match.

They agreed to play the game from multiple moves at seven different points, the first two of which were mutually agreed upon. So when they came to a difficult spot in their game they agreed to play two games from the same player position. They then split the game again when they both agreed to produce three games in the middle of play. And from that point in any one of the games, each player could split the game again, twice each, to ultimately produce seven games branching out from the original. The winner of the match had to win four of those games.

The first time they engaged in this approach the games had been suspended until the next day, but Fielding slept for more than 11 hours. After a few such events she noticed the pattern of sleep coming after great mental efforts. She started to note the sleep patterns of all on board.

Ho Yang, as overall commander, was lightly in charge, as all the astronauts knew their responsibilities and maintained them with nearly military precision. Such an attitude was part of the DNA of anyone chosen for such a mission.

Ho Yang listened. He listened to his mates, he listened to their talk and banter especially sensitive to any change in routine or mental approach. But more than anything, he listened to the craft. The six travellers were moving fast in an untested spacecraft and were far from any help should something go wrong. Ho Yang knew just how precarious their situation was and tried to maintain calm in the face of strange noises, strange readings and strange happenings.

Bolrenko first noticed it and brought Donohue into his confidence. Donohue acknowledged that he had noticed Ho Yang's edginess and agreed with Bolrenko that they should both help Ho Yang in his concern for their ship but do so quietly. There was no value in hyper sensitivity but a real need to maintain vigilance.

After a proximity alarm nearly caused Ho Yang a stroke in his concern, Bolrenko and Donohue made sure they found the invader, a chunk of rock about the size of a desk, which had passed behind and below them by a kilometer or so. Bolrenko rigged up the radar on one of the Landers to be used to scan their nearby space as an early warning. They did a scan every day as part of their routine and reported the result to Ho Yang.

They knew that making any change in course would make their trip very much more difficult as they were on a direct course for the source of the signal found by Overholt, but simply knowing that such a course of action was available was enough to take some weight of worry from Ho Yang's shoulders.

All of the astronauts were aware of long term studies of weightlessness that had shown there was a huge specific toll on the human body after prolonged time without gravity. Hard core exercise took much of their time, as it was necessary to maintain muscle mass far exceeding the muscle mass necessary for life in space. It was really easy to slide on this effort as pumping muscles far beyond the need for them was uncomfortable and time consuming in their limited space environment.

The astronauts understood that a minimum standard was necessary so they could work up to the necessary standard they would need to explore and leave the ship. There was no need to keep that mass active for their entire trip, but there was a need to keep their recovery time within reason. And recovery in the final months prior to getting to their destination would not be easy in the close confines of the ship. Conducting their body maintenance this way also saved on the amount of food and protein they required and had to bring with them. Ten years worth of food for six people was a large requirement. Some had argued they might be able to replenish supplies at their destination but they knew they couldn't count on that and had to prepare for a return trip.

Mission planners had grappled with sending six or four astronauts especially given the much larger size of ship necessary for the additional travellers. In the end the extra astronauts were added as much to stabilize a crew that may encounter psychological issues during the long trip. The possibility of one of the travellers dying along the way was very real and enough astronauts were required to make sure there was no shortage during the critical parts of the mission.

It also allowed for a broader spectrum of people to be represented. Ho Yang was chosen commander of the mission. He was a Chinese national, but educated in the United States making him acceptable to all. He was also an engineering generalist so he could fill in for most of the specialties should something befall one of the other astronauts.

Life on Earth resumed its course not long after the ship left. Everyone understood that this great leap forward for humankind was being conducted in slow motion, with little to be known for more than a decade.

Unbeknownst to scientists on Earth, eventually the travellers were able to confirm suspicions that the broadcast beacon was coming from a mid-sized asteroid orbiting a medium-large sun. It's wide orbit would take it far beyond the 5.3 light years away from Earth that it currently was. As they neared the asteroid they were able to follow the continuing stream of light pulses headed to Earth. These signals did not vary from the original pattern.

Overholt and Harendez had cashed in on their notoriety and settled into comfortable lives. The story of First Contact was cold, though many on Earth wondered if there would be other contacts with aliens in the intervening years - while they waited for news of the ship. A small industry had grown around the mission and its eventual return.

Chapter Four

All the while the ship plodded on through the emptiness of space without much reference to the speed they were moving nor the distance covered, except their inability to see home. First the visual dimmed. Then the details visible through a telescope faded until only the light of the sun remained obvious. Existing without a visual of Earth was more affecting than any of the travellers had expected. Only the slimmest of tethers remained.

Looking ahead, there was that feeling of driving to the horizon in the far distance and never actually appearing to gain ground, except there was no horizon and there was no ground falling away around them. Only the variation in the flight of the ball they launched gave them any sense of motion.

Time was their only real dimension, and that acquired a stretched and compressed quality that made it very difficult to even feel hungry or tired at any logical time in their routine. They worked hard to maintain some form of structure to their existence and found that eventually they had to adapt significantly to each person's inner clock and specific needs. They eventually found a bit of rhythm with the younger members of the crew requiring more sleep and the older members needing less sustenance.

They tracked the source of the light signals and prepared to rendezvous. At the proscribed time they fired their reverse thrusters to begin the process of slowing manoeuvres to bring the ship into human control for small scale movements around the asteroid they chased.

In flight, they monitored the light wave transmission from its source. It continued in the same monotonous pattern as it had for as long as they flew. Once they slowed they were treated to better views of the asteroid source of the signals, and excitement grew among the crew. It was the first evidence in a long time that they were actually moving through space, save their lost ability to communicate with Earth. Once the craft slowed, the more proscribed rhythms of civilization returned almost without being noticed by the crew.

Eventually they were close enough to the asteroid to manually adjust their course to engage the medium sized body, really an asteroid with an atmosphere, which partly burned off when the comet approached its star, giving it the characteristic comet's tail. At this point in its orbit around its star it was far away from the star's influence and was just another cold rock in space.

"Chalk one up for NASA," said Mike Donohue. "The guys I talked to said they were pretty confident the signals came from an asteroid."

"My cosmonaut friends also thought it would be coming from an asteroid," said Russian Ivan Bolrenko.

"As did our own space agencies," said Jimmy Ho Yang, while

pointing at Japanese communications officer Mika Oh. She nodded.

"Perhaps it's not the revelation they thought it would be," smiled Donohue. "Did they give you any rationale or just odds on your money?"

Mika looked confused. Jimmy laughed while Renaud and Ivan simply shook their heads.

"My agency had people saying everything, in strict confidence only, that way they could be right no matter where the signals came from," said Ivan. "But I will deny everything."

"Our guys were pretty confident due I think to the lack of amplitude or break in the stream of numbers. Had it been coming from a planet sized body it's rotation would likely have been evident in the broadcast stream."

"Unless it is coming from a satellite in orbit. Our teams never gave an explanation, or if they did I didn't hear it. I just wanted the bottom line, there was so much to deal with in the rush to launch," said Renaud.

"It should be fairly easy to set us down on a mid-sized rock. Gravity is less of an issue and hopefully rotation isn't too much to overcome."

"If its spinning rapidly it might be a problem, but that's what computers are for," said the Frenchman. "Besides, I'm driving and if you can handle traffic in Paris, navigating a parking spot here should be easy."

"You know Renaud, I've had to park in a lot of difficult places, but this time I think you're right. I'm glad we picked the right man for the job. I've stood watching traffic in the Place Concorde, and you have to think like a fighter pilot to handle it."

The effort to slow down from their near light speed took several months. As the nearness of their arrival at their destination became apparent, work arrangements started to resemble the frenzied activity they sometimes managed on Earth, as routines were shifted as much work was required to be done in advance of the planned landing. Work that couldn't be done in advance without knowing the specifics of the landing.

As they gathered telemetry, they were able to confirm Martin's speculation that the beacon signal was coming from a very small satellite which maintained a geosynchronous orbit above the asteroid.

Donohue studied the satellite that broadcast the signal. It seemed odd in its configuration and orbital attitude. And then it hit him, he sat bolt upright. "Oh my," he said.

The broadcast signal, the light beam that had been detected from Earth, had been sending a signal in multiple directions. He told the rest of the crew.

The news hit them almost as hard as the original news of first contact. Could there be other civilizations to encounter beyond the single one they had found?

Additional analysis confirmed the multiple signals and provided a revelation.

The signal that reached Earth appeared to have been directed to the Earth's moon, and more specifically it was aimed at the side of the moon that faced deep space - the dark side of the moon - dark from Earth as it never presented its face to be seen from Earth.

"Did the aliens know that the signal would hit the Moon? Did they also know that it would from time to time hit the Earth, as the moon's orbit assured that a signal contact could not be maintained through that huge distance of space?"

"Remember, the signal was found trailing the moon's orbital path, a part of the sky not usually scanned because of the light pollution from the Moon and because the orbital motion makes long term scans impossible."

"That confirms the direction of the Earth signal but where do all these other signals go and what do they mean?"

"That's part of what we are here to find out. With luck there will be someone or something down there to tell us."

"Well if there is someone down there, they are likely aware of us," said Fielding. "They haven't said hello yet, have they Renaud?"

He shook his head. And Mika, who had been monitoring radio signals also gave a slow shake, having encountered nothing unusual.

They sent out a mirror transmission of the same outward signal, by light and radio. They collectively held their breath expecting a return acknowledgement . . . but it did not come.

They were equipped with a small Lander, actually two Landers, one of which was going to drop to the asteroid, once the main ship was moving in unison with it. The second Lander was a stripped down back-up and there for parts, emergency, or even a second landing should that be necessary. They were not copies of each other with the second machine a much sparser version, really an operable parts wagon, not intended for use except in an emergency. Three astronauts, Jenn Fielding the American cipher expert, Ivan Bolrenko, a Russian civil engineer, and Frenchman Renaud Martin an electrical engineer, would make the trip down to the surface. Martin was the Lander pilot.

The second Lander was switched on and off, ready if needed. Ho Yang was the designated emergency pilot, being the crew member with the most experience in space and the most practice at Mission Control prior to blast off. The first Lander was boarded and powered up.

"Alright Houston we are detaching from the Nautilus and moving to the drop co-ordinates."

"Houston? Really?"

"It's a joke Mika," said Fielding. "You're our mission control."

"I prefer calling them 'Kremlin'," said Bolrenko.

"Really, your mission control was in The Kremlin? I thought you launched from Kazakhstan?"

"Everything in Russia goes through the Kremlin," said a straight faced Bolrenko with a exaggerated accent, before breaking into a giant grin. "I am joking with you Jennifer."

Martin sat in the captain's chair with Fielding acting as co-pilot. Both were expert pilots on Earth, as was Bolrenko. Martin came through French military ranks and Fielding got her wings first as a crop duster in her teens, and then a search and rescue pilot, a job she used to finance her mathematical studies. She had spent several years in the military before the opportunity for this mission came. Her father had been a military pilot and then worked on civilian aircraft and Fielding had been around planes of various sorts her entire life. She had been involved with military flights as well, mostly as a navigator and remote pilot, controlling unmanned drones.

It had been a strange way to serve. She and a dozen or more 'pilots' would gather in a windowless room in a non-descript building on base, check in for their shift and then enter their noiseless pods and take control of drones that could be flying anywhere on Earth. Sometimes they would take over in mid-flight as one drone pilot's shift ended and theirs began.

Most often these flights were strictly 'eyes in the sky' and usually they were done with a very low profile. They also were equipped with microphones to pick up any audio information that could be passed on to ground forces or intelligence units. On a couple of occasions for Fielding her mission had been active duty in a restricted or combat zone. She had always flown drones with live fire capabilities, as almost all military drones had defensive capabilities. In the combat work some drones were heavily armed for forward, aggressive uses.

Piloting them was like playing a video game except that the screen resolutions were far advanced, the satellite provided highly detailed real time views in daylight; the ordinance was real, and you didn't get a chance to respawn for a second life. She had seen that first hand when drones on mission with her had been downed and the pilots left grasping at their controls wanting back in the fight immediately.

Fielding had had it demonstrated to her that return fire could be damaging. She had once guided her drone back to base even though it had technically not been able to fly, at least according to its operational tolerances.

That feat had gotten her noticed by her commanding officer who passed on the details in his weekly reports to brass. Fielding had a remarkable, in fact, an unheard of capacity to concentrate. It was noticed by her fellow pilots and commanders. When she was relieved mid-flight she had trouble detaching herself from the mission, so much so that she alone was allowed to fly past pilot fatigue tolerances if she chose. And she always did.

Her record was a 22 hour reconnaissance mission into Afghanistan in support of a group of Special Forces who had been secretly dropped into the country to affect several hit and run raids on important Taliban targets.

The Special Forces would conduct their manoeuvres according to plan using the drones as their forward eyes and their backward eyes during their withdrawals after a raid. Fielding's experience and attention to detail in these missions had more than once saved the ground force from unexpected firefights. Twice she had led Taliban searchers away from the Special Forces bivouac in very hostile territory. Once, she had laid waste to a Taliban group laying in wait for US forces to move through a pinch point. They were hidden high up a valley in a cave. She spotted them and used one of her defensive missiles to destroy the cave and kill the ambush.

She had pioneered the tactic of slow flybys of territory in the days and weeks prior to a mission so she could have familiarity with ground concerns rather than simply relying on satellite imagery. Some drone commanders felt that this tactic might tip off the Special Forces' interest in a target but Fielding showed them how to maintain a very low profile in her reconnaissance flights by flying a smaller drone and going in very early in the morning, being very conscious of any shadows the drone might throw, by using the sonar and by flying at about rooftop level, high enough to stay hidden but low enough to get a much better street view. She varied that altitude during reconnaissance depending on surrounding geography from perhaps as low as 20 meters to as high as 100 meters and of course much higher when necessary.

In space, the mission Lander was equipped with a small drone, less than a meter across, with audio and visual pick-ups in the event that it was needed - Mission Control could not anticipate all possibilities and a drone would provide some level of forward sight during explorations. it was equipped to fly in both atmospheric conditions and in a vacuum. Without an atmosphere the drone would have limited uses. For the descent to the surface Fielding was officially the Lander's co-pilot.

In a nod to Jules Verne, the command craft had been dubbed Nautilus by the crew. It was a bit more descriptive than JIC-1, for Joint Investigation Craft - Number 1, the only name the bureaucrats of the multinational effort could agree upon before the project launched.

The Nautilus was a string of several modules from a crew perspective on the inside, but it was really a number of tubes with the ability to shut off each section from the others in an emergency.

The Lander was similar as it was two compartments, actually three if the equipment areas was considered. A pilot house with a bit of extra space sat on top of a crew room with storage of everyday items and other necessities. Once they landed the equipment room would be emptied and then used to haul back anything interesting that they found.

The Lander itself was not modular and was built inside a dense web of springs and motion absorption material used to anticipate a rough landing. The craft was structurally capable of a bounce landing if the terrain or gravity demanded use of the tactic. The crew had trained for such a landing but they hoped it was not necessary as there had been injuries in every single training run. Minor injuries yes, but even those presented a more sinister aspect with only the most basic medical facilities. Mika Oh was a medical doctor, but she had not practiced medicine for several years. And she was not going to the surface.

Tests upon approach to the comet suggested a thicker atmosphere than they originally anticipated and more gravity than the size of the object would suggest. That suggested the bounce technique was not necessary. Fielding breathed a sigh of relief - her ability to withstand the bounce landings had not gone well in their training, though she smiled through it for the sake of getting assigned to the mission. Despite being immobilized for the jarring landings she had felt concussed on more than one occasion after training.

The asteroid must have been made of mostly heavy metals but curiously the astronauts found those signatures were difficult to detect despite multiple scans.

The comet was vaguely a long rectangular box shape though very irregular, even elliptical, and about 50 kilometers around the narrow axis but perhaps three times that size on the wider axis. This was no small stone.

As they had approached what they now called Rugby, because of its shape, they had photos of some type of regular construction as evidence of intelligent activity on the surface. It's spin was along the long axis and fairly rapid, making a complete rotation in about 10 hours.

They first tried to orient the command ship Nautilus to match the spin of the asteroid but were unsuccessful due to the oddities in is attitude. It spun with a significant lopsidedness, sort of like a badly thrown football, one end with a tighter spin than the other. They settled for a regular orbit around the asteroid about a third of the way along its length.

After much discussion it was decided that the Lander, now referred to as Spike, though the Americans managed to avoid explaining to their colleagues the real reason for this reference, would try to mimic the spin as it orbited prior to landing. Civil engineer Mike Donahue just started referring to it as Spike saying it was because it would pin down their presence on Rugby with an exact location.

"I'm going to nail the landing," said Martin, with an innocent look at his co-pilot.

Fielding was sure he was referring to the celebration after a touch-down score in American football where the ball is thrown hard into the ground, much as the Lander would likely do in its touchdown on the surface of the asteroid. She grimaced and smiled at the same time. The idea of a hard landing was not pleasant, as she knew from training experience, but the oddities of Rugby suggested it was very possible. Martin was aware of the possibility and kept the bounce landing in the back of his mind should they have trouble orienting to the rapid spin of the asteroid. The Lander was built with a hard touchdown in mind.

"We are taking her down to an altitude of five kilometers prior to our orientation exercise with the surface," said Renaud.

"Roger that, Spike. Moving toward the surface and orienting with the axial rotation."

Spike was small compared to Nautilus and it moved smoothly through space. Perhaps 12 meters in diameter, it was an egg shaped sphere, and sported several rocket cones attached for various manoeuvres and protective structures for those cones. It included a number of spiked legs to help slow it if it tumbled out of control. After a number of thrusts and counterthrusts by the small rockets, the Lander was in a geosynchronous orbit around the spinning asteroid nearly above the point where the apparent structures were located.

"Hey, that wasn't so hard," said Martin. "Funny, just as I thought we had it with the last bit of thrust, we seemed to lock in. Almost as if I was docking with the Nautilus, just that little bit of complementary motion that completes the maneuver. When your brain registers that both bodies are moving in perfect unison."

"Spike, please stay in place for a few minutes and let me reorient the computer navigation and the communications," said Mika. "We are now over the same surface location as you but we are in a slight backward orbit, moving against the spin of the asteroid. You will lose communication with us for about half of each 10 hour rotation. If we went the other direction our orbits would take longer as the asteroid would be chasing us and we would be out of contact for many hours on each rotation."

"We talked about this," said Fielding. "And with an orbit in the same direction as the comet's spin you would also be in contact with us for much longer on each rotation. It's a choice. I was outvoted."

"I see the value in that now," said Martin with a smile in his voice. "And when we rotate out of communication you might see the value in my preference. Certainly the members in Nautilus will."

"And I thought we should have matching orbits, even if it takes a bit of extra work to achieve, so we stay in constant communication," said Bolrenko, his voice echoing from a compartment below the pilot house. "I don't know why that was lost in this debate?"

Martin shook his head, "Because Mr. Bolrenko, we decided that it would be a waste of time in the initial stages and could be accomplished at the leisure of the mother ship's command once we had departed."

"I must have missed that. Oh, and I would prefer to be addressed as Colonel."
"We also addressed that, I believe about six years ago before we left Earth. Military rank is reserved for members of the same military - being an international group, military rank has little meaning

among us. Only Commander Ho Yang has that distinction among us, as he is the overall mission commander."

"Mr. Bolrenko just doesn't have the necessary gravity."

"Ah, but it appears that Rugby does; have the necessary gravity, I mean. Indications are the atmosphere is very thick, in fact too thick for the size of this asteroid. It must be artificial."

A few hours passed as the Lander used its cameras to search the surface for signs of intelligent life and a possible landing area. As the asteroid remained steady beneath them Martin's voice crackled, "We've found a spot fairly close to what have been identified as structures and will begin our descent."

"Copy that Spike."

Watching intently as the asteroid and the Lander rotated beneath them, the crew in Nautilus watched as Martin put the Lander through a short series of manoeuvres calculated to take the Lander down in a controlled descent, with only the slightest forward movement in relation to the rotation of the asteroid Rugby.

"We are nearing the surface, angling in slowly, in the event a bump and roll landing is necessary. Instruments say 20 meters, 18, 15, 22 that's odd . . ." said Martin. "Now 12, 10 must have been a ravine or rift or something - why did our sensors not pick that up?"

"Visual agrees," said Fielding. "It was a little track cut in the surface which ended at a cluster of rocks. Probably too small to show up on general scans."

"Then let's get more detailed scans, this is not a simulation," said a tense Martin.

Mika was scanning the tracking instruments.

"They are down," said Mika in the Nautilus.

"We are down," said Martin.

It was a remarkable feat of flying as Spike landed so softly that only a slight flower of dust was released when it touched down.

"Thought you were supposed to bounce it in? At least that's what Spike was designed for," said Mika with a hint of awe in her voice. "That was one pretty landing. Our sensors recorded almost no resistance upon touchdown."

"Copy that Houston, though we should have a proper rugby touchdown for this particular landing," said Fielding and then she flipped off the comm and turned to Martin. "Once we got close it just seemed easy."

"It was the same feeling when we hit the geosynchronous orbit, like we got locked in the last little bit and dropped like a feather."

"Yeah, I know, I could feel it in the controls," said Martin. "Once we hit about five meters above the surface it felt almost like something locked onto us and eased us down with a little cushion at touchdown."

Fielding opened the comm. "Houston we are down and secure. Systems are operating normally."

"Activating legs and sensors," she said, choosing a series of pyramid shaped metal spikes extended from parts of the sphere nearest the surface and extending into it upon activation. Soon they fixed on resistance in the rock and the Lander was lifted slightly off the surface. The spikes held sensors which tested the soil and its density, chemical make-up and looked for the presence of organic material and water. The tests would take a bit of time, enough that they could orient themselves to their landing area.

The view immediately in front of the pilot house was bleak, not unlike the pictures of other extra-terrestrial landscapes, rocky, uneven with little to note and a slope away towards the horizon. In this case, due to the small size of the asteroid the horizon appeared to run up quickly from the Lander and then fall away to nothing. There were no mountain majesties to frame the distance, there just wasn't any distance anymore once the horizon was met, except a narrow band of yellow, seeming to rise from the surface, a product of the starlight encountering the atmosphere. And then there was the inky black of space, presumably where the atmosphere was too thin to reflect enough starlight to make a difference to human eyes.

There was little natural starlight, but the light from a not too distant star was enough to cast a weak watery shadow, stark but slight. The rest of the light was generated by the Lander, two spot lights which could be controlled for brightness and direction.

They had been on from the start of the landing. Fielding aimed them along the surface and fixed them in a wide angle illumination from the two main view ports of the Lander.

Martin moved to a window beside his left hand seat and was scanning the surface. Fielding moved to the opposite side of the Lander to look out another window. Bolrenko was below in his compartment position as landing mission leader, now the primary focus of the mission, as he was responsible for everything that occurred on the surface.

"That landing was very soft. The shock absorbers on the surface vehicle barely registered a bounce," said Bolrenko.

"Yeah, amazing. It felt as if we were touched down gently. Sort of like . . . "

Fielding spoke while gazing out the window. Her voice trailed off.

"It's actually pretty bleak out there, no real colour but there looks to be some evidence that someone was here or still is. There are some bits of equipment and evidence of shafts, what appear to be entrances into the interior of the asteroid," said Martin.

"Are you using full magnification?"

"No, no magnification. We are actually pretty close to it, let me turn up the..."

"You had better come to this side first Renaud and look out."

"What is it? enquired Mika from the radio, a little bit of fear in her voice.

"Oh my god," said Renaud's voice through the comm. "It's a town, or at least a village or something."

"What we saw from orbit as a collection of manmade objects, due mostly to their unnatural regularity, appears to be a collection of buildings, none larger than a double garage on earth, though it's hard to tell from here how far away we are. They look to be less than a kilometer away, perhaps closer," said Fielding with a bit more composure than Martin, who did not have the benefit of regarding the structures as long as the American. "The odd shape of Rugby is playing games with distance perception. The horizon is very odd given it is very near in one direction and much further away with a 90 degree change of perspective. Where the two sections meet, at about 40 degrees it is almost impossible to fathom. Very disorienting."

"We will need to get out and look about," said Renaud. "I must say when we saw that from above, I thought it was a natural rock formation, like the Giant's Causeway in Ireland, just basalt rocks formed at the same time in the same shape. There is no evidence of any actual life forms, but there is overwhelming evidence of intelligence and life having been here. In fact, given the structures, I half expect to see some advertising billboards or logos on the buildings. They are very Earth-like."

The Russian engineer had joined the pilots in the control room of the Lander, having secured the rest of the ship after landing.

"Could it be an Earth settlement that we have not been informed about?" asked the Russian. "After all you Americans have been here and there without us before?"

Fielding was nonplussed. "And you Russians have been places that you haven't publicised. If my government had sent me on an 12-year wild goose chase when they knew what was here, I don't think they would survive when I return, either electorally nor personally. And the Treasury would be hearing from my lawyers. No, this isn't American, though it does have the corrugated tin look that is so popular in farm country. It looks cheap, light, strong and easy to work with."

The Frenchman and Russian both nodded as if they had seen this type of construction before.

"It looks like rural areas I've seen in the States," said Bolrenko. "Though I must say the material looks . . . space age, I guess." He smiled. "How's that for my use of English?"

Fielding looked at him. There was more to the Russian than he let on. She wracked her memories for what she knew of him, stuff picked up on pre-flight briefings. It was mostly his personality that shone through during the flight - he didn't speak of himself or his experiences at all. Though she thought she had heard him talk of home and his youth, she realized that is was mostly the Frenchman who waxed on about his life and the loveliness of his native land.

Bolrenko had been born in St. Petersburg, educated in Moscow and taken into the space program through the military despite his civil engineering background. In fact he had designed and supervised construction of a huge bridge span over the Volga River in the south before it emptied into the Caspian Sea. His military background and organizational skills got the project completed in about two-thirds of the time allotted for construction.

Bolrenko had made a name for himself in command. First stemming from his control of the bridge engineering project and afterward in several large civil engineering and logistics projects. He was a very capable organizer and according to the dossier, inspired loyalty in those who worked with and for him.

Around the ship he had proved to have a dry sense of humor which contrasted with his no nonsense personality - in fact he often played himself against type to get a laugh or a smile. It took the other astronauts some time to cotton on to his personal quirks and mannerisms.

After about a year in space he and Mika Oh would often spend time together in the exercise room and seemed to enjoy each other's company - at first volunteering to work together to be the expedition's diet monitors and "cooks" and soon thereafter taking time to help each other with their side experiments.

By the end of the third year they announced their 'marriage' to the rest of the crew who had already come to see their togetherness as a fait accompli. They even asked Commander Ho Yang to officiate at the ceremony, though they had to convince him that as

Commander he had the traditional authority to perform the service. Having come from a different tradition he was unaware.

Still, according to the mission plan they were to serve in different roles during the delicate landing phase as Bolrenko was the commander of the landing party and responsible for the exploration of the asteroid, while Oh was the communication and information specialist making sure images were stored, computer files backed up and all necessary telemetry was completed and stored for future analysis. She was also the chief medical officer and monitored all of the crew's health and vitals. She served as the voice of the Nautilus while it remained in orbit and was determined to keep all communications on a completely professional level.

Bolrenko's bulky appearance belied his physical dexterity and natural strength. He was quick and precise in his movements with an efficiency that was apparent to even the most casual observer. Mika had commented on it with awe in the early stages of the voyage. Bolrenko was a leader in the astronauts' exercise schedules, pushing them to retain muscle mass necessary for exploratory missions and for a quick recovery once they returned to Earth. He pushed them hard once they began their braking maneuver in preparation for the landing.

He quietly told stories of Russian cosmonauts who had been in space for long periods and the difficulties they had regaining the use of their limbs due to loss of muscle. He was able to put a lot of fear into the astronauts with his grim descriptions of cosmonauts taking months or even years to fully recover and telling tales of pain, disfigurement and difficult physical challenges due to lack of diligence with exercises in weightlessness. He knew how easy it was to let the hard physical exercise leak away when it appeared in the moment to be so unnecessary.

"Houston, we are going in for a look on foot. We can return to

Spike and retrieve the surface vehicle if our estimations on distance prove to be wrong," Bolrenko said to the command ship.

The three astronauts suited up. The atmosphere was thicker than expected but did not contain any oxygen forcing the explorers to wear complete atmospheric protection and carry their breathing apparatus. They had a small four wheeled vehicle which they could use if necessary, though it required a bit of assembly. It had been broken down in storage to save space on the Lander.

They did take it out of storage and set the solar collector in place to begin to charge the vehicle's battery. If necessary they could assemble it for transportation within a few hours.

"There is no way this atmosphere is natural," said Fielding. "The gravity is stronger than it should be on a rock this size, so it must be artificially generated too. Why would the atmosphere be primarily non-reactive gases like Argon and Neon?"

"Occam's Razor says the simple answer is usually the correct guess," said Martin. "Either that's what the aliens breathe or there is some other good reason to engineer the atmosphere that way. It's speculation, but if they are mining or conducting heavy industrial work here, a non-reactive atmosphere would pretty much stifle any chance of fire or explosion. Could be merely a safety concern." The group walked on, rapidly getting nearer to the collection of huts.

"Remember smooth, steady breathing. Anything else will cause you to have to return to Spike earlier than desired. We are on a survey mission this time. Check out the structures, map them out in some detail and look for any signs of life. Something might be living below the surface if those shafts mean anything," said Bolrenko, who was in charge of the landing mission.

"We travel together," said Martin. "We can spread beyond a few steps but never out of sight of each other."

"Yes. At least in tandem and preferably with all of us together. As soon as I see any English writing I will be in touch with the Kremlin."

Fielding laughed. "Me too, but I'll put a call into the White House, but we won't hear from them for a long while." Bolrenko smiled.

"Tell us what you are doing and seeing," said Mika's voice, trembling slightly in their helmets. "We are quite concerned and curious here above you. We need a bit of step by step description up here. Silence is worrisome."

"We are just preparing to leave the airlock. Have you managed to reorient your orbit?"

"Yes, for the most part. There seems to be little reason to orient it strictly due to the oddity of the asteroid's spin but we will remain above you in orbit for the duration of your stay, though we will be required to make minor orbital adjustments every day or two, Earth time, that is."

The burly Russian fastened his suit lock, gave the thumbs up, which was returned by Martin and Fielding. He waited for the green 'go' light indicating all the atmosphere in the ship had been withdrawn to the main crew quarters, leaving the airlock a vacuum. When the indicator light blinked green he glanced at the others and gingerly opened the air lock to the surface. There was a hiss of gas entering the chamber.

"This place looks a lot like the outskirts of a small town in Tennessee near where I trained in river dam construction," said Bolrenko. "It's all so very lonely, ba-by" he hiccupped with an Elvis warble, then added the tune. "It's just so lonely, I could die."

"Be careful what you wish for," said Fielding with a smile.

As the slit in the doors widened the astronauts could see the village or whatever it was quite clearly. The horizon seemed very close due to the size and shape of the asteroid. Martin looked back at the structures he had first seen and estimated they were only about 300 meters away in the opposite direction of the building structures.

The astronauts began to walk toward the structures. First with a bouncing type step common in low gravity and then with a bit more of a stride.

"Hey, gravity is really much stronger than I expected here," said Fielding. "It seems to have gotten stronger as we approached the structures. I am feeling only a bit light in my boots."

"You are right. I feel like I forgot to eat the last few days and have almost the same weight as Earth. Remember that we have not experienced gravity in some time. It is probably much weaker than Earth even if there is some kind of artificial gravity field being generated. There was no indication of this in the Nautilus nor in Spike," said Bolrenko. "This is unusual. Look at the horizon. We are on a fairly small bit of geography."

They approached the structures. And found they were actually closer than they thought. There appeared to be three sizes of building. One was quite small, topping out at less than two meters in height. The next were larger, topping out at perhaps six meters in height and the third the largest were about eight meters tall.

"This appears to be a little town - I'm calling it Memphis," said Bolrenko with an air of finality. "It's down at the end of Lonely

Street - it's Heartbreak Hotel," he sang.

"Russians are Elvis fans?" commented Fielding.

"We ain't nothing but hound dogs, drinking Vodka all the time . . ." he sang. "It's from my days at the Institute. We were young and things from the West were decadent. You know."

"Yeah, I guess I do. In my time it was things from the Southern US that were decadent. At least a lot of people thought Elvis was decadent. Though that is history to me. And now, he's a legend, widely acclaimed, often imitated, but, and I will remind you, never duplicated."

"Oh, I don't know," said Martin as they walked. "Ivan has a certain Elvis swagger."

"Thank you , thank you very much," he deadpanned.

"Well here we are, and this time Elvis is looking to get into the building."

They had reached the perimeter of the cluster of buildings and began to walk around and between the structures which had been arranged smallest to largest from their vantage point, giving the impression of a more uniform height and further distance from the Lander.

"Do not try to enter anything yet. Let's get a strong sense of the whole collection of structures before we try to get inside one," said Bolrenko, who was leaning in for a closer look at one of the buildings. "Look at the material, it has a tin look but you can see a web of reinforcement, like a wire pattern embedded in the metal. It's very intricate and looks almost three dimensional. The metal has a visible depth to it."

He took a tool from his belt and ran it gently along the broadside of the metal wall. He would feel the wire mesh reinforcement as he brushed the wall. He knocked with his gloved knuckles on the wall, testing it for thickness. It felt very solid, with no hint of hollowness, but the size of the buildings suggested the walls would not likely be unusually thick.

"It appears to be metal, likely a steel or tin derivative, with some wire reinforcement. The material seems very dense, almost bunker -like," he spoke his thought aloud for the benefit of those in the orbiting ship. "The buildings are standing on some sort of pre-made platform a few centimeters above the surface of the ground. He thrust his touch tool into the ground at the base of the platform and flicked some dirt outward from the base. A few thrusts and he still hadn't reached the bottom of the material.

"Well, it's a least 10 centimeters deep, without any change in the material. It looks like concrete but it's something different as clearly the water in concrete would explode in this atmosphere."

He took a slotted tool and chipped at the edge of the platform a few times. He was unable to dent or scratch the surface. In fact the metal of his tool edge was being ground down through the touch.

"The base material is also very dense."

They took pictures of the buildings which were arranged quite regularly and spaced about 5 meters apart. They used a combina-tion holographic laser camera to scan and read everything around them. The readings would later be recreated into a 3-D view of the building group.

They took detailed atmospheric readings finding it was composed almost entirely of neutral gases, Helium, Neon, Argon and Xenon, gases that do not react chemically. This atmosphere supported a drone which Fielding piloted in and around the buildings to complete their survey. That done, they retreated with the intention of returning to the Lander to sort through their findings. Facing the small cluster of shaft doorways on the return trip to the Lander, they decided to take a side trip to the shaft structures that Martin had first seen upon landing.

The structures stood at the end of a very straight trench which pointed back to the collection of metal buildings. Martin's hunch proved correct as the small buildings were just three sided entrances to shafts below the surface. It was unclear at first if they were seeing several entrances to one underground complex or if there were several independent tunnels under the surface.

"Okay, let's do an experiment here. Jenn you go into that entrance, I'll take this one," Bolrenko said pointing to his right and then straight ahead of him, "and you Mr. Martin, take the other one on the left."

"How far do we explore?"

"Let's each get inside and see what is going on. First I'd like to determine if they are connected into one large set of tunnels below us, or if they are separate entrances. So we stay inside for no more than a minute and report back here. We'll decide on a plan of action once we return to Spike, based on what we see. Go."

Bolrenko jumped and strode towards the central entrance door. Like all the tunnel doors it did not have a lock nor was it completely closed.

"Why even have a door if it can't close?"

The others moved toward their assignments. Jenn noticed the same ill fitting door that would not close. She pulled it open and saw a set of stairs going down into the blackness. She switched on a light source strapped to her chest, the small personal camera was already activated to record her movements.

She looked down to see a significant stairway heading down a fairly narrow passage. She went down and counted 55 steps before she reached the bottom where she saw that the passage opened up to the left into a much larger room. She stood in the entrance area and passed her light around the space noting some machinery, some other passages and some shafts in the floor.

Her minute was up and satisfied she had seen what was necessary she started back up the stairway. Two steps up and out of sight of the larger room, she heard a loud series of clicks and light blazed in the tunnel. Momentarily surprised she let out a 'Wow' but received no response to her communication. The radio was not operating between her colleagues at this depth.

She quickly regained her objectivity and moved back down the steps to see the entire room lit up. It revealed more detail than she had seen, but did not show her anything she had not previous recorded. She let the camera take a scan of the space and she moved quickly up the stair. By the time she was within a few steps of the top she glanced back and saw the light click out.

As she neared the top she began to receive the voices of Martin and Bolrenko, expressing concern. Before she could reply she emerged from the doorway to see her two colleagues standing there with looks of relief on their faces.
"We were just planning our rescue mission. You took more than two minutes. Find something interesting?"

"Yes, about 20 meters down there is a large control type room with machinery and more shafts leading straight down. I was headed back up when the lights clicked on down there. They went off as I neared the surface - maybe a timer of some kind with a motion sensor?"

Both men looked surprised. "Maybe we weren't down long enough to trigger anything?" said Martin.

Martin related that his shaft also went down about 20 meters but it had two side shafts that he poked his head into to scan. One was a smallish room with a table in it and some machinery. The other appeared to be a passage, as it was about 15 meters long with doors on each side.

"I looked, the doors were shut tightly. My time was up so I returned. There was no automatic light source. You can see when we review my camera's scans."

Bolrenko said that his doorway led down only about five meters to a moderately sized room full of desks and machinery. I took a walk around it but didn't trigger any lights. It looked like an office space to me."

The three compared notes for a few minutes and resolved to return to do a more thorough scan of the spaces and perhaps try to get some of the equipment to operate. They all agreed that it was fairly obviously a mining operation of some kind.

"Okay, let's get cleaned up and get our rations and take a few minutes to process what we've seen before we talk about it and decide what to do next," said Bolrenko.
"It's obvious that we need to enter the shafts and the buildings," said Martin.

"Wait!" said Bolrenko with more than a bit of irritation in his voice. "Think on what you've seen, then we will talk. You may well be right, but we draw no conclusions until we have had time to process what we've seen."

The three crew members returned to the Lander, exited their suits, repacked them for another trip outside the Lander and prepared for their meal. They transmitted all their video and audio recordings to the Nautilus for analysis. At Bolrenko's insistence, they did not speak. They settled in over their rations, made a few abstract comments about the food and resumed the silence.

"Now, any observations? What is our next step?"

"It's obvious we need to enter the shafts and buildings," said Martin with a sly smile. Bolrenko tilted his head, not at all amused. "Well, it's obvious," continued Renaud.

Bolrenko gave him a withering look which slowly transmuted into a grin. "Perhaps but first we need to be in contact with the Nautilus to see if they can add to our knowledge. Perhaps their surveys of the asteroid have turned up other places more worthy of exploration. I remind you both that this is not Tennessee, or a Black Sea resort or even a training exercise. We must maintain caution and deliberation. I for one would like to get home."

"So far no little green men have snuck up on us," said Fielding. "I'm guessing we are alone."

"Don't guess. I agree with your supposition, but you must have been caught a bit off guard when those lights came on. What if there was a room full of aliens? What would you have done?"
"Sing 'Suspicious Minds'?"

Bolrenko laughed. "From what I've seen so far, it's more like 'In The Ghetto'."

Contact with the Nautilus was made.

"Ships' computers say the signals are coming from the surface, from a location within the building sites you've seen and apparently a couple of others on the asteroid itself. We are investigating those locations," Mika said.

"They are broadcast to the small satellite that Mike found orbiting the asteroid. From there the signals are broadcast by laser in a number of directions, about 20 at last count. We are trying to follow the beams to see where the destinations are. So far we've identified one exo-planet in the Goldilocks zone around its star about 2.2 light years from here, and we've identified four other beams aimed at nearby asteroids all within a light year of this location. What is interesting is that the signal that has been broadcast to Earth the entire time we have been travelling here, ceased immediately upon Spike touching down," Mika added. "Before it stopped Mike confirmed that the signal sent to Earth would have been significantly hindered by the orbit of our Moon."

"Could that have been part of their plan?"

"There isn't enough information to tell at this point," said Mika.

"We wondered if you could help us on that one. Have you found anything else worth exploring during your scans of the surface?"

"Yes, two more 'settlements' exactly like the one you are near almost exactly the same distance from each other as they are to you. It's where the other signals are coming from to the satellite."
"So a geosynchronous triangle. Anything else unusual about them?"

"Not really, only that visual scans suggest they are older than your Memphis location, as there is a light layer of dust on the structures, making scans of them a bit difficult. We find the signal being sent to the orbiting satellite, same as there is from your location. It

allows for continuous broadcast despite the rotation of the asteroid. All three places are near outcrops of rock likely thrown up by
meteor impacts and all three have shown traces of lithium on our
scans. It looks like you are right where you outta be."

"There is a remarkable coincidence that all these places are config-
ured exactly the same. Or no coincidence at all."

"We have to go inside the buildings at Memphis and explore," said
Martin. "If the signals stopped the moment we locked into our
touchdown then it's fair to suggest that the beacon was set to
draw someone in and once they demonstrated interest the beacon
was turned off."

"Why would they want us to come here. It's not a mayday beacon.
There is no evidence of anyone here. Why would the beacon be
set for us?" Bolrenko asked.

"That's what we are here to find out," said Jimmy Ho Yang, his
voice coming from the com, while he completed his scans of the
surface. "Maybe it wasn't set for us."

"Ja, we should begin a systematic exploration of each building,"
said Bolrenko. "I think one of us should stay here in Spike as a
rotating safety valve. Two exploring Memphis at a time and one
here sifting whatever we find to improve the efficiency of our
exploration while staying in contact with Nautilus. We can proceed
as necessary."
After a rest period Bolrenko and Fielding made for the buildings
with Martin configuring the data they had already collected to plan
future expeditions. The away team decided to explore the two
buildings nearest the Lander in case they need help quickly. They
stayed together to see how they could gain entrance. The first
building was only about three meters in height and did not have an
obvious door. After a bit of exploration around the perimeter

Fielding found five rounded buttons, almost indistinguishable from the rivets which were found in a regular pattern around the conical building. They were about half a meter off the ground.

"Here, these appear to be buttons," she said, leaning over and pushing one. Nothing.

"It's almost like a key pad. Perhaps it's a combination lock," said Bolrenko.

"Do you think they would have to lock up their property here?"

"Perhaps not. Still, there seems no other indication on how to get inside."

As Bolrenko pushed at the sides of the building trying to find an entrance, Fielding pushed the buttons. Nothing. Then she tried several combinations - the first button and then the second, the first and third and continued on that path for a while without success.

"Hey, let's do this," said Bolrenko, who moved up to the buttons and pushed the third button three times. There was a hiss, and the outline of a small door appeared, perhaps a meter in height. It popped open. Bolrenko gave it a light push and clicked inward and then swung open.

"How did you know that?"
"It was part of the code that was sent. Remember three 3s, then 9 nines."

"I wonder what the 9 nines are for?"

He shone a light inside and waved Fielding over to see as well. Inside there were several low benches, a double stack of low platforms with material on them and some equipment with what appeared to be screens and some interface device.

Bolrenko boldly stepped inside, or at least as boldly as one could when doubled over to little more than a meter in height. He asked Fielding to watch for snags on his space suit and to make sure the door stayed open. He went directly to some of the equipment and as he touched it a picture appeared, a hologram centered between small poles which looked like antenna. After a moment it focussed and displayed what appeared to be a tunnel with a machine inside and a large bucket half full of rocks.

"Exploration party? Do you read?" crackled the comm. Bolrenko acknowledged.

"Lights have been activated in the shaft areas on the other side of the Lander. We are picking up transmissions but are unsure of what they are."

"Yes, we have found some equipment and have activated it. I have a broadcast hologram of a tunnel with some devices in it - frankly, it looks like a mine."
"It appears that this is some confirmation of an alien mining camp, given those pictures and the shafts we explored," said Fielding.

"It sure has that look. We will have to explore further. The settlement does appear to be abandoned, so why would it send a strong laser light signal towards our Earth. Are we the closest? Did they need help?

"We need to conduct an extensive survey of whatever is here. Perhaps they had mined out the lithium and Earth was the next closest identified source."

"Well, maybe, but you don't set up a laser signal to no one, they signalled in their fashion for a reason."

The next day they began the exploration in earnest, and noticed that the gravity on Rugby had lessened significantly. They were back to bobbing around like they were using particularly efficient pogo sticks. In fact, while exploring the smaller buildings they had perfected a technique of squatting, and then launching themselves forward feet-first through the low doors, while swinging their feet underneath their bodies to catch themselves before they fell.

After two weeks of rotating missions to the various buildings and to the tunnel entrances it became apparent that the settlement was indeed a mining camp. It appeared to have been mining for lithium, most of which was gone leaving only small traces. The camp and the others on this asteroid were likely abandoned when there was no more lithium. Like the small buildings, much of the equipment was at one half Earth scale.

"We have seen only traces of lithium left, but there are no traces of anything else. I find that odd," said Ho Yang during a full crew communication session. "Could it be that they used the lithium as a catalyst in whatever operation they were conducting. There are no other heavy metals here, not even traces that you might expect."

"Except the whole asteroid is made of iron and lead."

"Okay they wanted everything here but that. Otherwise they would have not left any asteroid, and simply consumed the whole thing."

"Could that be their intention, maybe they've used lithium as a catalyst to sweep the asteroid of anything except the iron and lead and now they can use it for whatever purposes they have?"

"I guess that is possible, but it doesn't seem efficient to sweep every little trace element and leave only the base iron and lead. Unless of course this asteroid only contained large amounts of a few elements. I expect they would have seen cadmium and thorium at least with the other two and maybe even a bit of mercury - but they aren't here and either is anything else, except the gases in the atmosphere."

"It is strange," said Ho Yang. "Elements don't naturally separate themselves so much."

"This isn't Kansas anymore, Jimmy."

"Could they be capable of towing the asteroid to process it now that it has been swept down to base metals? Or could they have readied it to be processed in place?"

Explorations of the various sizes of buildings suggested the stature of the inhabitants was significantly smaller than Earth humans with many humanoids under a meter in height who appeared to run the camp, and did most of the administrative work. The assumption by the evidence was that the mining was done mostly by machine. There were several volumes of hand inscribed ledgers and Bolrenko was able to conjure up similar records on a holographic display he had managed to get turned on.

None of the other similar screens could be operated as they all appeared to need a security code to start. That led Fielding to surmise they were personal devices.

It appeared that the retreat from this place was orderly as very little was left behind save a few machines and devices that were large and heavy. Wandering around the camp they did find a small cemetery like area, with markers partly buried in the ground. The markers were inscribed with the same characters they had seen in other places in the settlement, an almost hieroglyphic looking script. They discussed disinterring anything that might be buried. If it was a cemetery they might desecrate the graves and lead who-ever dug them to be very angry. And if they found something what exactly would they do?

They did have hand held metal scanners but did not have any ground sonar that they could use. Scans of the area were negative. Martin pointed out that their scan settings might not allow them to pick up anything that might lay there, as the composition of the asteroid was heavily metallic.

After discussing the situation they decided to try to dig gently in three potential plots. If they found anything they would photo-graph it and scan it without moving it and then rebury it when they were done. They began digging in earnest, going down more than three meters. Digging revealed no bodies or evidence that any had lain there.

"Doesn't it strike you as odd that a culture with a technology apparently quite a bit ahead of ours still has some of the same approaches to things that we do currently, perhaps a bit more streamlined but essentially just upgrades of what we use?"

"I was thinking much the same thing. Though it struck me that Earth bound cultures going back thousands of years have some of the same concerns for the dead and thought processes that moderns have. Isn't that what we've determined to be the hallmark of civilization? This alien culture could be similar to ours but their technology could be anywhere, though it doesn't seem light years ahead of our own. I mean, we managed to travel here. They com-municate much as we do. They appear to have much the same social networks."

"We have to be careful, we might be projecting our own values and experiences on what we find. Further investigation might prove things are much different," said Mika.

"Do you really believe that Mika?" asked Donohue.

"Yes, I am trained to believe it. And it makes good sense to avoid prejudging what we find."

"You are right as usual, Mika. But everything we see and experience is done through our own experiences. Even if I go to Japan or China, life is very different compared to Texas, but pared down to its essence, its identical. We both eat, we both procreate and have family concerns, we both build our lives and we both have community contacts and issues. Successful civilizations are implicitly concerned about these things, about building up and not tearing down."

"So how do we ascertain that approach here?"

"It's evident just from the mining. But also in the apparent personal devices that exist and the fact that there are no bodies of any dead left behind."
The exploration continued, slowly at first but more rapidly as they became familiar with the settlement and its details.

Perhaps the oddest finding was that the largest of the buildings, those measuring up to eight meters in height, were dormitories. But they did not house larger numbers of the small beings, they apparently housed the same number of humanoids as the smallest buildings did, but the bunk areas and desk chairs were built much larger, for beings that were perhaps more than five meters in height. The doors matched this apparent difference but the technical equipment did not, it remained standard at about one-half Earth size across the entire settlement.

These living areas had fewer of the screen devices in them. The buildings that were medium in height, about five meters tall, appeared to be mostly storage units. They contained shelving, some machines and machine parts.

"These ledgers are most interesting," said Fielding. "I would like to get back to the Nautilus and reference my library to see if I can figure out what they mean. The devices also display some of the same script and more besides. Is it possible to take the device with us and have it still operational?"

"Bolrenko thinks not, that it is tied into some power source and we would not be able to make it work," said Martin. "I'd like to try to gerry-rig an electrical power source and feed it into one of these things. If we can get it to work we are in business, it would be worth taking one or two home with us. I'm not even sure they work electrically. It might be some other power source that we are not familiar with. Prior to trying to jump the power you should take photos of the screen display and get a sense of what is there so you can try to decode it if things go wrong. Once that is done I'll make my effort, failing will make no difference at that point, though we will not have saved all the effort recording the screenshots."

"Yes, I suppose that is the only way to proceed," said Fielding. "I can't help but think this language looks very similar to something I've seen. It is very cubic, almost runic, especially in the ledgers, though there are some rune combinations that look hieroglyphic where it appears to be entered by hand. Perhaps a short form. The screen characters are more rounded and regular, not at all for certain the same language. Though likely they are the formal, more precise version of it - like our handwriting and printed letters and words."

"Surely there are only so many cuts or slash type marks that can be made in any runic language, they must all appear to be the same, or at least similar?"

"Yes, they are, but I can only discern the eight cardinal directions in these and there appear to be only a few special characters or multiples of character. I'll have to take a closer look," she said. She ran the types of runic languages through her mind. She thought of hieroglyphic languages like Egyptian where the glyphs are more like Chinese characters, one symbol to one idea, thought or action. This didn't seem to be like that, the glyphs were too simple. So perhaps she thought, it was a runic language where the runes were all the same and their relationship to each other is what gave meaning. Again, a quick scan suggested that the marks themselves had some differences and were simple, more like a very simplistic alphabet, where each symbol represented a sound, and sounds were combined for produce words and meaning.

She knew deciphering the runes would be difficult without some sort of Rosetta Stone to help. Even if it were simply two alien languages which said the same thing, it would be a starting place to help decipher the meaning which lay hidden in the symbols.

After searching out the whole settlement area the team concentrated on the mine operation. Much of the heavy machinery was left in place, though there was evidence that some had been removed.

There was no evidence of how the mine workers moved the material to the surface nor how it was processed into a pure form.

"Surely they didn't carry the ore up by hand and then transport it off the asteroid in that form," said Bolrenko. "There must be mine tailings and some evidence of how they moved it around. They must have processed it here. The effort to get it from here precludes the ability to refine it and take it away in a pure form."

"Don't forget, they appear to have tamed gravity somehow. They may have simply used machines to dig and process before they used some anti-gravity device to transport it out of the mine and off world," said Martin. "Maybe they simply processed it out of the ground - like sucking on a straw, taking the purified elements out with antigravity?"

The explorers did find large platforms of a similar material to that which was used as a foundation for the buildings in the settlement area. Given their random locations, it was evident that these platforms moved in some way. Martin studied them for a time but was unable to ascertain what they were made of, though they did have traces of lithium on them.

"Up! Go! Start!" Martin tried various commands to get the platforms to operate. "Abracadabra!" The platforms were un-moved.

"Nice try Renaud, but I'm guessing if they move at all, they are not calibrated to English commands."

"Everything else is," said a clearly annoyed Martin.

"That's only on Earth," said Bolrenko, with a smile. "English has clear advantages. The English speakers don't have to learn another language."

"C'est la vie," said Martin. "The platforms are clearly some kind of alloy I think but the lithium is only a trace on the surface, it isn't part of the alloyed material. I guess we shouldn't be too surprised to find things that confound us, amongst the leftovers of an alien civilization."

The Lander team completed their surveys and their exploration and they broadcast their findings back to the Nautilus and thence back to Earth, knowing the signals would only precede them by a short time.

Martin prepared Spike to leave the surface. They had found the source of the signals which appeared to be a beacon of some kind, though they were still at a loss to know why the signal had been sent, other than surmising that they were signaling that the asteroid had been completely mined out. The signal had been sent in 22 specific directions, with a laser light beam, which was aimed at several planets spread through space and also aimed at a number of asteroids in the same immediate area. Earth was the furthest body from the source of these signals. Donohue confirmed that the Moon's orbit around the Earth intersected the signal far more often than it intersected with Earth. In fact it was a rare chance that the signal had been seen on Earth at all.

The four other signals were directed at planets, all of which appeared to be in the Goldilock's zone around their various stars. The planets were of varying size but never more than 102 million miles from their star, nor closer than 86 million miles. Other than that there was nothing particularly exceptional about the exo-planets. Studies of the light array they presented suggested mostly oxygen and nitrogen and a combination of smaller concentrations of neutral gases in their atmosphere.

The astronauts discovered what appeared to be a stone tablet with an inscription which displayed the runic type of text they had seen on some of the screen schematics.

Fielding had taken photos of that and any other text on doorways or on cabinets as well as a huge number of shots of the holographic screen displays in order to begin an systematic attempt to decipher the language.

She had spent quite a bit of time trying to understand the symbols. Deciphering the language before they left the asteroid would have been a huge advantage in their explorations. So while the others toiled on the surface exploring, Fielding was left most often in the

Lander to monitor the others progress by radio and through drone operations while she worked on decoding the language. It was frustrating work with very little to go on. Where specific things in the settlement were labeled she first tried to ascertain if the label was a short form or a pictograph or a hieroglyph of whatever apparent function was labelled.

It appeared from their studies of the settlements that there were a number of very large humanoids, up to four meters tall with massive bodies and likely a corresponding huge strength.

According to records in the memory banks, where photos existed, they appeared to have done much of the heavy work necessary on the outpost. The aliens themselves presented in photos and video as extremely human-like with the same relative make up as beings on Earth - in fact remarkably so, except for the huge variation in height, and some minor differences in detail, just unusual enough to remain outside of normal Earth parameters, such as an extra crease in the ear lobe, or very small palms in relation to finger length.

It also appeared that the huge beings were not overly intelligent as there were images of them in what appeared to be classroom settings - learning very elementary things like counting and simple written language. Some of the background in the images suggested how the runic language was constructed but the pictures were incomplete and only hinted at the composition of the forms and how they were used. Still, it was valuable information.

The rest of the humanoids were quite small in stature, not much more than a meter in height, and they were slight of build, strong enough compared to their size but wholly unable to master the huge bulky tasks of the larger beings.

"The Larges and the Smalls," said Bolrenko. "The Smalls seem to be the administrators and did the fine and more complex work, like accounting and machinery mechanics, while the Larges were the worker bees. Were the large beings slaves?"

"It seems as if their society here was something everybody was familiar with, there was no sense of pressure on the Larges, at least that I can see. No evidence of punishment or security systems. I do not think they were slaves, though they appear to be an underclass."

"On Earth there developed a single kind of human, with enough variations that it has caused strife and tension among them. This society, whoever they are, seems to have developed more than one kind of humanoid but there is no tension between them," said Martin. "They look like us. Perhaps not exactly in the same proportions but they would not look out of place on Earth, except for their sizes."

"Don't forget the Neanderthals," said Mika Oh from the Nautilus. "Earth had different humanoids but they did not survive into the modern era. It appears that wherever these people originated that was not the case."

"So we have determined that these aliens did not originate on this asteroid?"

"There is no evidence of long habitation, nor any evidence of agriculture or farming on any scale. The population at its height, if every settlement was being used at the same time, was probably no more than 1,000 and that was divided between the Larges and the Smalls perhaps 60-40 with the Larges predominating."

"It's obvious this was a mining camp where they collected lithium or what they mined left a lithium residue," said Jimmy Ho Yang, the Chinese engineer who remained on the Nautilus. His voice was processed and transmitted very clearly. He might as well have been in the same room.

"In China such an outlier camp would maximize its resources. So the bunks would be at least double shared and the output would be larger. People here would likely sign on for a term. Given the distances to any of the potential home planets, that term could be a decade or more in length. I would estimate the population at least double the previous determination, assuming resources were being utilized to their fullest."

"An interesting take on it Jimmy," said Donahue. "They must have some other method to attract people to work in these camps, and be away from their homes for years."

"It's not always money or resources that induces people to make their choices, my fine American friend," said Jimmy through clenched teeth.

"Aye, you are right. Could this have been a prison where the mining was incidental? Surely those kinds of incentives have been known before," he looked innocently at Jimmy.

"Certainly that's a possibility but there is no evidence of coercion, or security, not even real locks on the doors. We got into the buildings easily. The entry code was the same on all buildings and really was more a function of opening the airlock, which you would not likely want to do accidentally. And the screen images show no suggestion of punishment. Everyone seems to be hard at work and doing so quite willingly," said Mika.

"We are out in space - years of sophisticated travel from any potential civilization. If this was a prison it is pretty secure in itself. Sort of like Siberia, right Ivan?"

"Or Australia," he shot back.

"Touche," said Martin.

"Or Devil's Island," said Jimmy.

"Alright, I think we've established the desire for secure prisons. I just don't see any real evidence that this was a prison, unless the Larges or the Smalls were the prison population and the other were the guards. And the ratio between them doesn't make sense if it's a prison. But that seems to be the only divide."

The surface team continued to gather evidence of the settlements and took hundreds of thousands of photos, and 3D scans until virtually every inch of all three settlements were recorded. Donahue directed the surface team to explore the information storage device and its power source. They took as many screen shots as possible, and once having completed that, explored the workings of the device.

Bolrenko found the device used a power cell of unknown intricacy. They removed it from the device and were able to reconnect it, as it merely slid into a slot in the machine. The machine was tethered to some network and once it was severed it would conduct power but it would not operate as it had before. They decided to stow it and the power source card on the Lander to bring back to Earth. They reasoned that there was the possibility of a technological advancement in that machine.

"What seems odd is that we are not seeing a lot of high end technology which would be expected from a interstellar intelligence."

"Yeah, I'd been thinking the same thing. But how would that technology look if we weren't seeing it being used?"

"Right. However, there aren't a lot of machines lying around that we cannot see the obvious use for. In the mines themselves there are a few obvious earth cutters and tunnel diggers. Perhaps they took all the most interesting technology with them when they left?"

"They must have. There does appear to be a manipulation of gravity which is still operable. And the materials used in construction have an immense density. It must be a new technology for creating metals of highly dense alloy. There is nothing but the info terminals left in the crew quarters areas of the storage buildings. They must have had machines for nourishment and space suits for surface travel, if the scans of the other connected planets are right in showing a much different atmosphere with oxygen."

The Lander team continued to puzzle out the basis of the settlements and found things remarkably similar in the other two settlements on the asteroid. In fact, so similar that it appeared that the settlements were pre-fabricated to match each other. Only the placements of things inside the buildings or the mines were different from the original.
"If we are calling the first 'town' we visited Memphis, what are the other two?" asked Jimmy.

"Well we didn't linger in those places very long once it became obvious they were copies of Memphis. Do they really need names?"

"As identifiers, it's necessary. So, as bored as I am here in Nautilus waiting for your return, perhaps we can try to name them. I'm thinking we keep with the themes. So it's either places in Tennessee, Egyptian cities, very lonely places or perhaps lonely places in Tennessee with Egyptian names?"

"You have too much time on your hands, Commander. You need a hobby."

"All the same, start thinking. While I wait, this is my hobby."

The team had been on Spike for almost two months of Earth time when they decided they had everything they could carry and photos of everything they could not.

"Now the real work begins trying to piece this all together. We have time on our hands, at least. It would be great if we could return to Earth with all the answers."

"Yes it would, but let's first consider immediate issues. I'm leaning to Luxor and Alexandria but I could be convinced otherwise. Maybe Nashville and Tupelo?"

"Tupelo is in Arkansas."

"Shouldn't we be concentrating on the task at hand?"

"I thought this was the task at hand . . . surely we have plenty of time to consider all the other stuff. Like five years. I don't know about you but I will need some down time between exploratory revelations."

Mika sighed. "Yes, of course, you are right. Something lighthearted for a while then we will switch to real work."

"Ah Mika, you need to take a break from work sometimes."

"That's what my professors said. My parents however, disagreed."

While the group pondered the naming question they were checking source information to continue their inquiries into what they had discovered.

"We have telemetry on the four other laser beams that were

directed at planets. It appears from information in the local storage system that one was their home planet. Located about 1.8 light years away from the present position of the asteroid. Our orbital data suggests it is only a short while past its closest point of about 1.4 light years and balloons out to about three light years distant at the most, given the orbit of this asteroid as well. Interestingly our studies show it travels quite slowly, so it completes an orbit of the same star as the home planet, in about 20 years," said Donahue.

"That suggests people could shuttle out to the asteroid in only a year or three. With travel times like that you would be more in-clined to stay for a while. However, these were likely two way trips," said Jimmy.

I've also noticed that the probable home planet is quite large by Earth standards, perhaps as much as two or 2.5 times the size of Earth and scans indicate the surface has liquid water."

"What about the other lasers and the planets they pointed to?"
"Remarkably the same. In this little section of the galaxy there are three more planets in the Goldilocks Zone that are all roughly the same size. What appears to be the home planet is the largest but the other three are only a bit smaller than the home planet."

"It stands to reason that Earth is the only other water and oxygen planet in the Goldilocks Zone that they've found at least within the distance that our Earth is from their home planet, at about 4.8 light years distant."

"We've been beaming our intel back to Earth, where it will arrive a bit before us, so our research in the interim will be valuable. Now we have to prepare for our return."

"And the laser directed at Earth was really directed to our Moon," said Jimmy. "Could there be a mining colony on the Moon? And why were the lasers maintaining contact - the light would take years to reach their destinations, so it cannot be a communications source."

"Not in the sense of a conversation," said Donohue. "However, perhaps it is just a system of contacts showing themselves where they've already been?"

"Or an early warning system that their little group of planets has been compromised from the outside," said Fielding. "Remember, the signal beacon stopped once we reached the surface. It might take a while for anyone to take note, but that would be an indication that someone had stopped by."

Spike was prepared for a lift off. Outside of the settlement areas the asteroid had little of its own gravity and for a little while the settlements appeared to be generating some gravity of their own, or at least in their own vicinity. That lasted only a day or two after the Lander settled. Calculations were made based on the effect of the existing local gravity on the surface team, with the possibility that the higher gravity would be restarted by the actions of their take off from the surface. The rocket engines were set to provide enough lift.

"Okay, everybody set," he looked at the control panel. "Check."

"Everything secured, settings corrected, rocket thrust set and ready for activation? Check."

"Deactivating the landing spikes to disengage," she flicked a switch and the Lander rocked slightly, tilting a touch to one side.

"Throttling up."

The spherical ship rocked gently and lifted slowly. Fielding looked at Martin with a furrowed brow. He remained concentrated on the instrument panel. Spike should have been rising faster.

Martin frowned, immediately thinking that take-off had activated the higher level of gravity near Memphis. He increased the power to the engines. The veins in his neck started to bulge as if he was exerting the effort of the rocket engines and not just the worry of unexpected resistance.

The Lander was not pulling free of the gravity. It was climbing from the surface but not at the steady speed necessary. After a minute of thrust and perhaps 50 meters gained in altitude Martin throttled back. He could feel the Lander lock into a steady descent though he was afraid to give in to the pull entirely and provided a bit of upward thrust to ensure a very soft landing. He activated the lateral thrusters to move the Lander away from Memphis. They travelled several kilometers, thinking that this would get them out of the artificial gravity's range.

"We need more thrust, in the event the artificial gravity has more range than you anticipate."

"I can feel a bit of pull on us, more than the artificial gravity. We didn't see any reference to a gravity hold or a tractor beam? I'm going to recalibrate and try again."

"I have seen evidence of the gravity in their records but nothing about how it is generated or where it is, or how it might affect spacecraft on takeoff," said Fielding. "In fact the effect was so slight on landing that I'd almost forgotten about it."

"Yeah, but remember the reduction in gravity from our first away mission to the second, there was a distinct shift. Okay, here we go," said Martin as he powered up. This time the Lander shook more violently, obviously fighting an increase in strength of the artificial gravity. The Frenchman strained and applied more power, as if the gravity had a hold on him rather than the ship he controlled. Now Spike was heavily engaged in trying to break free and the asteroid was gearing up its hold to match the increasing thrust.

"Reserve power levels are dropping, 50 per cent, 45 per cent, 40 . . ." said Bolrenko. "If we don't go full thrust now we might have only one more chance to escape Asteroid Rugby."

Martin had to make a quick decision. A few seconds ticked by. It seemed much longer as the fear of being stuck on the asteroid welled up in each member of the landing party.

Bolrenko and Fielding were on edge. The ship was shaking violently, on the verge of dangerously vibrating past structural tolerance. A vial of fluid, strapped to a cabinet, shook loose and fell, breaking on the floor. The liquid inside seemed ready to lose its integrity as the hold of gravity on it was so slight. Fielding threw a large absorbent towel over it as she could not leave her chair. She wondered why the gravity on the fluid was negligible but on the Lander itself it was immense.

Then all the tension drained from Martin's face, his decision made. He pulled back gently on the thrust and let the Lander drift into the gravity lock. Spike was about 100 meters above the surface and was sinking back slowly. Martin fiddled with some of the attitude controls. At 20 meters, Martin quickly engaged the thrusters, and threw the Lander into a quick but controlled 180 degree spin. The Lander stopped descending. Martin grinned. He increased the thrust gently and the Lander soared smoothly away from the surface, devoid of the gravitational pull of the asteroid and was quickly several miles above Rugby and moving to the Nautilus.

"Houston we have broken free of the gravity pull and will begin orbit matching manoeuvres upon reaching your orbital plane," said Martin. "Spike will initiate docking with Nautilus as soon as we can attain the necessary position."

"Acknowledged Spike."

Fielding was staring at Martin, still in shock, waiting for him to acknowledge what had just happened. He did not look at her but was awaiting her comments. She was waiting for him to acknowledge the results. He wanted to remain cool in command but inside he was shaken.

Finally Martin, feeling her stare on his face, turned to her. He tried to remain impassive but he could not stop himself from flashing something between a smirk and a knowing grin.

"That was quite the demonstration of flying by feel. I haven't seen that since my crop duster days," said Fielding. "What tipped you off to the need to turn?"

Martin turned away and refocused on the controls, monitoring the readings.

"You know, I'd love to have some wonderful explanation that pointed to my flying experience, but for some reason it just seemed the right thing to do."

"Maybe that is your flying experience."

"With the hold on us continuing once we left the surface and even beyond the point that we first felt it when we landed, I figured there had to be some easy way to release it. The lack of gravity on that broken vial made me think the gravity pull was on the Lander only. The spin turn was my immediate choice. It made more sense than a somersault," he laughed.

Once the gravity was released the towel on the floor began to absorb the now weightless spilt vial of liquid and held the glass shards fairly close together until Fielding and Bolrenko could shed their safety harnesses and move about the Lander in zero gravity. The spill was quickly cleaned up with the remnants bagged and the Lander inspected for damages inside an out.

"I'm not sure we would have had enough power for another attempted take off," said Bolrenko as he inspected the readouts. "We are down to 25 per cent, plenty for what we need to do now, but not enough to punch through that gravity generator. There must be some sort of significant power generator on the asteroid that we did not see."

"Or that we did see but didn't know what it was."

"I'm not sure that all our power would have punched through. That feeling we had of being grabbed and locked into our orbit and then landing must be real. It would be good technology to have. If most accidents take place on takeoff and landing, having a grip on aircraft during these critical times would vastly reduce accidents.

"That's the pilot in you talking. Imagine all the other applications of a zero gravity field, or the ability to turn up the gravity effect at will."

The Nautilus reported that they were sending a steady stream of data back to Earth and would join that data stream when they docked with Spike and initiated the return flight.

"So as we fly back to Earth, about six years will go by and our data will arrive almost all at once just before we do? Essentially they will begin to get the telemetry and information we provide only a few days before we arrive?"

"Sort of, more like a few months. With our speed up and slow down manoeuvres, we will arrive a few months after most of the data. We have begun sending the data and we will soon commence our return flight, broadcasting our findings all the while. We've been sending our data transmissions during this time and will continue to send. Eventually they will reach Earth and mission control there will know about our progress and will expect us to arrive a year or so after they receive the first transmissions at the beginning of our investigation of the asteroid. All the travel times are expected as was the amount of time we took to investigate. They will be prepared for us though the timing will be a bit hit and miss as we will not arrive until about a year after they begin to receive our data from Spike. It's all about the acceleration up to light speed and the gearing down that takes time. That's why our efforts over the next six years will be the investigative jump they need. Earth scientists will have a little time with the data just before we arrive, having just sent them the results of our six years of study."

"Remember, we aren't exactly five light years away. It's actually a bit less. The problem is we have to gear up to light speed and we have to slow down from light speed. Each maneuver will take several months of the time we travel, just like it did on the way here."

"So they will actually have some of our telemetry a little quicker?"

"Yeah, ultimately as we slow down they will get our transmissions quicker as the transmissions are moving faster than we are - the data stream will stretch out and be received more slowly. Assuming of course that we are still transmitting data. And I suppose we will at least be sending results of our own experiments and research into our travels. It doesn't make much difference though as we will have much more time to study this data than they will before we arrive."

"And remember for us, about two years will have passed. If Einstein was right, and all indications are that he is, our friends and relatives will be about 12 - 14 years older in physiological terms. That will take a bit of getting used to."

Chapter Five

The Nautilus began its long journey home. And the astronauts settled into their personal routines, sandwiched around their flight and research duties.

Fielding began a systematic study of the runic language that she found on the asteroid. There were many sources of text as the aliens had labelled many installations and places. Correlating the runes to the places and their apparent functions seemed a good way to start.

She would have plenty of time to try to decipher the language through the thousands upon thousands of photos she had acquired. Some were photos of installations and others were screen shots of the information output from the device they were able to operate. Many had pictures attached which gave some hint to the language used to describe them.

"With all the ways to convey information you have to be partial to print, even if it seems drab compared to film, holograms, music and theatre among others. At the end of the day, printed language is the only thing with any permanence. Look at our storage systems, even for print, I cannot easily get a copy of a file I wrote even 20 years ago as the retrieval system has changed so much. In fact, if I didn't know what old storage systems looked like I could easily overlook them and all the knowledge they contain."

"So you think that what we thought was a chair on the surface was really a hard drive?"

Fielding shot him an exasperated look.

"So it's not really about print, or the mode of holding information, it's actually about the storage system?"

"Yeah, in the end the good old book is still king. The book is actually the storage system. All that's required is an education in reading the code, or words. Gutenberg for all his faults beats Steve Jobs as an innovator."

"Print has its charms," said Renaud. "And I guess for pure information storage it is hard to beat, but what about video and still photos. A picture's worth a thousand words, right?"

"And what about song, music and words? The music evokes a mood or feeling that the words add to. In the end, the music or tune makes the words almost unforgettable," said Mika.

"I was talking about information storage, but I get both your points. Other formats have value. Though it could be argued that music is really a different kind of information. Now, what's the song about quantum physics again?"

"I could make one up if necessary. It has a beautiful melody."

"Yeah, but it would be about teaching basic concepts. The melody is really for memory. Would you use a song to pass on first run research?"

"I'm a bit of an iconoclast. I might do that," said Renaud. "In fact I did put my undergraduate thesis in avionics to music, or at least part of it."

"I didn't know that you were a composer."

"No, I'm not, I just changed the words to a bit of Sinatra. 'Fly me to the moon, take me to the stars . . . ' " he began to sing.

Fielding laughed, "Okay, I get it. Next thing you know you'll have Ivan crooning Elvis avionics bullet points."

"It ain't nothing but lift, the wind crying on the wings . . . "

"Nooo! Five years of this is too much. Perhaps your digressions will become the stuff of graduate students studies into the psychological affects of lengthy space flight."

Bolrenko was engaged in putting together a study of the settlements and the likely use of all the buildings and equipment. He had taken to calling the other settlements Nashville and Tupelo even though the only real distinguishing mark was the order in which they explored them. He tried to assign the largest of the buildings the name Graceland but it didn't really suit it and it didn't stick among the astronauts, as too many buildings looked too much alike. On occasion they referred to the larger buildings as the Graceland size but even that really didn't play.

Martin was working on trying to understand the technology they had encountered, the gravity generator, the screen based information systems, the power sources, the high density construction materials and the mining equipment. Ho Yang joined him.

"The anti-gravity thing must have been big. There is no evidence of wheels anywhere. The mining containers don't have them. There is nothing anywhere that has wheels.

"Maybe they are like the Inca - no wheels."

"Maybe they are the Inca."

"No the Inca civilization fell, it's more likely the Maya. They just disappeared in the middle of dinner."

"Or more likely were interrupted by invaders in the middle of dinner and didn't have a chance to come back for their aperitif," said Martin with a grin.

"Now we French, we always have time to consider our future over a glass of wine and a plate of cheeses."

"The Maya had corn bread."

"So did Elvis. And grits."

"Ever have grits?"

"Yes, and once was enough."

"You are hereby banned from the South."

"Except for Florida."

"That means no bouillabaisse?"

"In Florida?"

"No in Nice."

"Is it nice in Nice?"

"Shut up."

"Ferme la bouche? It's the only French I know."

"I'm sure you know more. Oui?"

"Okay, Renaud, you win. I know much French. Like Paris. Capeche?"

"That's Italian."

"So was my grandmother."

"You two realize that your words will be recorded for those who study the mission," said Mika.

"I know. I want them to understand my heritage and my quick wit," said Fielding with a smile.

"They will never understand your French," said Martin.

"Ah Renaud, you are my favorite Martin," she said.

He thought for a moment, "And I Dream of Jenni-fer."

Mika Oh was primarily responsible for communications and was beaming evidence and hypothesis to Earth. She wondered if the mission telemetry went at the same time as their private conversations. Perhaps these conversations were to be used to understand the strains of lengthy space travel and collected only after they returned to Earth. Everyone had their moments of stir

115

crazy. The fact they didn't all go off at the same time seemed to lend the episodes an air of amusement rather than foreboding. Usually a sharp word or two was all it took to bring things on board back to reality. That and a good night's sleep.

Fielding was pouring over her ciphers. She was actually going over stored texts on the art and history of runic languages as she had hit a brick wall in terms of deciphering the runic language found at the alien site.

She often worked in the central part of the astronauts living area, mostly because she didn't mind the interruptions, they helped clear her mind as she referenced some other difficult cipher jobs, trying to see if the key to the success of those jobs could be used for this one. Once it was evident that any quick and easy translation was not going to happen, Fielding had taken a long term, systematic approach to her task - she knew she had the time available.

"Damn it, I just can't see it. We have access to huge amounts of written language, this shouldn't be so hard. I feel like an idiot on my first experience breaking a code," she said out loud.

Unaccustomed to her saying anything about her project the other astronauts looked at her and then at each other.

"You are not an idiot, it's a totally alien language. It likely does not conform to Earth based languages," said Jimmy. "It's kind of like Marco Polo trying to understand Chinese characters."

Fielding looked at him, almost as if she hadn't opened the door to his comment, like she had been unaware she voiced her frustrations aloud.

"At least Chinese is an Earth language. The things they describe are the same even if the culture is not. There is a huge field of language theory and code breaking that I presume you are unaware of," she said. "I have tried to reacquaint myself with this background stuff. Our current problem is very frustrating. Even Italians had a vague understanding of Chinese character pictographs."

"And that was acquired by people over time who were exposed to the Chinese. All I'm saying is that we are all smart; intelligent within the expertise we bring to this group. If you can't do it, none of us here could do it."

"Oh, I don't know," said Donohue. "I'm not a cipher expert but likely we've all been exposed to it. Sometimes all that knowledge and intelligence clogs up the synapses and clouds the solution. Someone else can cut through the clutter and see a clear path."

"There's the Zen again," said Fielding sardonically but with a slight, sly smile. Mika furrowed her brow.

"Are we all intelligent? Yes I would guess that all of us have tested and proven in the field that we are significantly more intelligent than the average person - else we wouldn't have been selected," said Donohue.

"That's not why we were chosen though, Mike," said Mika. "We all bring much more to the table than just intelligence. Some is quantifiable and much of it is simply out of the realm of brain power. Age, experience, professional background, fitness, mental probity, and maybe a bit of family connections, luck or good timing has much to do with it."

"How many here have fathers who served in the military?"

Everyone in the lounge space raised a hand.

"And Renaud Martin down in the storeroom does too. How many

of your father's ended their military careers as Colonels or Generals?" All raised their hands.

"And how many of your father's were supreme commanders of their national forces, the equivalent of a Major General in the States or a Field Marshall in some European countries?"

Nobody raised their hands.

"Curious humm," said Mika. "We are all children of soldiers with exceptional service records, people who rose very highly in the ranks and people who are proven and capable. Do you think that is an accident?"

"Then why is nobody here attached to the top guys?"

"I expected that. They wanted people who were comfortable in leadership positions, as we are all leaders of some aspect of this mission. They wanted people whose background suggested stability and levelheadedness, and they wanted people who were not at the top of the generational heap. Either because those people were not expendable or they would not work well in collaboration with others. It's almost as if the leaders of tomorrow had already been chosen."

"But what is intelligence? Obviously in putting this mission together, intelligence was not the highest priority," said Donohue.

"That's quite a conclusion to draw. I could be insulted," said Mika.

"Intelligence isn't smarts, book smarts that is. Book smarts are just study, repetition, memory and belief. Intelligence isn't just the ability to think on your feet or problem solve or put together patterns of unalike things," said Fielding.

"You'd never know it from intelligence tests."

"Then what is it? What is the essence of intelligence?"

"Well, it could be all those things and more, but I've never given it much thought," said Mika with a shy smile. "But if pressed, I'd say it is related to self-awareness. Also, it's related to consciousness - in that there is an innate intelligence in every human but that level increases hugely when people are more aware of their place in the universe. Some people are just wired to use more of their brains."

"So that explains the sometimes random flash of intelligence in otherwise unexceptional people. But what about those who are always functioning at a higher level. Are we really the most intelligent people from Earth? Isn't that what Mike was trying to say," said Fielding.

"No, he said we were picked to join the mission because we are the most intelligent, or have demonstrated the ability to be intelligent consistently on a regular basis. I'm saying because we have this experience we will arrive back on Earth as the most intelligent due to this experience," Mika said.

"So, like I said intelligence isn't just being book smart, it's about background experience," said Donohue.

Commander Ho Yang was listening to the discussion. These types of exchanges were common. He rarely joined in as he felt it necessary to maintain some distance from the others as the Commander of the mission.

He was responsible primarily for piloting the ship and constantly watching its operations. Any problems among the crew were his to deal with. He had intervened quietly as it became apparent that Bolrenko and Oh were establishing a personal relationship. He did not forbid it, but asked that it be kept quiet and not made obvious to the other crew for some time. Such a lengthy voyage required co-operation and professionalism for the entire time.

He was responsible for everyone and everything on the Nautilus. He did not sleep well most of the time, though he did take a measure of calm when large amounts of data were transmitted. At least if something happened to them on the return trip, much of what they had learned would be in the hands of Earth scientists and their efforts would count for something.

His only slip had been to engage Renaud Martin on Indochina policy. Martin's grandfather and great uncle had died in unrest during the French adventures in Indochina. He was not sympathetic to the Chinese view of the area. Martin wasn't sympathetic to anyone's view of the area and wasn't going to let Ho Yang's intransigence and rank stop him from battling. Donohue and Fielding managed to remain out of the fray.

Eventually Martin became so agitated that he took a swing at Ho Yang who did not back down. The two grappled momentarily in zero gravity, and when Martin landed a heavy punch into Ho Yang's solar plexus it seemed the Frenchman had triumphed only to have the zero gravity affect the punch as a pushing off motion, rocketing Martin to the other side of the crew cabin and leaving Ho Yang surprised but unhurt, moving at equal speed in the opposite direction.

Martin started to laugh. Ho Yang, still angry with the issue at hand, and Martin's foolishness at turning such a disagreement physical, eventually laughed as well at the ridiculousness of the situation.

"If I could only land that shot to your guts, then French policy in Indochina would be vindicated and the entire Chinese civilization would have to admit I was right," said a straight-faced Martin.

Ho Yang stared at him confused by the sudden outburst. Martin cracked a smile, and Ho Yang, quite uncharacteristically, cracked up.

"The French are odd people, at least to my Chinese sensibilities," said Ho Yang. "If you went to Indochina and were so passionate, I understand why you did not last there. As different as they are to Chinese, they are more like us than you, and they take a very pragmatic view."

"We should have figured that out before we tried to get involved in Southeast Asia. We had plenty of that same experience in hundreds of years with the English," said Martin.

"And the Germans, too," said Fielding.

"Especially the Germans."

The crew decided that their experience of releasing a ball outside the ship to help them track their progress was a good idea from a morale standpoint so they undertook the effort again. Once they reached their full speed they readied the task. This time they were even more careful in the ball's release, trying to align it better with the ship's flight path in hopes of keeping it alongside them for longer.

However, while the ball at first seemed to run alongside them perfectly, after a couple of months travel it was evident that the free moving ball was ever so slightly misaligned and would intersect their own flight path at some point in the future.

"When? asked a worried Ho Yang.

"I've done the calculations based on the measurements of its angle of flight and . . . . "

"When?" asked Ho Yang sharply.

"I expect the ball to touch the side of our hull in three years time, right about the time we are required to begin our slowdown manoeuvres."

"Okay, that's not so bad. I think we need to brainstorm over what to do. It appears possible that if our speed reduction is done prior to contact we might avoid any collision. Please think on how else we can fix this problem," said Ho Yang. "It appears for now that we have a very interesting problem and our hope to observe the object has now been cast as an imperative to understand its exact position."

"I'll keep up the tracking measurements and report back to you about any changes to my current calculations," said Martin. "I expect we have to slow down at the necessary time to avoid contact. And if that is a bit early, no harm. If it is a lot early, the expectation of our arrival home could be out by some time - weeks or perhaps months."

"Don't speculate Renaud. Let us deal in facts. Keep up the ball's tracking and think on it - other solutions are welcome. You can all demonstrate your apparent intelligence."

Chapter Six

Flash, United Nations . . . (New York, Geneva) The United Nations released a report from its probe to a distant asteroid from which mathematical and obviously intelligent signals were received more than 12 years ago.

Astronauts report evidence of what appears to be an abandoned mining camp on the asteroid.

Astronauts named the asteroid Rugby due to its shape and spin which resembled a rugby ball, ovoid and spinning generally along its longest axis, much like a rugby ball in flight.

Reports from the returning ship say there was evidence that at one time there were two types of humanoid, with an appearance very like humans on Earth who lived on the asteroid. These groups appeared to live in harmony, though the precise nature of their interaction is unknown.

There was no life form on the asteroid when it was visited by Earth astronauts.

One type of being was large in stature and very strong. The other was perhaps only a half to a third as large and obviously not as physically strong as the larger type. Both humanoids were quite similar physiologically, possessing the same basic anatomy and body structure, which is quite similar to Earth populations.

There was evidence of technological advances in gravity manipulation and energy generation but according to reports from the explorers they were unable to understand or replicate the technology and can only verify its existence.

The space ship is expected to return to earth in a few months. Preparations are being made for landing and recovery of the astronauts. According to reports the six astronauts are all well, though they are significantly weaker due to the lack of use of their large muscle groups. They will be taken to Geneva for debriefing and rest before being presented to the public , a process expected to take several months.

In the meantime more information will be provided as it is delivered to Earth. The precise landing date will be known several days in advance."

-END-

Information from the mission began to trickle to Earth scientists after being redirected from mission control which began receiving a stream of data from the Nautilus several months prior to its touchdown. They all worked feverishly to decipher the known results of the mission. Technological specifications of some of the alien equipment found on the asteroid were also provided to Earth scientists for analysis.

Newspapers reported that the alien presence on the asteroid suggested a significant command of gravity, enhanced building techniques and materials, power resources and agriculture or at least food preservation and possibly space travel.

Earth scientists learned that the alien information systems appeared unremarkable technologically, though their language was thus far impenetrable. There was no evidence of medical issues, in fact it was remarkable only in the fact that there was so few references to medical issues and no instances of infirmity or age related concerns among any of the records retrieved.

They lived a remarkably Earth-like existence with obvious references to family relations on distant planets. Only the smaller stature of the beings compared to Earthlings and presence of the large version of the aliens, significantly larger than humans on Earth, seemed to be different from the style of living on Earth.

In the months prior to the landing, Earth media were inundated with bits of news, which they dutifully reported, but without details or analysis. Details were being held back until there was a greater understanding of the implications. While the public had now long been aware of the likelihood of extra-terrestrials and civilizations out in space, the confirmation of this fact was significant enough to occupy information and media outlets.

The general public was not given the information that the beacon laser beam had been aimed at the Moon. The space agency set up for the interstellar mission reconvened to arrange an exploratory mission to the dark side of the Moon. There was a high expectation that they would find a mining camp. Opinion was split as to whether that camp would be occupied. The mission was expected to launch several months after the other trip had concluded, once preliminary findings had been verified and some study completed. Astronauts were chosen and the craft built. Earth's Moon was a distant place but not unknown. Planning such a trip was fairly simple but creating it out of nothing required time.

Results coming back from the first mission suggested that First Contact had morphed into second contact, that is actual evidence of a civilization that was not from Earth. There was a strong sense that the third kind of contact had to be approached, and that was an actual face to face meeting with this alien civilization. And that might occur on the far side of the Moon.

Known photos of the region were scanned without much success. There were several possibilities for manmade objects but if there was a colony on the Moon it was likely built under the surface. Astrophysicists were excited, or as excited as another year long delay would allow. Various national intelligence services were nervous and counselled an exercise of caution. Much media speculation centered on technological advances.

That civilization and conditions on Earth were about to shift dramatically kept anyone with a stake in it very tense. And while the man on the street sensed the shift, it was those with hands-on responsibilities who worried the most. Unpredictability was not their chosen condition.

"I can see the advantages in the new technology, especially the anti-gravity stuff, but what about the potential down side?"

John Overholt was sitting with some friends in The Little Smoke-house Restaurant in Flagstaff waiting for their meals. Service was slow, but they didn't notice, it helped grease the conversation.

Allie sat across the table from him, but one over, beside Ethan, who was across from John, with a doctor friend of hers straight across the table, beside John. Ethan had been visiting John as the two had been asked to participate in a documentary financed by NASA regarding the imminent return of the space mission. Public relations were going to be managed and the curiosity built up for the moon mission.

They had kept in touch, as much from the necessity of their shared discovery as from the long friendship that had grown out of it.

"So what's it like living in paradise, Ethan?"

Allie's friend Katerina perked up.

"The heat is inconsistent. It's warm and sometimes really humid which is most uncomfortable, especially after living in the desert. The sea keeps that to a minimum though. At the top of the mountain it can be downright cold. And given the location it's always a little remote unfortunately. I will say life in my Hawaii is nice. I do like getting to Oahu once in a while, the charms of the city, you know. But returning to the Big Island is calming. It helps to focus my mind. That's how I know I'm having the full rack of ribs," he said closing his menu. "It's that Hawaiian ability to concentrate."

"I had never heard that about Hawaiians," Katerina said. "I've always wondered if it would be constricting to live on an island?"

"A string of islands, and it's pretty easy to get from one to another, though too expensive to do it very frequently," said Ethan. "But you know, I had forgotten the charms of the desert - no humidity, warm with cool nights and the feeling that anything you want is within reach. Okay, several days drive, but still within reach, sort of."

"Downside?" asked Allie, shifting Ethan back to John's serious question. "The alien technological advances cannot have a serious downside for us, can they?"

"I suppose they could Allie, but that's not what I was referring to. I agree the technology appears to be only a bit, though a significant bit, ahead of ours. It's the fact that we will miss the slower shift in culture if our societies had discovered these things themselves. The aliens have some period of time on us growing into what they have become. The difficulty in our adjusting might be directly correlated to how long that actually is or was. If there is a lengthy difference, the social aspect of change for us might be quite jarring."

"Unfortunately that is a difficult thing. Once the door is opened you cannot go back, unless you're Amish or something," Ethan laughed.

"Even the Amish move along with technology. They are perhaps properly in awe of how technology can change the social structure. So they move with very deliberate caution."

"So you're a social scientist now, John? So do we need to take the Amish approach with any alien tech?"

"Me, not really. But who knows," said John. "There may be medical advances that put you out of a job Allie. Me too. Word from NASA is there are some huge advances in controlling gravity. Mind blowing stuff which alone could transform our transportation sector and lead to who knows what unexpected, or unintentional consequences."

"Anything else you can share?" asked Allie's colleague.

"Apparently they have a much improved materials technology where they've found a new alloy technique with implications in building materials, and pretty much anything manufactured."

"Wow, I can see those things leading to major social change. So why is it unmanageable?"

"Once the word is out, and it already is, that human life can take a giant step, the pressure to provide these things wins out. And social consequences be damned," said John. "People have fought wars over far less."

"I can hardly wait," said Allie, "With some sort of gravity machine, I guess my ride up 11 floors to the hospital administration will be a bunch quicker."

"Think of all the applications of zero gravity in medicine."

"Imaging would be more precise, as the patients could be more easily positioned for readings. Moving people around the hospital just became simple, perhaps automated and gentler. Surgery could be improved without the force of gravity to contend with. It's not even my field, I expect you two could easily add to the list."

"I was with Allie, getting up a few floors would be easier and maybe I wouldn't be run off my feet. Though it strikes me that the elevator is really just a rudimentary anti-gravity device."

"I do find it interesting that as we find easier and easier ways to travel and move about, we are forced to contend with the reduction in our own locomotion and the need to keep our bodies moving. Old timey people moved enough in their daily lives so they didn't need additional exercise to stay healthy. Perhaps that is what led to the rise of adults remaining interested in kids sports well into their middle age."

"Hey, I just like playing tennis that's all," said Katerina.

"It will be interesting to see what exactly is going on with the discoveries and then what the next steps will be. I'm sure there is much more than we are getting. They need to spool it out slowly for social consumption. I cannot imagine that we will not pursue a face to face meeting with these aliens."

"Do you know that as an insider? Or is that just your personal speculation?" Ethan widened his eyes but said nothing.

"Funny thing is," said Ethan, "nothing much has really changed in the 12 or so years since the aliens were found. A few advancements of our own seem to be more directed to efficiency and reliability of manufactured goods, rather than some new mind-blowing tech that will change the world."

"The world has changed though," said John. "It's subtle - it's the understanding that things will change and change dramatically at some near date. It's like nobody is innovating; they are simply making those things we have and those things we use more efficient and of better quality. They all lay in wait for the other technological shoe to drop."

"Sort of like my mother," said Allie.

"Now we've been through that Allie. It will happen when it's meant to happen."

Allie nodded, but she thought it would have happened a few years ago; waiting had almost become unbearable.

Everyone had taken an uncomfortable breath. And then their food came - sparking a flush of relief from everyone at the table.

"They really take their time smoking all their meat," said John. "They have a real thing about quality."

He took a deep pull on his drink. They don't cut corners, he thought to himself. Perhaps Allie was right, There was a point where waiting would not improve the outcome.

"Are you ready?" he asked her.

"Yes, my steak should have been done by now."

"I mean really ready . . . " She stared at him, and gave a tiny, barely perceptible nod. He nodded back, ever so slightly.

Chapter Seven

Splash down had gone flawlessly. The astronauts were picked up by the nearest ship, a French aircraft carrier in the South Pacific, on a tour of French possessions in the Pacific and Indian oceans. The ship, La Marseilles had visited Reunion Island and New Caledonia and was moving eastward into the Pacific when the call came that they were it.

There had been an argument between the various space agencies regarding the method of retrieval. The Americans were split between a sea landing and a controlled re-entry, while the Russians preferred a landing on terra firma. The Chinese mirrored the Americans' options but pushed the sea landing citing concerns about the astronauts brittle bodies after so long a time in space. Outfitting the ship for a controlled re-entry would have been difficult anyway, as they would have needed to carry the necessary fuel the entire trip or make arrangements for a refueling in Earth orbit prior to landing. At that point simply transferring the astronauts and their goodies to the docking ship was considered but ultimately rejected as the need to strip down the technical specifications of the ship would take too long.

Once it was obvious that the French ship would be doing the honors of pick up, American, Chinese, Russian and Japanese space agencies sent their representatives to be on hand.

The six astronauts were taken aboard ship, isolated in a makeshift area, subjected to a battery of medical tests, and given a few days to reorient themselves to gravity while they awaited transport to Geneva. It was evident quickly that the reintroduction of gravity on the space travellers bodies was going to be a problem and that it wouldn't be solved on board a ship. Trying to buy time, the UN issued a series of communiqués outlining the discoveries made by the expedition.

Citizens of Earth, already aware since the asteroid's discovery some 13 years before, that they were not alone in the universe, had already made most of the philosophical adjustments in the intervening time since the expedition was first announced.

Fears of religious collapse had proven false. Religions had simply adjusted their terrestrial boundaries accepting God's creation as interstellar rather than merely planetary. In fact several sects decided that God had been away helping other alien civilizations and that was why things had gone to hell on Earth.

There were suggestions that alien creation stories were similar to those on Earth and it may have occurred in much the same way in other places in the galaxy. While this sparked some theological arguments, it seemed to revitalize moribund religious thinking rather than explode generations of belief structures. It never seemed to dawn on the true believers that the fact that there were different creation stories on Earth lent potential creation stories on alien worlds as much credence as anything.

Business had long since adjusted and after a few days of speculative swings, the markets had settled down by the time the expedition returned. Hints about the possibilities of new technology in
the investigations by the astronauts led to some wild speculations in
the markets as nothing was beyond the imagination of Earthlings,
but there was nothing to base value on, and investors quickly
snapped back to reality. That didn't stop the dreamers from trying
to cash in.

Various political groups took up the cause of the larger stature
Giants who appeared subservient to the less numerous Smalls, but
with no one there on the asteroid anymore to demonstrate
against, the whole thing died quickly. College students turned their
attention elsewhere.

News outlets wanted a piece of the astronauts but they were
secreted away in debriefings for many months with limited press
access, mostly due to their individual medical situations and the
reintegration of their lives back into their personal histories.

Mike Donohue noticed it first as one of the debriefers in Geneva
was an old friend.

"Hey Mark, nice to see you."

"How are the limbs?"
"My arms are still a bit swollen but essentially fine. They hurt a bit
for the first few days, nothing debilitating just a bit of pain in the
joints. But my legs, a completely different story. They are still very
swollen. In fact I can't really get out of this chair easily, though I am
told to get at least 20 minutes exercise per day and push it a bit."

"I can see. It looks like tissue and joint issues."

"It is, mostly in the lower extremities, as gravity is a bit of a new thing. In fact they have me lying down for a prescribed amount of time and even tilted with my legs significantly above my head. I'm told that my blood pressure is fairly low thanks to the prolonged anti-gravity. When we first landed I had a huge headache for a couple of days. Almost like a concussion. But it passed fairly quickly."

Donohue had immediately noticed Mark Ellison was now a Colonel and was significantly older than he remembered. At first he put it down to the fact he hadn't seen him in several years even prior to the mission. And clues in their conversation to the passing of time had not really hit Donohue as he had experienced much the same time as they flew. In fact, given his disabilities during his recovery, he actually felt older than his friend. But Ellison's very gray hair, the stiff gait and thick glasses were a tip off of a much older man.

Debriefers were very conscious of the gap of time, and recommended a short course in recent history to the returnees. The astronauts were given long lessons in recent Earth history and shifts in popular culture. They were entirely out of touch with Earth and its timeline since they left and needed to be brought up to speed on local and national politics, entertainment including which notables had died, who had married, and who had receded from public view. Scandals were gently explained and slowly the astronauts were brought back to being full citizens again.

The feeling of newness lingered. Donohue remembered trips away from home before leaving Earth, and the feeling of seeing the familiar things again gave them a shiny newness that he under- stood they did not have. And yet, fueled by minor changes and unexpected differences, seeing them again even after a short absence gave a jarring sense of unreality to things that were really quite familiar. Even the angle of the sun a few weeks on, changed the way things were perceived. After many months it could be quite jarring. After years and years, he wasn't sure how he would react. He made a mental note not to blurt out every difference he noticed once he was back in the wild again. For now he was confined to base and the jarring effect was only evident in photos. Somehow he knew that travelling through the most familiar territory was going to be the most difficult experience of his reorientation.

The changes made the astronauts feel like aliens themselves. They were also given the opportunity to get up to speed on their professional lives and personal hobbies and interests. There was a concern that they needed to be able to reintegrate into society and could not do so without that background. It was necessary as much for the returnees as it was for those who knew them who would expect them to be conversant in specific areas of knowledge.

Donohue had been in his mid-40s when they left and was now officially 59 years old. Ellison looked like he was over 60, which he probably was, with years of desk work in the Pentagon aging him prematurely. And despite his infirmities Donohue's image in the mirror looked unchanged, like he was still on the good side of 50.

"You are looking good," said Ellison. "I think there must be something to that relativity stuff. You look just like your picture from the mission briefing before take-off."

"Well, I don't feel it," said Donohue with a grin. "It must be the haircut. First decent one I've had in 12 years. Let me try to walk a bit, if you don't mind spotting me. I haven't gone over yet, but I haven't walked too far either."

He pushed himself up with his arms, trying not to wince at the pain in his wrists and shoulders. Fully upright he straightened his shoulders, jiggled back and forth on his feet and took a step. Without pain he took another, and then two more.

"Hey, this is going pretty good."

He then took another two quick steps but had to catch himself on the door handle. Ellison steadied him at the shoulder.

"Whoa. I got a little ahead of myself there. It's just like the leg muscles stopped working."

He took a moment to regain his balance, shuffled around and took enough slow deliberate steps to get him back to his chair.

"It's getting better."

"I'm told you should be ambulatory in maybe two weeks, give or take, and depending upon what the definition of ambulatory is," Ellison laughed.

"I could always count on you to be straight to the point. How long is our debrief?"

"As long as it needs to be. At this point you aren't going anywhere anyway. I'd like to talk as much as possible but I understand it might be a touch difficult so please stop me if you need to. We can take a break, a lengthier rest, or just put it off for a day."

All the astronauts had been assigned a particular debrief specialist, in several cases it was someone they knew, who had been recruited to the task a few years before the landing, provided the necessary training and been readied for the task.

Brass wanted to take everything very slowly as the nature of this mission was unlike anything they had ever dealt with. Astronauts were separated for their initial debriefs under the guise of medical care. There was a concern that all the stories and information be delivered to various national governments without taint, without corroboration by their fellow astronauts and not subject to censure or correction by any member of the team.

The briefing details would be corroborated by the debriefing team and then the reports from all astronauts would be bound together and passed to all necessary national and international agencies. From those reports the United Nations would make recommendations of a possible follow up. They had already determined that the mission to the moon was a go.

The first finding was essentially medical. On top of the higher than expected medical issues surrounding a return to gravity it was fairly obvious that Einstein's theory of relativity had been proven correct with an even more pronounced difference in time elapsed than had been expected. When the astronauts emerged after almost 13 years of travel, much of it at the speed of light, they had barely aged in a medical sense, but their parents and siblings, the best comparators, had aged significantly.

Four of the astronauts were fitted with pacemakers as their hearts could not pump enough blood in full Earth gravity. Tests on their hearts showed an increased capacity when pushed but the long flight in zero gravity had weakened the muscle's pumping power. That was expected to improve with time.

It was not immediately released to the public but Mika Oh had suffered almost no ill effects from the weightlessness. Jenn Fielding too, had managed to escape the lengthy recovery period. She was pretty much back to normal after just over a week in regular gravity. The science teams poured over their results but given the small sample size were unable to draw definite conclusions.

Both women recovered quickly. The older the participant the slower was the recovery. In addition the larger the participant the slower was the recovery. Donohue was a bit bigger than average at a touch over six feet in height but he was also of average weight at 180 pounds. His age seemed to be the key to his slow recovery.

Bolrenko, was a bit heavier but an inch shorter and he also had a slow recovery, while Jimmy Ho Yang came around fairly quickly perhaps due to his wiry build. Renaud Martin, recovered a bit quicker as he was significantly younger that Bolrenko and Donohue.

The first story in the press was heavily managed by the joint Space Agency which nominally held control over the joint mission.

Ivan Bolenko's parents had died in the interim in a car accident about five years before the ship returned.

Bolrenko had asked for his sister to be allowed in to see him during his recovery and debriefing. They had spent several days together cleaning up the loose ends of their family. The astronauts were all chosen because they had no spouses or children so there was no need to meet with immediate families. They did initiate back and forth contact with their surviving parents and siblings.

'Bolrenko discovers truth about aliens', and 'Russian leads alien exploration team' were headlines in Russia after the press cornered Stazia Bolrenko - Ivanov who heard first-hand about some of the mission details from her brother.

The leak was annoying to some in the space agency but inevitable and in the end the trickle of information probably kept the press off of the astronauts while they recovered.

The French press leaped forward with 'French commander averts Lander crash and saves mission' and the American press joined in with 'Americans puzzle out alien truth'. The Japanese and Chinese media were much more circumspect about the contributions of their nationals. Though the Chinese constantly referred to 'Commander' Yang due to his overall responsibility for the ship. Mika Oh was portrayed in the Japanese press as the conscience of the mission with praise for her efficiency and demeanor under pressure.

Bolrenko tried to set the record straight but of course that just provided more fuel for the media speculators.

In the end Mike Donohue proved to be the best spokesman for the group. He was articulate, engaging, self-deprecating and circumspect enough that the mission handlers were not only pleased with his slow release of relevant information, they actually consulted him on when and how bits should be released.

The astronauts had all been in their late 30s and 40s when they left Earth. They returned at least 50 years old with several almost 60 by Earth's chronology but functionally and physiologically only a few years older than when they left. Only Bolrenko's parents and Mike Donohue's mother had died in the intervening years. Alice Donohue died of cancer in her mid-80s a few years before the mission returned. Nieces and nephews had become young adults and a few had been born since the departure. Family connections were rekindled.

Information about the mission trickled out forcing the United Nations to hold a joint news conference two months after the landing with all the astronauts. There they provided a complete release of mission accomplishments. The public was shocked at the lack of aging demonstrated by before launch photographs and by the physical difficulties encountered by the returnees, still evident even two months after they came home.

Some press reports referred to their expedition as "The Flight of the Dorian Grey."

The press conference dominated the world media for weeks and stories continued for months as details emerged. The world discovered details of the mining colony, the remarkably familiar humanoid form of the aliens, and got more details about the two similar races of aliens, one gigantic in stature and the other quite small by Earth standards. The press conference outlined the power generating technology and the existence of a home planet. They did not mention some of the finer points, including the existence of several other colonized planets, deeming that information unnecessary at the time of the press conference.

The two types of aliens and the discovery of a home planet soon captured even more of the public imagination than the potential technological advances. Several large corporations formed new divisions to try to exploit the alien technological advances into desirable products.

The astronauts had been hard at work during the long return journey. Bolrenko, Jimmy Ho Yang and Mika Oh had all worked hard to understand the power generating card. It appeared to be a compact super-storage battery, holding a vast amount of power, enough to power an entire neighborhood for a year or more. There was a lithium component but analysis suggested a new type of alloy, one with an isotope of thorium they were unfamiliar with and a new type of engineering to produce the alloy, where the chemical bonds were somehow loosened so the electrical storage and conductivity was increased exponentially. Of course that led to speculation that the alien mining community was after the lithium which appeared at all three mining sights as a residue. Others wondered if that residue was somehow tied to use of the lithium in high energy mining operations. The power generating card itself appeared to be made primarily of thorium and mercury with some minor trace elements.

The secret appeared to be in the alloy of the two metals with lithium and a solid form of argon with several higher level elements like cadmium, held in stasis by the electrical charge, that produced the storage capacity by supercharging the pack. The higher levels of argon in the air in which the super-conductors operated appeared to be the key to its efficient operation.

In fact when the team on the return flight had figured it out, Ho Yang slapped himself on the forehead with a laugh. "Of course this configuration works, it's actually so simple that I cannot believe that chemists did not discover this on earth decades ago."

In fact, the astronauts had a small wager that Earth science would discover the technology by the time they returned. Donahue was the only one who said they wouldn't yet have it and he collected a nice bonus from each member of the team, all of whom had nearly 13 years of salary waiting for them.

"Okay Mike, how did you know?"

"Necessity is the mother of invention," said Donohue, tapping his temple. "I figured Earth wouldn't need this technology in the time we were gone and so would not have invented it." He offered to use the money he won for the good of mankind telling everyone he would pay for the dinner at their five year reunion.

"Well that's awfully nice of you Mike but I'm guessing we will remain in close contact for at least that long trying to decipher all the mission details," said Fielding with a smirk.

"It won't be that long unless you are unable to decode their writing. Nearly six years and powerful computers and all your expertise and you haven't managed to get too far on that. I figured you'd have it pretty quick given all the cross references that existed and the known use of language on doors and control panels and stuff," he said.

"Maybe it will take six minds one year to decode it rather than one mind going at it for six years," she said. "Sometimes with a puzzle you need to have a different perspective and it can fall into place quickly. That's why I tried to take some forced breaks on board ship when I was trying to puzzle it out."

"I don't know how many cipher experts they have working on it, and using your notes to speed the process, but in the six months since we've been back they have come no closer that you did. It seems to me that deciphering the language is the most important thing - it opens all the doors."

"It's like the Voynich Manuscript. It looks fairly easy to decipher but it is trickier than it appears. There must be some type of code to the writing, nothing that is there to hide the meaning but something that all native readers would know instinctively, like a transposition within the script that is part of its use," she tried to explain. "I don't know how else to explain it."

"The Voynich Manuscript? I think I've heard of that."

"It's quite famous in cipher circles. It's a large book from the 1500s which appears to be a descriptor of various plants and medicines decorated with a large number of pictures and drawings. The language is unknown and despite hundreds of attempts no one has cracked the code. Oh, and many of the drawings depict plants that are unknown in botany."

Well, good luck with that. We are all pulling for you, and glad it isn't us who are tasked with figuring it out. Particle physics seems so much easier, at least to me."

While the cipher breakers labored, samples of the reinforced metal used for most of the buildings was examined and found to be an ingenious use of existing elements, two of which were treated and processed differently than they had been on Earth. The resulting metal strings could be woven into a lattice work and embedded within the base layer of metal, sort of like a new kind of tin, with the alloy metals again treated differently in processing so the resulting metal was far more malleable, airtight, light and very strong.

Earth scientists had their hands full testing all the other elements for their potential uses just by treating them as the aliens had in the processing. A whole new branch of materials science opened up as this method and others were experimented with to produce new materials and new properties in old ones.

After a time the furor of the mission and its aftermath died down and the general public realized that aliens would not walk among them, or land a giant rocket ship in Tiananmen Square, the Place Concorde or Central Park. Life went back to its familiar rhythms with anticipation of the moon mission replacing the excitement of alien discovery.

There was some hope that alien technology could be applied to the moon mission, to explore the destination of the alien signal. However with the mission set to go only a bit more than a year after the return of the first mission there was not enough time to test and use any knowledge when the sensitivity of the mission required absolute precision and reliability. It was not a time to push the limits of existing technology.

The returning astronauts all had their duties with the International Space Agency to fulfill, but most of them also took prestigious spots at various universities, gave commencement addresses and in some cases accepted spots on corporate boards of directors where their insight and expertise was deemed valuable.

Mike Donohue was first to the corporate table. He was the oldest of the astronauts and after much of the public furor quieted down he was able to get back to his life. He quietly retired from active duty with NASA, took on an advisor's role with the International Space Agency, continued to help with analysis of the mission, though much of that from a logistics point of view rather than science or exploration. He joined the board of a new company dedicated to unravelling the anti-gravity production abilities found on the asteroid by exploiting the vast power resources that could be harnessed through the alien battery technology.

He was really on the board for show but did contribute some ideas as to the direction research should follow based on what he saw on the asteroid. His abilities in public speaking and media relations kept the issue alive in the public mind and with investors.

Ivan Bolrenko took on a university professorship in analysis techniques and leadership. He was raised to the rank of Field Marshall in the Russian Air Force prior to retiring to lead the Russian Research Institute, where he lay the course for future research projects.

Jimmy Ho Yang became more deeply embedded in the Chinese military though mostly as a figure head of international co-operation and Chinese leadership. He chaffed at the role which he believed to be more for propaganda reasons than for the inspiration of future Chinese astronauts.

He did manage to get on the boards of several corporations. His appointments were tacitly understood to be for public relations reasons for his first few terms, with the understanding that he might become more active once his public role was reduced. One of the companies he served with was constructing large agricultural stations in remote places in Africa and South America.

Mika Oh became involved with Japanese efforts to market their industrial products to the world - especially those efforts to have

Japanese companies build manufacturing plants in other countries, to harness tax advantages and calls to purchase locally. The Japanese promoted their brand of production and pride in their products, where the Chinese preferred to keep production local where possible to keep labour, environmental and social costs down. She moved to Moscow to be with her husband Ivan.

Renaud Martin joined a company determined to unlock the secrets of the gravity generators he had encountered on Rugby. More than just a figure head Martin had lined up financing, sold shares, and done much of the higher level hiring to get the company started. He served as the first president, ostensibly to guide the start up in its infancy but he refused a desire by his peers to become Chairman of the Board.

He liked the swashbuckling business approach to the research and development parts of the project but very much disliked the financial aspects and the need to continue to show actual hard and fast progress in the research. He supplemented his income with a position in theoretical engineering and physics at the Sorbonne, while maintaining ties to the European Space Agency. It was his ideas and approach which helped to create the materials science industries founded on alien technology.

And then there was Jenn Fielding who turned down a number of potential income sources to focus on breaking the code of the alien language. She worked out of Florida State University where she had taught before landing her position with the mission. She was the closest to the continuing mission with her research and connections to NASA.

It was understood that a breakthrough in the language would completely open up the alien culture and its science to Earth scrutiny and it served her bloody mindedness to endure on the project as she felt she had so much time invested. Given all the work she had done she refused to quit believing that walking away would sent the entire project back years. She was convinced that she needed to find only one key, a key letter or symbol that would start the blocks tumbling into place to unlock the language and expose the alien's secrets and accomplishments. Other cipher experts had taken other approaches but no one had managed any success.

If third level contact was going to happen then Earth needed to understand the alien language. Knowing such a meeting was inevitable, perhaps as soon as the Moon mission, she worked relentlessly to solve the puzzle.

With the pressure of the Moon mission Fielding was too busy to get home to California to visit her parents and her siblings who were too busy in their own lives to do much more than have a few long conversations. They did communicate regularly and she promised to head home for a visit when she found a good time for a break in her language research. She could feel the pressure. And constantly she had to fend off incursions into her time where other researchers decided to do all of the preliminary work she had already covered, and asked her advice on how to proceed. It took her a while but she realized that they had to cover the old ground to try to break new ground. She was years ahead of them, and it was on her to keep pushing or the secret would take years longer to find.

She plodded on with her research and took on very few teaching duties at the university, content to lecture to students about her work and the background approaches to her research. Those lectures helped her organize her research and gave her a bit of a break.

John Overholt and Ethan Harendez had already cashed in on their notoriety due to their connection to the alien discovery. As the astronauts were bound by non-disclosure rules it fell to them to be the unofficial face of the issue in many media interviews and broadcast documentaries.

Harendez and Overholt took to spending some time to piece together a documentary about the science behind the discoveries and the potential advantages to humankind that face-to-face contact with aliens might provide. They had received a treasure trove of data from Overholt's experiments on board the mission and from the telescope mounted to the frame of the ship.

"John, we can cash in a bit more than the usual interview fee. I'm thinking a four or five part documentary outlining the science, the mission to the asteroid, the research on what was found and the technology which might come of it and then a final piece on the face to face contact - you know four or five shows at two hours each. PBS will be all over this."

"Yeah, sure they will."

"I've talked to them, well, okay a friend of mine has talked to them. It's 30-30-30 for you and me and my friend who is a documentary producer."

"Okay, two things . . . that's only 90 per cent and how do you know this producer?"

"The extra 10 usually goes to the cost of production. Like we can save some money upfront by giving points on the profits. And this guy is attached to the University of Hawaii. He first came to me about a documentary on the work of the telescope. It worked out well. He made some money, the University made some money and the telescope was able to point out to the government about its social contributions. Everybody wins."
"Except you."

"No, I won too. A win for the scope is a win for me. But yeah, I wondered about a bigger win for me, us, just at about the same time Peter, the filmmaker, realized I was 'that' Ethan Harendez.

"Thought it would be nice if we cemented our place in the history of this thing. The victors write the history and all that. I will be in LA in a few weeks. We should get together and see if we can put something together."

"Okay Ethan, I'm all ears. A little bit of good publicity can go a long way in our careers. Let's both draw something up and we can hash it out when you come to California."

" In the mean time I'll tip my producer friend."

"I like your way of thinking. But I'll be in Arizona."

"Maybe we can meet in Vegas. Contact me when you have an agenda. I'm sure we can figure it out."

" I'm not sure Vegas is the right destination. If we need to be in LA I will manage to get there. Allie and the baby might appreciate a bit of a holiday. We'll figure it out once you know more about your own trip. Remember how much you like the desert?"

John had followed through with his family revelation and he and Allie were proud parents of a nearly year old girl. They had toyed with a number of spacey names but in the end settled on Allie's grandmother's name - Laurel. At the time John thought it appropriate as a reminder of his professional success but soon realized that Laurel was and even bigger success than anything he'd managed among the stars.

Allie worshipped the little one and Allie's mother had stopped pestering her about family. They were both young enough to add to the family. And Allie, with her natural inclination of concern to the well-being of her patients, was attentive to the needs of her daughter. John wondered why he had wanted to wait for so long.

Chapter Eight

"War!" Shouted the headlines on every media newsfeed. The focus of world attention shifted to immediate international issues.

A few months after the return to Earth of a space mission to uncover the truth about an alien contact, a little niggle in a remote outpost in Brazil, started a chain of events which saw armies marching, weapons trained on targets and much of the world on edge.

Aliens and off world issues were pushed back as concerns of the here and now took center stage in international circles. People around the world followed the events as they transpired over several months.

Chinese globalism, a movement of China to branch out across the globe in search of resources, living space and economic hegemony had been building for a generation. That growing movement was being challenged by locals in several nations. The Chinese response had been swift, defensively offensive and pushed the fear of a modern Chinese imperium into places that had never considered it.

China had continued its purchases of land in Central Africa and western Brazil, where they cleared 10s of thousands of acres of jungle and converted it into farms to feed their millions. Columbian rebels kept crossing the border with Brazil to raid these settlements to resupply their guerilla efforts against the Columbian government. They used the wild spaces between the border and Chinese farms as safe havens. The Chinese had sent in a few military missions to root out the rebels and the Columbians did the same, but the efforts were half-hearted on both sides as neither wanted to chance killing anyone except the rebels. Diplomatic considerations of the border forced both governments into halting the most aggressive activity for fear of crossing the border.

And then the rebels made a blunder. Caught by a small Chinese security team in the midst of a raid, the rebels killed 83 Chinese, mostly civilians defending their crops and businesses. Several security personal were also killed.

The Chinese responded two weeks later with a large co-ordinated attack on rebel positions deep within Colombia. Initially sympathetic, the Columbians made the usual diplomatic challenges for the breach of their sovereignty through the usual diplomatic channels. Functionally, the Columbians were content to let the Chinese take on the expense and difficulties of battling the rebels. The Chinese insisted upon more co-operation from the Columbians, who were more talk than action.

With continued Chinese activity crossing the border, the Columbian military was forced to eventually respond. But instead of co-ordinating attacks on the rebels they ordered the Chinese out of their country and their airspace so they could take on the rebels alone.

The Chinese became engaged with Columbian military units who sought to restore sovereignty. A three way battle commenced with both the Columbians and the Chinese attacking rebel positions and the Columbians attacking Chinese military incursions with the Chinese returning fire. The Columbians shot down two Chinese fighter jets and an airborne fuel tanker. In retaliation the Chinese shot up a Columbian military airport.

Angry recriminations came on both sides with the Chinese accusing the Columbians of assisting the rebels to raid their farms, while the Columbians accused the Chinese of supplying the rebels and giving them safe haven. In the meantime most of the rebels moved by night east into southern Venezuela and dispersed among the population. Some decided to hide in plain sight posing as poor Brazilians looking for work on Chinese farms.

After a few weeks of stand-off, diplomatic back and forth, and no action taken by the Columbians to root out the rebel menace, the Chinese attacked on a wide front, finding mostly abandoned rebel camps and a few hidden heavy weapons.

The Columbians made a show of rooting out several senior military leaders who were apparently sympathetic to the rebel groups. The Chinese were unimpressed, calling the Columbian efforts a smoke screen. They maintained their positions inside Columbia and continued their search and destroy missions seeking out rebel groups in the jungle.

Having made a stab at a diplomatic peace the Columbians were incensed by the continuing Chinese aggression and tacit belief that the Chinese had regarding the Columbian inability to manage their own affairs. They attacked Chinese supply positions inside Brazil killing several hundred and laying waste to many years of Chinese agricultural effort.

The Brazilians had been warning the Columbians they considered any attack on Chinese positions to be an attack on their sovereignty and countered with an attack on Colombian military bases for breaching promises to remain outside of Brazil with military personnel. The attacks were aimed more at the airbase's infrastructure and operations than any personnel. The Brazilians were ostensibly allied with the Chinese but not officially so, therefore military responses between the two countries were not coordinated.

Privately the Brazilians were appalled at the Chinese militarization of their farming operations. They had an agreement that no Chinese military would be in the region, but that was quickly brushed aside once the Columbians failed to destroy the rebel menace to the Chinese farms. The Brazilians protested to the Chinese who said they were operating in self defence and the Brazilians were welcome to help them protect Brazilian sovereignty.

Chastised but still annoyed the Brazilians decided to co-operate with the Chinese. The hard currency they earned from the Chinese leases of land was too good to ignore.

Venezuela was walking a very narrow path allowing the Chinese to root out any rebels they could find that had escaped eastward and in doing so allowing the Brazilians much the same latitude.

Venezuela was fearful of a de facto Chinese takeover of its south-western province which cut deep south with Brazilian borders on three sides. The Chinese were fed up with the foot dragging by all the South Americans and only paid lip service to their relationship with the Brazilians who were worried the Chinese would leave and deprive them of significant hard currency, employment of locals, and defence of their territory.

Both sides had been careful to focus their attacks on the narrow strip of land primarily on the Columbian side of the border, though they did not get too concerned about the actual location once tensions and attack levels had risen. If a few missions moved into Venezuela the government of that country decided to simply let minor transgressions go. Army staff and the national leadership spent many days deciding when they would post a diplomatic protest and when they would insist upon Chinese co-operation. How far they might go to defend their nation was not a question, the issue was when should they engage in it.

And then the Chinese widened their military attacks into Venezuela once they determined that many of the rebels had fled there and were maintaining camps in the remote southern mountains near the Brazilian border. The Venezuelans posted a mild diplomatic protest. The Chinese ignored them and co-ordinated a ground assault many miles into Venezuelan territory. Caracas protested to the United Nations, which asked the Chinese for a joint military force to root out the terrorist rebels. The Chinese agreed but while the makeup of such a force was being debated they engaged in an all out attack on any position that the rebels might hold across the entire southwestern province. Finally, facing pressure from nationalists the Venezuelans attacked Chinese positions in Columbia and Brazil. These attacks were initiated to hurt the Chinese infrastructure while staying away from killing people as much as possible.

The Chinese widened their attacks to military bases, especially airfields in the wake of Venezuelan counter attacks. Attacks on Venezuelan and Colombian military bases in and near Caracas and Bogota signalled a new phase of what was rapidly becoming a full scale war. It was evident the Chinese were not going to back down. The rebels had effectively melted away until the heat died down. The Brazilians saw the opportunity to take a couple of free shots at Colombia and position threats against Venezuela should justification for a wider conflict be required. They expected the Chinese would stay but didn't want to antagonize their neighbors should the Chinese decide to withdraw.

In the months that this drama was playing out, Chinese lands that had been rented and purchased in Africa came under attack from locals who resented the large and successful Chinese farms and mining operations and the lack of jobs they provided to locals. As in Brazil, the Chinese were much more comfortable employing Chinese workers which also helped combat unemployment in China, gave them cultural equivalence and provided a means to keep the workers productive and complacent. There were many thousands of Chinese workers managing the African enterprises for precisely the same reasons.

Having had success pushing generations of European settlement out of Africa through a combination of economic pressure, coercion and turning a blind eye to local violence, several African leaders began to pursue the same policies against the Chinese enterprises.

The African situation began to mirror the South American one when rebel groups, ostensibly backed by African governments, began raiding Chinese operations. Local military units were called in but as the rebels were quietly being supported by the local governments the military defence was naturally largely ineffective.

The Chinese military responded to the rebel attacks, leading to several major skirmishes and at least one large battle with heavy weapons. With a few aircraft shot down the Chinese fortified their holdings, expanded them into a large contiguous area and declared they would defend them vigorously. They adopted a siege mentality, insisting that all Africans leave the territory unless otherwise authorized and moved ruthlessly and aggressively against anyone who appeared hostile. Most were hostile, in response to the Chinese territorial aggression; and with the attacks in defense of Chinese territory, they became more frequently aggressive.

The resulting refugee problem created more tensions in the border areas near the lands under Chinese control.

The Africans were intent on nationalizing the Chinese farms and mining operations and the Chinese were not going to let go of their land purchases or all the equity they had built in the operations. The Chinese made a statement that their land holdings in Central Africa were one step short of sovereign Chinese territory, and made diplomatic overtures while making public military preparations to consolidate it.

The Republic of Congo was in the way, geographically and in opposition of Chinese plans. Much of the Chinese land had been purchased or leased and improved for long term use from Congo, as well as Central African Republic and Cameroon in the north, and from Congo and Zambia and Tanzania in the south and east. The bulk of eastern Congo stood in the way of these two zones and in between lay the wildest and most uncivilized parts of Congo and perhaps the world.

The Chinese managed several attacks that drove deep into Congo but refrained from taking a more concrete approach to the problem. They threatened through private diplomatic circles to take all the areas north and east of the Congo and Labala Rivers, a vast swath of territory.

Many countries including the United States and Japan had managed to remain neutral, though they didn't mind seeing Chinese ambitions around the world blunted. In addition, the repressed ambitions of a number of smaller countries seemed to swell as the major powers were otherwise engaged. The prevailing opinion was that if China had to defend its interests in many parts of the world at the same time it might back down on its aggressive expansionist policies elsewhere. Knowing this, the Chinese were keen to avoid even a whiff of their fear or trepidation of a wider conflict, so they carried on in a fully aggressive posture. North Korea rekindled its desire and rhetoric to strike and reclaim the South.

Iran, Turkey and Russia were all on alert as restless agitators began to stir in Central Asia.

Europe joined the more powerful economic nations and remained outside looking in as they tried to address their internal problems of economic decay, massive immigration and social change as well as a public very divided on the path to the future.

Eventually, after a number of months and multiple attacks occurring in Africa without any substantive help from local governments the Chinese identified local governments as hostile parties, declared areas east of the Congo and Labala Rivers as the new nation of Eastern Congo, installed a Chinese friendly government into the newly sovereign territory and diplomatically recognized the new nation. They supported the new nation militarily and lined up several Chinese friendly nations to do the same.

Several nations declared they were studying the developments in lieu of recognition but privately berated the Chinese government for taking such dramatic action.

The Chinese had fully embraced a kind of imperialism that they had avoided for a millennia. Having arranged for the establishment of East Congo, they took measures to ensure its sovereignty and poured money, resources, weapons and people into the region.

They aggressively expanded their operations in the area and equally aggressively removed any threats or opposition to their plans, declaring a non-aggression zone around the new country and a policy of attacking any potential threat within that zone.

The Chinese pulled back into Brazil but maintained a very strong military presence in the region. They announced an end to their aggressive posture but made it very clear that they would take the same measures in South America that they had taken in Africa if local governments and local populations forced their hand. The South Americans took notice, with Columbia and Venezuela deciding that a co-operative peace was the best option against a very strong willed China.

The diplomats and chattering classes tried to make sense of it all. It was a constant topic of conversation in diplomatic circles - especially ones where the Chinese were not represented. Usually circumspect diplomats could speak of nothing else.

"And here we thought the discovery of extra-terrestrial civilizations would help reduce the fragmentation of Earth societies."

"Maybe it has. The Chinese are determined to consolidate their empire. If the Russians continue to try to do the same and the Americans are able to keep a hand on their loose confederation of like-minded nations, then a hodge-podge of different approaches to civilization on Earth, will be boiled down to three."

"You forget the Brazilians and the Indians. And the entire Middle East. Those are big, big countries and regions with a significant Diaspora."

"I'll give you the Indians, as they seem to be as dispersed as the Chinese, but the Brazilians are not dispersed in any numbers except in a very few places. Middle Easterners are dispersed but they are far from monolithic culturally. Heck, we have whole departments of 'experts' who haven't been able to figure out the relationships between national and religious groups in that region, despite years of trying."

"So we are waiting on the Russian shoe to drop. They seem to be taking the long view, more of a reconsolidation of their former empire in the cheapest way possible."
"History is filled with these types of back and forth of empires. All

161

the way back to the Fertile Crescent and the Middle Kingdom, empires wax and wane and often end up looking the same with the same geography and similar but rearranged histories."

"I wonder what the future holds for us with an off-world civilization influencing us?"

"I'm guessing that unless the aliens operate in a truly alien way, say like insects, with a collective hive mentality, then their historical concerns will be very much like ours only with different names."

"The whole of human history will simply play out on a wider and more dispersed stage. Like Shakespeare said 'all the universe is a stage' or was it 'galaxy'?"

"Has there been any decision on what our next step is with the aliens? Are we just waiting for them to show up?"

"Word from upstairs is that attempts to decipher the alien language have stalled. They figure it's much better to approach the aliens having some idea of what they are rather than simply blundering upon them. While we did receive the transmission there is no indication it was specifically directed to us, knowing that we were here. It's no secret that the signal was likely aimed at our Moon and that it only accidentally made its way to Earth. The aliens may not even know we know about them. In fact they may have never made contact with any other civilization and could feel the huge affects of their own First Contact. Wouldn't that be a bit of a shocker?"

"Yeah, I guess. But I think it's safe to assume that if they knew about our Moon they must have known about us. Any presence on the Moon is simply too close for them to ignore another habitable planet. I'd expect the Moon might be a jumping off point for them coming here."

"Reasonable analysis, except there is no evidence they are here, or even on the Moon, at least not yet."

"Oh, here comes Shen Wei, the Chinese Vice Ambassador, prepare to be schmoozed."

Chapter Nine

Bill Henderson was packing for a trip.

He had heard that voice in his head many times as an adult, though he couldn't remember hearing it as a child. It had never led him astray. It had only helped him, though admittedly the help it had provided was not monumental. This time felt different, like all the other times were merely preparation for this one.

The first time he heard it, he had been having dinner in a nice restaurant when a voice clearly told him to turn to his left and warn the waiter who was backing up with a very full tray, because he was about to have an accident. The tables in the restaurant had been shifted to accommodate Henderson's large group and the waiter had forgotten about the change in configuration.

Henderson had hesitated only a split second but quickly reacted to the helpful voice, turning and gently placing his hand on the waiters back and issuing a gentle word of warning. He had only thought back the word of warning before realizing he needed to say it out loud.

"Whoa there, watch out, we're back here today."

The waiter took the instruction, moved forward and distributed the dishes at the table before turning to Henderson with a still busy tray and thanking him for his attention.

For his part Henderson was completely surprised that no one else had moved to help before he realized that the warning had only been in his head. Was it something he had thought to himself after picking up the subtle clues that there might be a problem? No, he knew it had been a gentle command.

He scanned the room trying to pick out where the voice might have come from. On his second slow scan of the room, a small, unusual looking man three tables over caught his gaze and held it, before giving a small nod.

Henderson didn't know what to do, his face showing a quizzical look of someone thinking.

Then he heard it again. "Glad to have helped, that would have been quite the mess."

Henderson looked into his lap and then slid out of his chair, dropped to the ground, and walked stiffly through the tables while the man continued to watch him carefully.

"Did you say something to me?" he stammered at the man.

"I did, and I'm glad you heard me. Not everyone does. I think my voice is very highly pitched."

"Oh, that's it. I thought I was hearing you in my head not with my ears."

"Wouldn't that be something. Glad I could be of help."

Henderson thanked the man and awkwardly made his way back to his chair and climbed back in.

He was at a dinner with a group from his convention. Though still a young adult he attended it annually, the Little People of America convention held in Los Angeles, California. Given that Henderson was born and raised in suburban Los Angeles, attending the convention was fairly easy and routine.

Years before, he had learned at the convention, of the almost limitless employment opportunities that the movie industry had for Little People. He had pursued this line of work while also taking university courses to prepare for an alternative life should the jobs in Hollywood dry up. There were a few acting jobs but most of the employment was in support of productions that needed a human dressed up in character, or manning a prop, or filling a technical role that required someone who didn't take up a lot of space.

He had gotten to know many Hollywood people, not just the movers and shakers but the production people, set designers, make-up, costume, cameras, key grips and the rest of them. His experience helped them and their help made his experience on set much better. Movies are a very slow business, with a lot of hurrying to be ready and then waiting forever to perform. And then doing it again.

Henderson did not entirely dismiss the incident in the restaurant because he did not believe the man's reasoning that he had a voice at high frequencies. That the man was one of the Little People like himself was not unusual to him at the time, he was sitting with a

167

large group and was obviously attending the convention which attracted many people from across the country.

For a while he tried to project his thoughts at those around him, using simple commands like 'look up' or 'stand up' and things like that. It didn't appear to work.

And then one day he heard the command turned back on him.

'Look up', he had thought while looking at a middle aged woman, standing on the far side of the sound stage.

A female voice in his head said, "What for?"

He was startled and looked down to make sure his feet would not cause him to trip. Then he looked back at the middle aged woman who appeared to ignore him.

"I thought you said up, not down. 'Look up'. Isn't that what you wanted? What am I looking at?"

He very deliberately looked up. He remained looking up.

"That's it, I knew you could do it. And no, I'm not the woman in the green, I'm just behind her, in red."

Henderson wandered over to her. "I heard you speak."

"And I heard you."

"I've never really done this before."

"Oh, I do it all the time."

"So there are others who can speak this way? Can they all hear us, or is our conversation just between us?"

"It depends. I just direct it where I want it to go. You can too, I'd guess, if you practice."

"Who else can do this. You are the only one I know."

"Actually quite a lot of Little People can do it, though many like you, don't know they can. It's just something we keep to ourselves. I'm not sure why but it seems right. Other people find it un-settling."

Henderson practiced, and found more telepathic speakers. And soon he was speaking to people quite naturally without noise.

Los Angeles was a big city so he found a number of other telepathic speakers, though few seemed to know they had the ability until Henderson spoke to them. He often spent time with these people who usually had to be calmed down once their skill became apparent to them. In many cases it did explain a lifetime of odd voices in their heads and instructions from out of the blue about mostly mundane things.

And now it had come to this. He was a member in the club of LA telepathy, even if it had no meetings, no membership fees, no stationary nor any formal membership. He often thought it a joke that the others played on him, pretending only Little People could talk without speaking. One particular day he was speaking with one of his usual telepathic contacts when his world was changed.

"Mr. Henderson, do you know who you are? Do you know why some of us have this ability?" he was asked that day.

"I think I know me, my parents and family background. They didn't have this ability, or at least they never revealed it to me. Why do some of us have this ability?"

"The ability to communicate telepathically comes from our ancestors. Many Little People have it, as it is genetic as is our stature. We have maintained it as a direct link to our ancestors who all had it."

"So we hunted mastodons this way? Who was our common ancestor, where did he come from?" Henderson joked. He was uncomfortable.

"We are emigrants from Eiosia, even though our ancestors came here many hundreds, even thousands of years ago, and have fully integrated into the local population."

"Eiosia? I've never heard of it. Is it a region of Siberia, or Bavaria? Or Czechoslovakia?"

"Not exactly, a little further away than that. Eiosia is another world occupied by humans."

Henderson was stunned, he cocked his head. He was very conscious of his own blinking. At first he thought she was joking, playing him for a fool. It took quite a bit of convincing but eventually Henderson understood the truth. Some human civilization somewhere had seeded a number of Earth-like planets with intelligent life, enough that emigration from more technologically advanced worlds was possible, and a mixing with local populations was entirely inevitable.

In his limited telepathic experience the speaker had to have a line of sight to the spoken to. He wondered if it was a condition of the skill or merely a failing on his part to improve his abilities.

And then he received instructions to travel for a very important meeting. The voice came one evening when he was alone. And it come to him in a crowd but no-one acknowledged it until he was told the speaker was very far away. He asked why, as in his experience telepathic speakers did not hide their identities, at least from other telepathic speakers. His questions were answered. He was visited in person to calm his fears. Now he had to get moving to complete his assigned task.

Chapter Ten

Jenn Fielding would not give up. She had declined offers from universities, private industry and government, similar to those accepted by her fellow astronauts. She was determined to complete her mission and decode the runic markings found on the asteroid.

She had passed the project on to other experts in the field as well but knew that her lengthy time with the project put her years ahead. They would all take the same approach she had taken but her lack of success pushed her into searching for something unconventional. She had made all the mistakes and moved down a dozen promising roads of inquiry without success. Anyone late to the game had to take the same route, if only to ensure she had not missed anything.

Still she worked. She fiddled and transposed, she worked away for several months after the asteroid mission returned, and then, with the Moon mission launch date set a few months in the future, she had a revelation. Attempting to transpose the runic letters directly into modern English was not possible if they were very old, if English concepts as nouns and verbs and historical antecedents did not apply. The aliens were not using a dead language, it was a living language that was very old and likely incredibly different from its own forerunner.

"I am getting some progress, Phil." She spoke to her mentor, Florida State University Professor Emeritus, Philip O'Regan. "For most of the time I assumed this runic language was hieroglyphic, that symbols represented words rather than sounds, and that it was constructed like our language. That led nowhere. Several years of nowhere. Then I thought if it was a modern form of an older language what characteristics might it take?"

"Then it dawned on me that all our attempts to decipher language were approached as if the language was older than the language we are trying to translate it to. Or such language is a specifically created code of a modern language. Look at how different English is after only 500 years. English from that time is almost incomprehensible to modern speakers."

"In modern idiom we use some letters as code for longer concepts, such as initials like FSU for Florida State University. They might be doing the same especially for the bits of runic identifiers in a mining camp. Initials could stand for equipment, locations, places. Certainly we wouldn't label things in a very fundamental manner. We use Men's Room and Ladies Room rather than the more generic Wash Room or toilet, or even the more colloquial Water Closet or even WC."

"I took these concepts and overlaid the success I'd had in seeing like runes in like places and like runes labelling like things. Still no breakthrough. Of course that was while we were still on our return trip and I had access to many photographs of written language."

"Recently I hit on it. Language evolves. It maintains some old symbols, it evolves new ones and meanings change. I looked at translations of many of earth's runic languages and the meaning is pretty difficult to ascertain. I did a fairly comprehensive study of runic languages in Northern Europe and tried to burrow inside the minds of those actually using the language. I tried to think how they would evolve older concepts and symbols to new inventions and ideas. Of course much of what we have of that is carved into rocks and so likely much more formal that an everyday idiom."

"So I moved my search out a bit into the Middle East and started translating ancient Sumerian, a runic language, into ancient Babylonian. Then I took the result and translated that into Ancient Hebrew, then again with the result into a more modern Hebrew and so on. In fact I did this through several language strings and found the result quite satisfying in the sense that I was able to see the development of the language as it moved through time, through cultures, through technologies and through ancient traditions. Of course there were anomalies and bits that didn't fit as I couldn't easily account for invasions and jarring cultural changes, but generally I was able to ascertain the meaning. Especially in the most fundamental words and concepts, like mother, father, home, food and the like. And more importantly I was able to track the changes, large and small that occurred over time."

"So in the end I gathered text from the asteroid that I was able to get from the screenshots. I used mostly stuff that was more literary, lengthy descriptions or long strings of text and avoided anything that appeared to be technical in nature and the labels and identifiers by which I had been stymied. I updated the runic symbols into what they may have become in a more modern idiom including some basic technology terms and expected social changes. I took that and tried to translate the alien runes into Ancient Celtic and ancient Sumerian. There was little in common with the Celt and a bit more with the Sumerian. Then I tried Ancient Phoenician - the computer began to spit out text at a rapid rate. Where previous analysis had produced a word here or there that may or may not fit, with the modernized version the modified Phoenician wasn't just similar, the runes were essentially readable. It was a definitive match."

Professor O'Regan had been nodding and making short positive comments all through Fielding's explanation, mostly directed to her assumptions and eventual target action. He was taken completely aback.

"Are you telling me that Ancient Phoenician is essentially the same language as the alien runic script found on the asteroid more than five light years from Earth?" he smiled and shook his head at the impossibility of it.

"Yes," she said quietly. "If the Phoenician is modernized according to patterns that are common to other language strings in their movement from ancient languages to more mature uses. There is a huge amount of scholarship in working out those strings of language and programming the computer to analyse them in the right way. Doing it by hand would be so slow as to be a barrier. If I had done it that way, I would have understood I was on the right track earlier, but I also would have almost no actual text translated, just a few words and thoughts. Putting in the time to get the background work done right, has opened up the alien language all at once."

He was stunned. His breathing stopped and he didn't move. Then his eyes went wide, like he was having trouble focussing on his thoughts.

"Good God," have you presented your findings yet to anyone? This is a bit more than making a little progress. You've essentially solved the language riddle."

"Nobody else knows, I wanted to explain it to you first because once this is out there, after the initial shock the uninitiated in cipher and language construction will want to get some explanation that this is real, with real evidence and real fact. All the work I did in forcing the modernization through many generations will need to be reviewed. The review alone will take many months or more. They will be all over anyone who is an expert in these things. I can walk you through my entire 14 months of work since we returned and even the preliminary study I conducted while we were still in flight. I have checked and rechecked that I didn't introduce some sort of biased coding into the computers."

He took a deep breath. "How highly classified is your research?"

"You will need high level security clearances. Anyone else we bring on to double check the results will need them too. It will take a while just to arrange that. If you are willing and we can agree on the size and membership of a research team to test my results, I will go to my security contact and ask for a high level meeting to push this along. Please keep this between us at this time. Just think about who we might ask to help. This stuff is so classified that I should have really gotten you a clearance before even speaking about it. Though I did get a written assurance that our conversation was authorized."

"Wow. Ok, give me a couple of days. In the mean time I think you need to approach whoever and get me a proper clearance, especially now that I am involved against my will," he smiled. "Don't worry I'd be fighting for a chance to be involved if I knew about it. And I expect there are a few others I know who would feel the same way."

A few days of back and forth conversations occurred which

Fielding insisted were done in person and out of doors. She didn't want to seem too cloak and dagger but she didn't want to be knocked off the project either because she failed to respect the classified nature of the issues.

The Russians and Chinese were very interested in her work and insisted on top level and constant updates to her efforts. They also had their own people working on deciphering the alien language and wanted representation on the team formed to analyse the approach and the results.

"Okay, Phil, I've secured the authorization to speak with you and you have likely received your security paperwork and instructions. Another few days of investigation into your every move for the last 20-30 years and you'll be cleared. I'm quite hopeful that you didn't engage in anything that would raise red flags with investigators?"

He laughed. "I've engaged in most things that a campus dweller would engage in, but I can assure you and hopefully investigators, that they were all harmless and at least short lived."

"They are very thorough. I'm hoping that even the people you associate with or do business with regularly are clean too."

"Most of my colleagues are apolitical, especially as they got older and realized that minority protests and agitation were not going to change the world."

"I'm not talking just about your colleagues, I'm talking about where you buy gas, about where you shop and who you play pinochle with."

"I don't play pinochle."

"Well that is one area you pass with flying colors; though it's more a figure of speech, Phil."

"As for my gas station guys, they all appear to be immigrants."

"Lucky for you that describes every gas station in the South."

O'Regan had to endure two very lengthy interviews on his personal life and his public and academic life, and answered pointed and loaded questions on his integrity and associations. He was fed details about some of his associates which he had not known, and in fact questioned as perhaps leading bits of misinformation tailored to draw him out on certain topics.

He was wondering about further interviews and more disruption in his life, especially after two former colleagues called him to point out that they had been contacted by three different government agencies with regards to O'Regan and his life. They wondered what he was getting into. The clearance came.

He received a Fed-Ex package at his campus office first thing one morning which included a phone number and code instructions - not the code word, but instruction on how to create it out of info that only he would know.

He called the number after putting the code together and dutifully destroying the package. He managed to burn it a bit at a time in his office thanks to an old ashtray he used as a knick-knack holder and a fan that kept the smoke dispersed. He had included the latter precaution only because he had the fan to move the air in the notoriously stuffy faculty office building. He was glad he did, because even burning the material a small bit at a time, gave the fire alarms a reason to burp their claxon sound for a second. Such short bursts were not uncommon in the office block thanks to the number of people thereabouts who wanted a quick smoke in violation of the rules.

The call was picked up on the second ring. "Yes," said a machine voice on the other end.

"132-008-GAT-PAH-909-CST-005."

"Verified, continue," said the voice.

Following the instruction in the Fed Ex package he said, "243-119-HBU-QBI-010-DTU-116."

"Verified. Please go to your contact for further instructions." The phone went dead. His curiosity pushed him to redial the number but a check on his incoming calls showed a bizarre group of letters, numbers and symbols and he guessed the number would no longer be in service and would be untraceable.

O'Regan was at once surprised and secondly pleased he was considered a worthy security risk. He had been engaged in the usual leftist politics as a youth and still was friendly with one person he had met through those associations. The trail of other friends and colleagues that appeared to have sketchy lives was surprising and long.

There was even a reference to some of this graduate students over the years, two of which had been caught doing cipher work for a foreign power. That was news. Deep down he didn't really blame them, he wondered what they had been paid. The work was apparently a public contract so there was no security issue, only that they had taken work for an intelligence agency of another country. The interviewer didn't say if it was a hostile power or what the work entailed so it might have been translating almost anything - though one didn't call in cipher experts to translate French toothpaste tubes. Unless of course they were being used by intelligence agencies to send secret messages.

He shook his head. This intelligence stuff really got down inside you and could consume your thoughts with rings upon rings of supposition and potential concerns, he thought.

He left his office and crossed the campus into the mathematics department. He took the elevator to the third floor and moved down the narrow hall to the office of Jenn Fielding. Her door was open as if she was expecting him, or someone else.

"I was told to come here."

"I was told to be here."

The phone rang. Fielding picked it up, listened for a few moments, and put it down.

"We are to go out of the building and go directly to meet a red Escalade SUV in the front drive. It will take us to our meeting on the ciphers. We are to bring no personal communications devices with us - we will be searched. I'm told we will be back in approximately six hours depending upon the length of the meeting."

They gathered themselves, both reluctantly leaving their personal devices on Fielding's desk, closed and locked the door and left the building. Walking out the front doors a red Escalade glided up to the front of the circular drive. Through an open window a man in the front passenger seat made eye contact and with a slight twist of his head indicated they should get in the back. Inside, the second row of seats was empty. In the third row of seats sat a man in a dark suit and dark sunglasses. The door closed and the vehicle glided out of the driveway.

"Wow, this is really scary stuff," said O'Regan, trying to smile despite his discomfort.

"Not scary at all Professor," said the man behind them. "We are merely taking all the precautions we've been assigned to. This is about as secure as we get. You two are expected. There will be an opportunity to eat after the meeting." He waved a metal wand around both of them. There was no beep.

"How long will it take to get there? Where are we going?" asked Fielding.

"Sorry that is classified."

They drove for about 25 minutes, first on the nearby highway, then into the countryside before turning down a gravel road which disappeared through a grove of tall pine trees. They drove well back of the country road to a group of low buildings. Once they left the main arterial road from the highway there were no markings on any roads or buildings. They emerged from the pine copse and rumbled down the gravel road towards the buildings which were decidedly larger than expected when seen from a distance. Jenn looked at O'Regan who had furrowed his brow.

"This looks pretty remote," he said. "A secure location?"

"One of many."

The vehicle approached the buildings and slowed to a stop in front of a security gate which protected the road as it led between two of the buildings. Most of the buildings faced each other inside a wide oval. The buildings appeared to be made of corrugated steel with some concrete framing elements - very Florida like. There were some pillar emplacements with cameras and other equipment mounted on them on either side of the road. The obvious security meant there was likely a lot more security in place that could not be seen, thought O'Regan.

The driver's window slid down as a man approached from around the corner of one of the buildings. He was dressed casually in light cream colored khakis, a dark blue golf style shirt with a winged logo and a black baseball cap and the obligatory sunglasses. It was Florida after all.

"Here with our two for transit," the driver said. "Official authorization is Fielding 02-10-77431 and O'Regan 10-33-98341."

The driver handed the security man a plastic card. He scanned it into a reader on one of the pillars, which blinked green. The security man checked his list and handed back the card, as the gate sunk into the ground. He waived them through.

"Go to building Number 4 - the numbers are posted on the front, top center - and wait."

The vehicle slid forward and entered a large paved compound perhaps a 150 meters around and circled by industrial style buildings about 30 feet in height, all with small red numbers lodged at the top of the triangular gable which formed the roof.

As they rolled up to Building Number 4, it's wide front door began to roll upwards to open. Inside was a small commuter jet, painted white and red, with no other markings.

"There's our ride," came a voice from the back seat.

The jet door folded down to produce a few steps up into the fuselage. Inside there were several comfortable seats underneath a very low ceiling, requiring them to duck down until they were seated.

They were introduced by first names only to another two men in dark suits who were already aboard the plane. The man from the back seat of the SUV who appeared to be in charge, accompanied them on the plane. Once they were seated the plane began to roll out of the hangar, and moved to the western end of the building complex where it rolled between two buildings and turned directly onto a runway.

They took off quickly and smoothly and flew for 90 minutes in clear weather before landing at what was obviously a military airstrip. They never saw the four F-18s that flew escort for them. People on the ground who gazed skyward at the right time would have seen the formation and wondered who it was that was so important. The small jet was surrounded by the four fighters, one each above and below and one on either side. The F-18s landed after the passengers were down and prepared for the return trip.

The group took another pair of dark cars along with their security man and the other security detail onto a highway. Before long road signs made it obvious they were in northern Virginia headed toward Washington.

"Our cover is blown," said Fielding, trying to make light of the situation.

"Maybe," said the man in sunglasses, without emotion.

As the cars reached the city, they took a circuitous route through the streets, pausing at George Washington University to pick up another man, who introduced himself as George Evans, a professor of history and culture at the university. The detection wand was passed over Professor Evans without incident.

The car took a number of back streets, past the Lincoln Memorial and glided along beside the Tidal Basin apparently headed for some non-descript government office block on the south side of the National Mall. Fielding gazed at the Capitol Building in the distance. It was impressive. They wound their way among the office blocks and stopped at the Bureau of Printing and Engraving and were taken into the building and whisked onto an elevator.

Fielding, O'Regan, Evans and the security guard who had accompanied them from Florida State all stepped into the unusually oversized elevator. Fielding wondered why their small party required a freight elevator and then figured it was some security measure that she was unaware of.

The security man pushed a series of buttons and the elevator began to descend, which surprised three of the passengers, who assumed their high level meeting was with a high level official in a high office somewhere in the office block above them, with a nice view of the Mall and the water.

O'Regan was hungry but figured it wasn't worth noting amongst all the cloak and dagger precautions. He wondered what he had gotten himself into. Jenn Fielding didn't show any emotion or concerns and O'Regan wondered if she had travelled this route before.

The elevator bumped around a bit. There was no indication of what floor they were on or where they were going. It took some time during which all three academics seemed uncomfortable. Evans asked if they were there yet, to try to lighten the mood. It seemed they were travelling a long way down.

O'Regan pulled at his shirt collar, he was feeling quite warm. He wondered if the elevator had broken down. Fielding was inwardly puzzled. She was certain she detected a little sideways motion for a brief moment as the elevator jerked around in its ancient guide rails. And she too had a concern that the elevator had ceased to function properly. She looked at O'Regan and Evans and could see the strain of uncertainty on their faces.

As they puzzled, the elevator gently jerked again in a rattle of several directions and then stopped. The doors opened and they stepped out into the waiting arms of two well dressed, middle aged women who greeted them by name and took charge of them, moving to another elevator which climbed three floors as indicated on the light display above the door.

"Come, you are expected," said one of the women. "I understand you are famished. We will provide a light lunch, finger foods really, after the meeting."

They moved down a narrow hallway, decorated with many pictures above a finely milled wooden chair rail. They moved past a few office workers rushing about, through a set of doors and into another narrow hall. It was obviously an older building, not constructed to modern standards. They rounded a corner where another older woman was standing outside a large wooden door. She was obviously waiting for them, waving them towards her and then motioning them to stop as she opened the door.

Catching a glimpse inside Fielding could see the carpets were rich yet functional and left exposed a portion of black and tan herringbone hardwood floor with very wide planks. The wall she could see was covered with paintings and framed certificates. They were all richly decorated with wooden chair rails and milled oak woodwork. The woman opened the door and peaked in. "They have arrived sir."

A voice murmured something and she motioned them through the door and into the room.

A tall man stood behind a desk with his back to them, facing a large window. He buttoned his suit jacket to formalize the meeting. He continued to gazing out of the window behind the desk as if he had been waiting for them. His hands moved behind his back and he paused while they all shuffled into the room.

Fielding's knees felt weak. The room was a strange roundish office with a big desk and several sofas and high back chairs. On the floor was a thick wool carpet woven with the Great Seal of the United States of America. The women motioned for them to find seats.

The man turned from the window. "Welcome to the White House. I've always liked this office. But despite all my research on the matter, I have never received a truly satisfying answer as to why it was built as an oval. Apparently that was the style in the late 1700s and there was such a room in New York that General Washington used for an office and for ceremonial events in the early days of the Republic. Doesn't seem like a good enough reason to go to all this trouble though."

"Mr. President, this is a surprise, a pleasant surprise but very unexpected," said O'Regan who stood closest to the President, recovering his wits the quickest.

"Yeah, sorry about that little trip, but it's easier and less noticeable for you three to move about than for me. The press gallery freaks anytime I get up. If a glass of water isn't on my itinerary they want to know why I was thirsty. In fact you aren't on my itinerary at all, seems you just dropped by as I was getting a bit of paper to write a note on - what a curious co-incidence.

"When they said it was to be the highest level security meeting, I told them to use the Mall tunnel. It, like everything else about this meeting, including the fact that we are even having a meeting are absolutely classified as above top secret," he said with a purse of his lips and a nod which brought his chief of staff into the office. He enjoyed the power of his office in moments like this.

President Benjamin Mediros Anderson sat down behind his desk, despite his height he did not seem too large for the furniture, a lovely old oversized wooden desk and leather bound high back chair. He did fill the room however. He motioned his visitors to sit as well.

Mediros Anderson was in his second term, having just been re-elected in what was largely an informal election. He was very popular with most Americans and even the press had difficulty pushing him too hard. He had presided during a period of economic growth, in no small part due to the effects of anticipated alien technologies and due to the relative international calm there were few threats to the nation.

Of course the Chinese aggression in Africa and South America was troubling but Anderson and much of America understood the Chinese determination to defend themselves and they understood their decision to build a wider empire. So far the Chinese had remained outside of the sphere of interests of the United States and most of Western civilization. The only areas of contention were where Chinese interests and Western interests intersected - and that was rare.

Hong Kong had been a concern but China backed away from over-bearing political control. It had built several container ports and other installations in the South China Sea but had limited these to areas it already controlled by sea or air. Southeast Asia and the Philippines were concerned but as China showed no more aggression beyond trade, those fears were treated mildly by Washington. A sail through, every now and again, was enough to establish American claims that these areas were international waters. The Chinese issued their official protests and were watchful but other-wise chose to accept the new normal. American allies in the region were less sure. The Chinese radiated a fierce determination to con-trol events and affairs within their declared sphere of influence and were careful to keep that sphere only as big as they were willing to maintain.

Anderson sat down and beckoned the three academics to pull up chairs close to the desk. He leaned in and asked them what they had found out about the alien writing and what it meant. Fielding took the lead telling him that an updated, modernized Ancient Phoenician was a virtual match for the alien writing character by character, and provided a more alphabetic approach to the words than they had anticipated. The meaning of most words had remained though the use of the language for several millennia among the aliens had twisted some of the words and usage, distorting some of the meanings.

"Okay, I got that from my briefing. What types of information did you find in the writings taken from the photos of the holographic display used by the alien storage device?"

Evans chimed up. "As awesome as the idea that Ancient Phoenicians are somehow tied to this alien culture I have found some eye opening details."

Fielding looked at him, a bit surprised. This was her show. She still had not been provided with any background on Evans or about his place in the project. All she knew was that Evans had been included at the government's request as a language expert, not a cipher breaker. She spoke up.

"Mr. President to summarize, Ancient Phoenician appears to be tied to the alien culture. That alone is monumental in understanding Earth's cultural development and present place in the galaxy."

She let it sink in for a moment. And Evans took the cue.

"Sir, I was brought on board as a language expert and political analyst. And now that the language has been understood it has taken on a more political nature," he said. "The aliens have their home planet and have colonized two others. Two more distant planets have been visited. Earth is one. Another, about four light years from their home planet and about 14.7 light years from our Earth, is the other. The indication is that their visits on Earth had gone according to plan . . . "

"And what is that plan?"

"A moment. And the visits on the other planet had gone awry."

"In what way?"

"The two questions are related so I will try to answer both with what limited knowledge we have gained thanks to the work of Ms. Fielding. Remember, what we accessed is the information banks of a remote mining colony, not the inner workings of the alien civilization," said Evans. "Much of what we know is gleaned from references to events rather than directly to reports of the events themselves."

"It appears that Earth and this other planet were reached about the same time, perhaps 3000 Earth years ago, when the aliens came to understand a universal gravitational propulsion system that vastly reduced travel time between stars, allowing travel at faster than the speed of light. Initially the visits to Earth took place because the gravity enhancement waves they found in interstellar space led them here and to the other planet. I have more on that propulsion system in a minute and I think we should begin a research project on it."

The President nodded.

"However, first the gist of the situation. It appears that the aliens came to Earth and provided the Sumerians with a basic writing system about 3000 years ago, which appears to have spun away from the original system once it was let go on the wilds of Earth. The aliens returned, found the Sumerian civilization had turned in an unexpectedly violent direction, so they cut ties and support which led to a downward spiral of the Sumerians. The aliens started again by providing a more specific system to people on the eastern shore of the Mediterranean and that remained their writing system during their brief civilizational moment. The Phoenicians morphed and did not survive as a centralized civilization. The writing from that brief time did not evolve here on Earth so we are able to compare it easily to the alien writing."

"Surely the alien writing evolved?" commented Anderson.

"Absolutely, but if both systems had evolved independently of each other they may have been almost impossible to link. We were lucky in a way. The very short use of the Phoenician system meant that it did not evolve too much on Earth, for that reason it is more easily matched. The Phoenicians evolved into the Carthaginians who were then destroy by Rome."

He continued, "It seems as though the aliens, who were virtually physiologically the same as Homo Sapiens began to mix in with existing populations after they had been here for a very short time. Here's the catch - they are very small in stature because the gravity of their home planet is very much higher than here. While there appears to be an element of evolution involved, they remain small if they matured here but their progeny are virtually the same as us and so, if born here, they often mature to approximately the same height, given the same force of gravity on them is the same as it is on us."

"So Earthling dwarves and little people are somehow linked to the aliens?" asked the President. "Are we to be ruled by Munchkins?"

"Yes and no, not all dwarves are aliens but those aliens on Earth often are much smaller than the norm for Earth. So they are unusual but within Earth parameters for intelligent life.

"And there is more. The giants that were found at the asteroid site are the same species as the smaller aliens. Only they were born on the asteroid, they are the children of the alien miners. Because of the low gravity they grew to large sizes and were able to do the work of many men, a happy chance that eased the operations of the mining community."

"Their efforts here were interrupted by strife in other colonies. Thus they left their colonizers here for many centuries without contact and were able to grow with us, in fact become us, while on the other planet, colonized at the same time, there was knowledge of the alien arrival and ultimately resistance to the mixing and there has grown a war between the colonizers and the original alien colonizers. Leaving the Earth to attend to their other issues as we were left in the dark on this alien arrival."

"And what does this all lead to?" asked the President.

"The Moon. There is evidence that they have been engaged in mining activities on our Moon."

"So do we have to go find them or are they are coming to see us?"

Evans paused. He looked around the room at everyone before responding.

"They are already here."

The room was silent. Fielding and O'Regan had sat bolt upright at the news. The President actually relaxed a bit, though his tension was still visible in his wide-eyed gaze.

"That's a bit dramatic. When?"

"I don't know sir, all I know is that those who do not want to be assimilated into the alien culture know of us, and know that we have been developed, seeded perhaps by the aliens, but not fully integrated into their civilization. They want to approach us for help in their push for independence from the home planet."

"And you got all of this from the notes of a mining colony? So I should call the Joint Chiefs and run to the Situation Room?"

"No," he smiled, "but I think we best be considering our responses and ready our capabilities for when this happens. Given the propulsion system they have they might send a delegation here at almost any time."

"I would guess, as you have Professor Evans, that they are already here. At least in some capacity," said O'Regan.

"We must decode everything and unlock as much of their technology as we can," said the President.

"Yes, and we have to bring everyone into the reality of this while trying to figure out the fallout, the cultural revisions, the political ramifications, the religious connotations, historical understanding, the military; and perfect an international co-operation beyond anything attempted or achieved. It appears that this oneness in outlook and thinking are necessary to avoid an international civil war of planetary proportion."

"Oh that's all. There you go being dramatic again. I think Earth is already sinking into a huge international conflict with the Chinese aggression, though so far it appears to be outside of our immediate concerns. The inward looking Chinese are now outward looking in a big way. And now we might have an international civil war on top between pro-alien and pro-Earth factions. But this is all speculation and you cannot provide a timeline."

"We will keep researching what we know. Their gravitational propulsion appears to allow them to take more than 90 per cent of the expected travel time away from interstellar trips," said Evans.

"Any idea how many of the aliens are on Earth? Could they raise an army?"

"There is no way to tell, but given the numbers of Little People, I would guess it is small, though many of us may be related to them through their seeding operations many thousands of years ago. It appears that this research project has been going on for some time."

" Sir, where do I fit into this?" asked Fielding.

"Ms. Fielding, right now I don't know. If the alien script is actually Ancient Phoenician, it appears that most of it could be translated in a few days by computer thanks to your diligent efforts. However, would it be understandable as many technical terms and abbreviations are not known? They are not known in modern language. It will take us some time to sift through the millions of documents that were extracted, that you extracted from the alien mining community."

"And still no idea why we received the original transmission, which apparently was directed to us?"

"Correct, Mr. President. There are a number of speculations however, the first of which is that we were never meant to receive it, it was directed at our Moon."

"Perhaps you should be on the ship that goes to the Moon. We may need someone to speak on our behalf."

The President turned to his chief of staff. "We best be moving on this ASAP. Draw me a list of who needs briefings and security clearances to proceed on preparations and a very quick understanding of the alien culture. And we need some pictures of any installations they may have built on the Moon."

"Er, ah, Mr. President, ummm, there is something you should know . . . our astronauts in the 1970s actually encountered these aliens on the surface of the Moon."

Anderson tilted his head and looked at his National Security Advisor. "And I didn't know this . . . why?"

"Sir, there are some details in our security apparatus that are only revealed when an issue arises. They have been deemed by previous administrations to be available to the President on a 'need to know' basis only. The aliens have remained out of sight and out of contact. Such things are considered superfluous to the on-going concerns of the nation."

"All this talk of aliens and alien contact for what, 12 years or so, and only now does the security apparatus decide the Commander in Chief needs to know? Well thanks for that. So I guess I now need to know everything that I have not been briefed on that may be lying dormant waiting for events to warrant my attention."

"Yes, Mr. President."

"In the mean time get me the Joint Chiefs and set up a major briefing of this information."

Anderson calmly moved some papers from one side of his desk to the other. His anger was palpable.

"And exactly how much contact did we have with them?"

"Not a lot sir. As the Moon missions orbited the Moon they saw some indications of intelligent life on the far side, the one not visible from Earth. They attempted communication but received no return signal. Once on the surface they were visited by two aliens, who were dressed in space suits that were obviously built with a much higher technology than our bulky suits. The aliens greeted the astronauts and explained that they were engaged in mining activities on the far side, that they came from quite a distance and had no aggressive intentions. Quite the opposite in fact, that we were distant relatives, having had both our planets seeded from another alien culture, ancient even to them.

"They asked that we leave them alone and they would do the same to us, until such time as contact became necessary. Subsequently we did several scans of their locations on the far side of the Moon but then stopped going to the Moon, shortly after that encounter. The aliens had indicated that they were to be left alone or there would be unpleasant repercussions."

"I see," said Anderson. "I still want a full briefing, A-SAP. Funny how A-SAP has morphed into a word that no longer really means the same thing as the original acronym - As Soon As Possible - now is a two syllable word that means 'immediately'."

"Point taken sir." He scurried from the room.

Anderson watched him leave and turned to the academics.

"You three should think on this stuff and be prepared to attend several meetings and perhaps more in the next few days and weeks. Go home tonight and think on this. We will be in contact in a few days with a meeting itinerary to put plans into place and from there on your involvement will be on an 'as needed' basis.

And according to our security establishment, that could mean anything at this point.

"I hope I can count on your help in the short term and the long, should it be needed," he looked pointedly at Fielding.

They all nodded and were escorted from the office to a nearby room where a lunch had been laid out.

"Finally some grub," said O'Regan. "I haven't eaten at all today."

Once in the room, provisioned with lunch and comfortably seated, Fielding opened the conversation.

"Well, Professor Evans, you seem to have been kept right up to speed on my research. Why were we not put in contact before? I might have searched out documents that pertained to the political situation."

"I'm not sure Ms Fielding. I was getting all your translated documents, or at least I think I was, as soon as you forwarded them. Now that I think of it, I was getting a steady stream of political information. I am now going to guess there was much more that I did not receive?"

"Yes there was. Much of it relating to the culture and relationships between the miners and their families both on the asteroid and off. We tapped into their personal logs. We haven't figured out too much of the technical stuff related to mining yet, as much of that involves language that has been invented subsequently to the use of the original Phoenician source."

"And the relationship stuff, the talk between people, hasn't changed much. I guess that makes sense."

O'Regan had been tucking into a piece of fried chicken and listening. He swallowed.

"Perhaps that's where I fit in. Taking the original language and trying to figure out the technical terms. That exact thing was a part of my major doctoral thesis. It was the way that Latin evolved as the Empire grew, particularly how it changed to describe Roman engineering, military technology and their battle tactics."

"I haven't seen a lot of that stuff in the translations," said Fielding." It was a mining colony after all. Apparently they used lithium, and it was lithium and cadmium and thorium and mercury that they were after, in some alloy process as the basis of their energy infrastructure. I guess all those elements were rare or mined out of their planets. They must have thought they hit the mother lode here on Earth, those elements are quite abundant here, aren't they?"

"I think you've hit on something Jenn. If the aliens are here on Earth, I wonder if they are clustered around lithium sources and sources of the other minerals?"

"Perhaps that technology is too new for them to have searched out these elements when they first came to Earth."

"What about the Moon. Surely that is what they were mining for there."

"I'm guessing there will be some serious study going on regarding old scans and orbital maps of the dark side of the Moon, looking for clues about locations and activities, assuming all that stuff hasn't already been done and is in the President's new briefing materials."

"President Anderson looked . . . . annoyed, when he found out about the previous alien contact."

"Can't say as I blame him. And, his immediate conclusion that there is much more he has not been made privy to. It's hard to forge ahead not knowing all the background."

"I remember hearing that Armstrong actually communicated with the aliens on the moon - they showed up in large numbers and indicated that the Earth bound exploration should remain on the visible side only and continue only for a few years."

"All that stuff was put down to conspiracy theories and wild speculation. There must have been something to it."

"I've read that Armstrong was a very reliable and honorable man. Though rarely questioned on the point in public he refused to deny any contact. Other astronauts in the Apollo Program reacted similarly."

"And then there are the physical oddities of the Moon itself. It's relative size compared to Earth is unusual, it's orbit around Earth where it is perfectly in phase to only show one side to the surface of Earth, and its orbital position so that solar eclipses are perfect, with the Moon perfectly covering the sun in the sky. What are the odds of these things occurring naturally? There are many people who have suggested that the Moon is an artificial satellite. To me, only its large size suggests otherwise."

Chapter Eleven

Teams were assembled to take on the widening arc of the alien question. Teams of metallurgists worked on the alien materials technology. Several privately financed teams of gravity experts tried to unlock the secrets of gravity propulsion and anti-gravity technology, and sociologists tried to identify the keys to the alien culture. Fielding and her team kept producing text and fed it into the various knowledge threads. They hit the mother lode when they stumbled upon technological specifications for the maintenance and repair of various machines on the asteroid.

Finding and understanding the gravity propulsion system was a priority as any travel to the exo-planets that might harbour life would be lengthy and difficult without it. Any mention of it in the records of the mining colony was forwarded to the team as it was being translated.

It became apparent that the gravity fields were like rivers in space, where gravity was balanced between local stars and black holes to produce a river-like swath of gravitational stresses. They moved through space like the high altitude jet stream does in Earth's atmosphere or like the Gulf Stream does through the Atlantic. Apparently these gravity balance points could be used by a rapidly moving craft to navigate through space at a speed much faster than light. According to records found on the asteroid the effect was like a slingshot of gravity tension suddenly letting go, though it was also described it as a choke point in a river which produced a strong eddy of water fighting to get around a rock where the water pressure builds up and squirts the water past the choke point at a rate of speed higher than the actual current.

How it exactly worked was unknown, even the alien science gave no detailed background on how or why the gravitational propulsion worked or how they identified these rivers. The key seemed to be this ability to recognize its existence. Some Earth scientists speculated that the gravity streams folded back on themselves and allowed movement from one space-time slice of the galaxy into another adjoining one. It was only a theory and Earth scientists spent much time and effort trying to figure out how to even begin to research it.

John Overholt got a call. He was asked to speculate on how to attack the idea, or to provide a line of inquiry he thought had promise.

He was still thinking on it for several days, when his phone rang. It was Harendez.

"Did you get a strange call about gravity propulsion?"

"Yeah, but I'm not supposed to talk to anyone about it."

"Either am I, but if we both got the call, it must be okay."

Overholt and Harendez decided to meet. Face to face was much better than lengthy silences on the telephone while they were thinking, or crazy message strings that took forever to go nowhere, and doubled back on each other to correct grammar and spelling mistakes that altered meaning.

While the teams worked on how best to use the knowledge they'd gained , perhaps by sending a craft to the original planet of the aliens, others worked to figure out when the rebel's craft would arrive. Given that they had not yet uncovered the timing for the abandonment of the mining colony or details of anything still operating on the Moon, it was a long shot guess at best.

A number of scientists and teams worked on the various problems suggested by the research team. Some knew what they were working on and why. Others speculated that their hastily assembled and somewhat vague university research programs must be somehow attached to the project, while others had no idea.

Harendez arrived in Arizona a week later - they spent their time at the array as Overholt was filling in for a graduate student who was ill. He liked to spend some quiet time at the array several times each year. He found it allowed him to engage in deeper thinking sessions than at his office at the university because of the lack of interruptions. He also found that rather than deeper questions of light and motion he often found the time most useful for organizing the minutia of his life. It was a constant matter of his amazement that the stresses and organizational requirements of senior professorship existed to draw the universities best minds into paperwork and bureaucracy. And everyone seemed to believe that that approach was normal. It had occurred to him that perhaps he was not considered one of the university's best minds - or that his usefulness as a scientist had already come and gone. It played into his theory that successful people were hugely successful once only.

"What do you know Ethan?" said John Overholt, back at the array which was now doing triple duty looking at radio signals from deep space, checking the part of the sky where the asteroid signals were first detected for any more signals including light signatures and all the while was still on the SETI program. SETI had not shut down, in fact the discovery of an alien intelligence had fueled more money for the project.

"Think about it. If we got the signals from the abandoned mining camp five years and four months after they were set to broadcast. . . and they knew at that time that the rebel group was coming to Earth to try to align our Earth civilization to a more independent way of thinking, then they must have left no more than 14 months ago plus the six years it took us to go there and back."

Ethan looked at him, his eyes widening. "Don't forget they know how to use the gravity propulsion."

"That's true Ethan, but that's not the point."

"Okay, so what is the point, Junior genius John?"

"They're already here."

Ethan's look of realization was comical. He looked like he wanted to hide, perhaps barricade the door or at least and set a watch for a likely invasion. He mastered himself with some effort. John tried to look as stern as possible, while reclining in his chair.

"Remember, I'm no longer a Junior Genius, I am now a senior fellow, a tenured professor and the Newton Chair of some sciencey thing at a prestigious American University, or two. I think they made it up just for me."

"Remember they are like us, in fact they may be us."

"I've never thought of the university administration that way."

"Funny. The aliens are just us without being from here. Come to think of it, so is my cousin Miguel from Barcelona. The aliens are not really invading, just doing a little tourist thing. Kinda like the English coming to America and mixing in with the locals."

"Tell the native Americans that," said Ethan. "So if they are here now, and are trying to stir up some stuff, why haven't we heard about it?"

"Could be a number of reasons. First, they are dealing with other people, though apparently not our government; or the President is a great actor, or they didn't find a sympathetic ear when they got here, or they are still assessing their situation. Remember some of them were open to the assimilation, others were not. Our planet has not been sufficiently softened up to accept full assimilation. Hell, we hardly knew about them until just a year or so ago. Perhaps they are assessing our planetary co-operation government by government."

"Have you mentioned this in your reports?"

"Well, no. It's just a surmise on my part. Elementary logic really. I figure some of the tall heads up the ladder from us have probably figured it out. I'd like to sneak it into a report at the right time, make it sound like widely known stuff, so we don't look stupid for having thought it up this far along, sort of like it was a given. I'm working on that."

There was a knock on the door. Both men looked at each other. Nobody ever came to the remote location of the array who had to knock. If you wanted into the small block building it was because you were expected and had a key.
The knock came again - without urgency.

"Is it Hallowe'en? Ok, I'm coming. Whoever it is, is at least polite . . . "

He moved to the door slowly at first as if considering his options, and then took the last steps quickly and flung open the door.

"Oh, hello," said a voice apparently caught by surprise. John looked down on a very short man, a dwarf really. There was no sign of any vehicle which he had used. And it was a man; shorter than the normal range, perhaps a metre tall, maybe a bit more but a perfectly proportioned human except with large hands and long fingers and a very flat, odd looking nose, like he was a prizefighter with a really long losing streak.

"I think you've been expecting me."

"Ummmh, yeah, for about two minutes," said John.

"Or two years," said Ethan.

"Perhaps I can come in and we can talk. I did not want to approach people in a busier part of your project because of all the fuss they would cause. I can answer some of your questions and you can function as a go-between, at least until we have established some understanding between us all."

John opened the door wider to allow the visitor to enter. He motioned him to their lunch table. The small man dexterously jumped into a seat and swung around to face the two electron pulse telescope professors.

"I am William Henderson, my friends and acquaintances call me Bill, which I prefer."

"Well, I'm John and this is Ethan . . . Ethan Harendez and John Overholt."

"I am aware of who you are. My family has lived here for many generations. In fact I am related to General George Custer and Elijah Henderson who came to America on the Mayflower."

Ethan started, sitting up quickly. "What? Aren't you invaders?"

"No, no Mr. Harendez, a branch of my family has been on Earth for millenia. I guess everyone's has essentially, except for the few visitors we had come a few months ago. They came, knowing that you would find out about us through the asteroid investigation."

"They told me that one branch of the Hendersons were reseeded stock several generations ago. However, the aliens came to Earth thousands of years ago and colonized. The original indigenous people of Earth died out, largely because they were few in number and unwilling to join with us. There was some interbreeding but any vestiges of Earth's original population were subsumed into the main group of newcomers which expanded rapidly. You call them Homo Sapiens, identifiable due to their large cranial capacity. We are you, or you are us, depending on your point of view," he smiled. "That's why there has never been found a missing link in the evolutionary chain. Anyway our people came to Earth and mixed where possible with the very small local populations of humanoids who were very similar to us despite our divergent planets of origin. In fact, the similarities have led us to believe that all these planets were seeded long ago by an alien race, so we are all related through them."

"Some of us remained small despite the gravity change, almost an evolutionary difference. The vast majority had larger progeny thanks to the lesser gravity here."

"But if you know this, that you came to Earth as a species thousands of years ago, how come this isn't general knowledge?"

"A good question, Mr. Overholt. I have only recently been provided with the detailed information of these developments due to my family's more recent inclusion. There are only a very few of us who know and we have only recently been reminded of this knowledge by visitors from our wider culture. This world is about to become aware of its own history."

"I have been contacted by the rebels on Amorra, the fourth world that was colonized from our home planet, the one where assimilation has become a problem. They are aware of the situation on Earth, where individual cultures have arisen and animosity between them can be strong. They know the situation and will exploit it if it seems exploitable to achieve their own ends. They want an affiliation with the home culture but not a full assimilation."

"I'm told they want peace but separation."

"So what do we report up the ladder?"

"An astute conclusion Mr. Harendez," Henderson said. He smiled widely, "I do not need you to take me to your leader, I know where he lives. However, that kind of direct approach is not best. While my appearance is a bit unusual I am not so obviously alien enough to capture their attention.

"What I need is a balanced report to the President outlining what I've just said. He can relay any questions or set up a meeting through you. I will return in two nights to speak with you. I fully expect the area to be covered in surveillance, but let's try to keep the drama to a minimum. Maybe you don't mention my return time.

"Once we talk again, if the time is ripe for a face to face with the President and ultimately the United Nations, we can make that arrangement. I expect they will want some measure of proof of my claims. Representatives have also been in touch with the Secretary General of the United Nations, and the leaders of Russia and China. Other cultural leaders may have to be brought into this, I am aware. But this is our starting point."

And with that he slipped out of the seat and left through the outside door while the two researchers thought of another question to ask. John rushed for the door but Mr. Henderson was gone without a trace, despite the station being miles from anything save the road that serviced it. John stood outside the door in the dark, with nothing around him that suggested anyone or any travelling vehicle.

"I guess you now have your opening for your report."

"Yeah, we have spotted the enemy and they are us. Plus there are other enemies among us and we don't know who they are just that they want to encourage us to remain separate from the hive that we've only just learned exists on an alien planet half-a-decade distant unless we learn to gravity surf to get there quicker. Problem is, he didn't mention if he was on the side of the home planet or one of the rebels."

"Just another day at the office, right John?"

And then the telescope scanner started to ping. For the first time since it first picked up the alien light signals hidden in the laser bursts, the computer analyser pinged that something unusual was being picked up by the scopes.

"Take my message to your leader," read the print out in plain English. And appending the sentence was a smiley face. "I'll be back!"
"You know John, this is not how I figured we'd be colonized by aliens."

"An invasion appended by 'Have A Nice Day', never really crossed my mind."

"Maybe we should make up some t-shirts and stuff. This stuff is gold!"

"It's not all about cashing in Ethan. So how exactly does one call the President?"

"Just for the record we have both cashed in. Why stop now? As for how to proceed, why don't you call the office of your local Congressman and/or woman? You should probably let the University President know as well so they don't get caught off guard. This is as much public relations as it is interstellar cloak and dagger diplomacy. Oh, and don't forget to mention my name."

Chapter Twelve

The oval office was full of expectant staffers.

The President put down the loose pages of the report. He leaned forward in his chair, his head down as he centered the pages on the blotter on the top of his desk. Happy to have something to do, he squared up all the pages in all four corners and tapped them in the center, slightly moving the top sheet, which required him to square it up with the others again.

He pursed his lips, and gave a long stare at the emblem on the rug in the center of his oddly shaped office. The staffers in the room were silent but restless and full of expectation.

"Well that's a bit of news, isn't it?"

The others hadn't read the report, except the chief of staff who wrote it. He had been in touch directly with Overholt and Harendez. He urged the President to provide the news. The

President began to speak to his senior staff slowly outlining the meeting with Henderson and the two astrophysicists, while his mind poked among the details for a response.

"How can we verify this as truth? What are our options?"

"I have people making contact with the Russians and Chinese and the UN to ascertain the contacts were made there," said the Chief of Staff.

"This stuff appears to be leaking out to the media. We will need a response or cover story if we want to buy time. And that depends on how much time we want to buy."

"It appears as though things have changed drastically," said the President. "Our origins have been exposed. Our geopolitical position is about to change radically one way or another. We are about to be introduced to a completely new order in our universe."

"So, do we do this behind closed doors and present details once we have them? Or do we release details that we have and continue to keep the public updated? What do we know about this Henderson person?"

"I think we wait. We must move slowly or the public will rise," said Frank Ellis, the National Security Advisor. "There was a lot of abstraction to this stuff before. We should wait at least to fully ascertain the Russian and Chinese position. We may know very quickly if we are in the same situation as the fourth colonized planet. Perhaps some contact will be made from them."

"Isn't this Henderson fellow one of the rebels?"

"No, not for certain. This is a very strange situation. We really don't know. Let's try to be clear here. Henderson appears to be human, one of us, as it were, but somehow privy to direct alien contact from which he purports to know homo sapiens true origin. He claims contact with the aliens but we are not sure how often, how detailed or if it's even a two way contact. Certainly from his position it appears a one way thing. We are not even certain he's legit."

"It would be quite the hoax. So we've got some detail on this guy?"

"Yeah, just a little. He's a dwarf, and . . . "

"You've got a little information on a dwarf? Is that a joke?"

"Umm, er, no Sir, we've been doing our background checks on him and they are still on-going with a team of agents looking into his life. I should have a more complete dossier in a few hours. William Henderson has done some work in the entertainment industry, but as he got older he fell into a job as an insurance adjuster, usually for claims in the entertainment industry. There is no indication of anything unusual. He does not appear to be any more wealthy than might be expected, though he has resources due to a large inheritance."

"Okay, it was reported that after the conversation with our SETI researchers he simply vanished from sight, in a very remote location."

"Yeah, okay, that one has me scratching my head. Perhaps he has access to the alien technology. But the bottom line here is he appears genuine, his message isn't threatening, just a fair warning of widening talks. Early indications are that his claims about contacting Russian and Chinese officials appear genuine."

An aide gently knocked on the door and was admitted with a nod from the President. He handed the President a sealed envelope and withdrew.

"Gentlemen, we have been contacted by another person, who claims to represent the breakaway group on the fourth planet. He is requesting a sit down meeting."

"How do we really know all of this is legit? That it's not some elaborate prank? I mean, really, little men from another planet, asking politely if we are on-side with their imperial government or if we want to form a rebel alliance?"

A few of the Joint Chiefs started to chuckle.

"This isn't Star Wars, Frank. I too, think we should wait a while until we get foreign reaction and to see if there is significant evidence for this development. There is no suggestion of any need to hurry. Henderson said he would be back to speak to Overholt and Harendez in the near future. He's likely looking for some indication of where we stand before he makes contact again."

"Don't forget the alien transcriptions do back up this scenario," said Navy Chief Rear Admiral Elliot Chambers. "And the general public isn't really aware of that yet. The more we can get from the transcriptions the better we will feel."

"Why are we all nervous?" said Air Force Chief General David C. Tabler. "It appears an amicable split between two similar cultures, not unlike the American split from the English. We just wanted to go our own way."

"Don't forget the English did not want us to go, and there was a war; more than once."

"Yeah, but within a few generations the split was not a big issue."

"According to the report from the SETI researchers, Mr. Henderson called it a war, in other words a violent struggle to establish the dominant will between the participants."

"We need to know more about this, before we can choose sides."

"Why do we have to choose sides. It appears to me that we have our own issues here on this Earth rather than trying to parse out our position in this alien culture. Thousands of years that we've been apart will produce some changes in customs even if we are all essentially homo sapiens. Surely they will not require us to make an irrevocable choice on short notice without sufficient information."

Another aide whispered to the President that the Russian President was on the phone. President Anderson picked it up and identified himself.

"Good morning Mr. President what can . . . "

He stood holding the phone, his smile gradually slipping from his face and his expression moved from neutral to concerned. He put down the phone.

"It seems as if the Russians are extremely wary of the situation. They think we are pulling a joke or something more sinister. They want a Security Council meeting and presentation from this Henderson fellow with significant evidence produced to explain this. I'm inclined to agree, though the Russians appear very unhappy and uncooperative with this development."

"And the Chinese?"

"He mentioned that the Chinese were already on-side with the meeting."

The meeting was arranged between the UN security council and

Bill Henderson, a former bit actor, and current forensic accountant and insurance adjuster. In Hollywood it was important to have all those skills - sometimes the job required it.

Despite surveillance William Henderson arrived at the telescopic array in the Arizona desert without anyone seeing him. He spoke to Harendez and Overholt as he promised. They relayed the desire for a high level UN meeting a few days later. He agreed to attend and left without being seen, making those who were watching skeptical that he even arrived. Only his agreement to attend the meeting in New York advanced the issues.

There was no mention in the press. If it was a hoax key intelligence people from around the world would know soon, and only they would be embarrassed between themselves.

The UN wanted proof from Mr. Henderson that he was connected to the aliens. With the meeting opened he arrived unobserved among the hordes of aides and unnoticed until he rose and moved to the lectern at the appointed hour.

The room went suddenly quiet. He greeted everyone and gave a short synopsis of the situation. He offered his unusual appearance and ability to appear at the meeting unnoticed as proof of his legitimacy.

That was rejected by the Chinese delegate due to evidence, which he did not deny, that he had been born in Modesto, California. Henderson provided a number of photographs of an apparently alien city, which looked very much like a number of cities on Earth with some fluffed up details edited in. He launched into a deeper dissertation on alien politics and the details of the rebel split. The members of the Security Council remained unconvinced.

"This man is a crackpot," declared the Chinese representative.

"He is merely fashioning known details into a narrative to scare us. He is likely psychotic."

"Sir, some of these details are unknown to the general public," said Henderson. "I know about the laser beams to other outposts and planets. I have been asked by the Central Authority on the Home Planet of Eiosia to inform you of the situation. I am aware you have been contacted by people from Amorra, the fourth world that has been colonized. However, I take no sides, nor does the Central Authority. In fact our culture is one of inclusion, peaceful resolution, where everyone is equal and conflict is virtually unknown. The 'war' on Amorra is essentially a culture war. That was a poor choice of words by me when I spoke to Mr. Overholt and Mr. Harendez in Arizona. There is no 'war' as you understand it. There is no shooting, death, re-education camps or even propaganda. For us, those holding conflicting opinions are required to present both sides."

"As a member of neither side, as a member of Earth culture, I can understand the rebels determination to remain outside the home world culture, as they want to preserve their heritage and are fearful of a radical shift. I understand that on Amorra they do realize that with time they will become part of the larger whole. They simply want to ease into it, to give older generations some-thing that they understand to hold on to and to install ways to pass on their history and culture to their progeny."

"Surely the Chinese should understand that, as they refused in the Middle Ages to engage with the outside world. They concentrated their concerns on internal issues and stopped looking at the wider world. As I recall you pulled back and buried a wealth of information gleaned from naval expeditions and discoveries and remained will-fully ignorant of the world as a whole," said Henderson.

"Ignorance is usually part of the cause of conflict, and definitely why most conflicts carry on or linger.

"Straight and rapid assimilation is what occurred on the second and third planets that were colonized. When we speak of a 'war' between the sides it is a cultural war - the benefits of separatism for its own sake on one side rather than rigid centralism on the other. The only violence has been by radicals on the Amorra side, with some particularly taken with the idea of self-determination, and from others who see the inevitable and want its benefits, primarily technological, in their own lifetimes. Ultimately we aren't against self determination. We believe that allowing it will bring everyone on board. The issue is what to do when some large group of people want one thing and others, nearly as large in numbers, want another and the two things are impossible to provide at the same time. Providing some with assimilation and technology will affect those who would rather live without it."

"So which side are you on, which side do you represent?"

"We have not yet determined if he's sane or not," said the Chinese representative.

"I represent both sides, sir. I have been sent by the central authority but I have been charged by both factions to explain their position and to ask Earth cultures to consider making a choice. That is our way. That choice will govern how we proceed together in our mutual discovery of one another. As a member of the larger Home culture you will be given significant advances in technology and asked to join with the Central Council, where the concerns of the whole of our civilization are aired. Currently, future expansion of the culture on Earth and Amorra's situation are the dominate topics of discussion there."

"And if we side with the 'rebels', and do not want to be assimilated?"

"In truth, likely the same. They have their councils and their technology, they do not have the resources to move it as easily as the dominant culture. For my part I would urge you to take your time. There is no hurry here. There is no danger in remaining neutral until you are more comfortable with the new realities. There are two schools of thought on this however. Should the United States get the advantages of full membership in the wider culture if the Chinese or Russians refuse it?"

"Are you threatening a technological space race? What you say is reassuring on one hand. And the argument that may ensue from anything but a unanimous position from this world's cultures is equally distressing. But you still haven't proved your story."

"I had hoped it would not come to this, but I understand the human need to see with your own eyes, after all, I am human too."

He paused for a moment and then faded out of sight. The room exploded with chatter. About 15 seconds later, as the chatterers paused to catch their breath, William Henderson reappeared on the other side of the large circular chamber. The room went quiet as he was recognized. After a few moments a group of people appeared with him. Most of them were dwarves. People who had not been in the room before, or at least not been visible.

The quiet that Henderson's appearance had engendered became an explosion of voices when the group of people revealed themselves one by one around him. The actor in Henderson played the dramatic silence and the raucous chatter without moving or appearing to speak. He waited - timing was everything. The room eventually got quiet as nobody in the newly revealed group moved.

"It is a simple visual trick," Henderson said quietly. "We are equipped with a device that alters the light waves around us and renders us invisible to untrained eyes. It's more like a party trick once you know the technology, it is not hard to spot if you are looking for it. There are signature light shimmers that can be detected. These are people from both our home world of Eiosia, and from the fourth planet of Amorra. They represent both sides of the debate. When you are ready they will mingle with you and answer any additional questions you may have."

"A party trick. I'd like to go to that party," whispered the Chinese representative to an aide.

"You might think you were the only one there, sir."

Henderson spoke to the whole room.

"The technology of this civilization is light years ahead of Earth, especially in terms of energy acquisition and use. It appears that even though we are the same species, the Home world has had a lengthy time where they were able to develop a more peaceful approach to their domestic issues, essentially a live and let live approach. This might have been a result of technological prowess which ended the needs for survival and subsistence among people. With easily obtained resources there is little incentive to battle for those that are available," said Henderson to the nods of several of the newly revealed people in the room.

"So I'm not sure I see the point of any conflict," said the American representative. "So the Amorran rebels want to hold their culture a little closer rather than getting subsumed into the greater whole? That's it?"

A voice from the larger group of aliens spoke up.

"Yes, that is it. Remember, that maintaining our independence requires that we hold back on a number of potential technological advances that the Home world could provide. This is done to stave off the abrupt shift in culture that would result. However, as your own history shows rapid technological change can be much more dramatic than it appears and could lead to a split in any very self-contained culture. Your own history on this planet, and in fact our histories on other planets show this approach to be destructive to local development. We do not want to be rigid about the need to remain together, but we strongly believe it is the best approach and also believe that all parties will come to believe that in time. So we make no demands at this time, only that you do not step outside the bounds of your own considerations and weaken the long standing deep beliefs in our shared culture with those who have already accepted it."

"And we can send people to Eiosia to study your ways and bring technological innovation back to Earth?"

"Absolutely," said Henderson, "and the Amorrans have been encouraged to do the same thing. In fact, that is some of the solution to the conflict with various groups of people choosing to emigrate to the Home planet to avoid the stifling of technology attached to remaining culturally separate. The mere idea of cultural homogeneity is new and some time without any technological advances influencing change might help your divided world decide upon its shared cultural norms."

"We are you," said the Amorran representative. "Perhaps a bit ahead of you in terms of history and cultural development, but we are physiologically the same, save for a few small differences in evolution, such as Mr. Henderson's very flat nose and our general size. We have the same desires, needs and wants as you. It's just that we have largely achieved them and want to share. Frankly we would have waited for contact with you until you had advanced your technology and solved some of your internal problems with widely differing groups of people, with significantly different opinions and arrangement of government organization and religion. Your technology had advanced a bit quicker than your social development, giving you the opportunity to find us before we deemed you ready."

"And now we have to figure out how to present all of this to the billions on Earth who are awaiting some answers to the mysteries uncovered on the mining asteroid," said the UN secretary general.

"We suggest you provide the information a little at a time, always moving the interpretation of it in a way that forms a direct line from start to finish. Our experience suggests it is easier that way."

"Thank you for your presence. I think we will need to discuss these developments among ourselves and determine the proper approach. I do think that everyone here will agree that we need to send a joint expedition to Eiosia and perhaps to Amorra to better understand the issues."

"A question if I may, said the American ambassador. "You mentioned self-determination, does that mean you operate your society on democratic terms?"

"Yes and no. Much of our local governance and decisions are made by people elected by those who are governed. However, the council of the entire civilization is appointed and operates wider policy governance in the manner of a utility - highly efficient, highly centralized and extremely concerned with value and quality of services. Our technology has rendered resources a non-issue so there is really no corruption."

"Nobody has explained why the asteroid broadcast a message to us?" chimed up another voice from the American contingent.

Mr. Henderson shifted his feet. "It was an accident, I am told. The broadcast beacon was only in place to indicate the asteroid had been mined out and nobody was there. The beacon was aimed at several of our other mining camps and inhabited planets including another of our mining communities on your Moon. Only an error sent the signal to Earth and only a chance situation in Arizona allowed it to be discovered when it was."

"So beacons are set between all of your outposts - sort of like a fire beacon of ancient times?"

"Yes, I suppose. In our case it operated as much as an early warning system to us that our walls had been breached. The beacon goes out upon contact with off-worlders with our installations. That's how we know the aliens are coming."

"So we are aliens to you?"

"No, not really, just a figure of speech, but we did not know that it was you who had breached our settlement. We have not encountered any other intelligent beings save for those near us who appear to be us from a common ancestor. We were aware of you. So at least we have that understanding of a wider culture. But it is just the five of us at this point and who knows what is really out there."

"A lucky chance for us, then," said the Russian, forcing a smile to his face.

"Or not, sir. Your foreknowledge of this situation has changed things for us as well. We have a number of people who want to visit Earth much as your people like to visit native cultures and those that have maintained some of the old ways."

"We have many wonders to see in Russia. We welcome tourists."

"There are many billions on our four planets and given the

223

automation many would accept an opportunity to try to understand their own origins. Such an influx may be beyond your ability or willingness to cope."

"People would be willing to come to Earth in large numbers, a journey of several years, just to look around?" said the Chinese representative. "That sounds less like a tour group and more like an invading army."

"I imagine your people from Earth might want to do the same, and in large numbers. And that is why you need to think about your relationship with the Home world and its greater culture. It's not as if they will all come at once, but a trickle may become a flood. I can assure you we are not an invading army but you need to see and understand that first hand. After all, when Napoleon invaded Russia, many in the Russian nobility welcomed the French as enlightened cultural elite."

"Nobody said the Russians were too bright," said a member of the American contingent a bit louder than he wanted.

"I have always thought that the Russians were reaching out for the height of human evolution," said the head of the French delegation with only the hint of a smile.

The Russian delegation stirred in indignation but were quieted by the Frenchman.

"It was the French who travelled to Russia," said the Russian ambassador. "Who was reaching for who?"

"Any culture that drinks more wine than water is on the path to evolutionary greatness," said an Italian.

"Or civilizational cirrhosis."

Chapter Thirteen

The United Nations security council met in a closed door session. It was leaked to the press that the meeting was about a border dispute in Asia.

"I see no reason to make any decision on this immediately," said the Russian ambassador. "We should take the alien's advice and try to calm our local disputes while strengthening the UN. In the meantime we can slowly leak out the situation to our populations. Further meetings with these beings would help soothe our concerns."

With a large number of local disputes, especially in Central Asia, the Russians smelled an opportunity to solve many of their problems and solidify their position among nations.

"China believes people should know the full story now and we have no interest in making any decision on which side to take for the foreseeable future."

Ho Yang had advised this course to the Chinese government. If the alien technology had solved all that humans need for survival then consolidating the Chinese positions around the world was necessary to having a strong voice in any negotiations. Privately he advised the Chinese to accept any technology they could get without compromising their control over their territory.

"The United States is interested in exploring the situation and recommends no actions be taken until our expedition to the Moon returns, and we can assess the situation. We welcome international participation. We should make an effort to move towards full disclosure with our people, but at a rate that helps maintain calm."

President Anderson insisted upon an American push to Manifest Destiny. With the discovery of the alien culture, the United States was no longer bound by terrestrial limitations. His military men expressed grave concerns as their ability to remain in control of their areas of influence was teetering in the face of alien superior technology. Many in the upper echelons of the military strongly advised caution and cohesion in any dealings with the aliens. President Anderson was more interested in pushing American ideas on the alien worlds.

"Speaking for the Non-Aligned Nations we are generally in agreement with everyone," said Pradesh Naado, to general laughter from the assembly. "Wait and see, keep talking, release of info and a move to quell the conflicts around the world."

So the meeting ended without an announcement save that the Security Council would act as a third party mediator in 15 border disputes around the world. There was significant pressure on China to relinquish control of its African colony. The creation of the puppet state was not even cloaked in diplomatic language by most observers. China for its part ignored the references but continued to mention the unrest in north-western Brazil as a potential trouble spot for separatists. From the Chinese perspective deflecting world attention to another trouble spot seemed the best way to quell international issues with East Congo.

"We understand the need for China to defend its interests," said the US ambassador to his Russian counterpart. "However, there is a line which we will not allow them to cross when it comes to extending their influence into our sphere."

"That which was unspoken has now been breached," said the Russian. "We too have our concerns and a very long border with the People's Republic. Frankly I think this has been obvious among all of us, even among the smaller nations with regard to their local issues. And this creation of spheres of influence is only going to complicate our relations with our galactic neighbors. They want us thinking as one, not as three or more."

"Aye, but no matter how stable the geopolitical world appears, it is always in flux, shifting and growing every day. Crisis moments take time to form so we must stay vigilant on the Chinese and even each other as our interests shift and change."

"Have your scientists begun to understand some of the technology brought back by the asteroid mission?"

"Yes, we have. Several companies have formed. Farming it out to private industry through a licensing process has been valuable. And I think in that manner it will be available to all. A few companies have taken on the gravity propulsion issue but have not managed a break through. I think it prudent to ask the aliens to provide it to us so we can visit them. It would show good faith on their part, and at least for many years would only facilitate communication between us."

"Everyone needs to understand that even with the gravity

propulsion system the trip to meet the aliens will still take nearly four years if our people stay for a few months time."

"We need to assemble a qualified group to go. A group who can make the most of their time there. If this Henderson fellow is to be believed any adoption of their technology will change us dramatically. In fact I'm not sure how it can be slowed or stopped unless we are all steadfast in that regard and take the Amorran approach."

"There is more to this Henderson fellow than he's letting on," said the Russian. "Everybody seemed satisfied that he was the mouthpiece for the aliens however it is not clear to me how that has occurred. Has he been visited? Is there a full time presence on Earth by actual aliens? Are they in some communication with their Home World Eiosia?"

"I guess in the end the mechanism is of little importance as long as we are sure there is one, and that Henderson is on the level."

"He's legitimate or the greatest magician in history."

"What I'm trying to figure out is why all of their worlds appear to be unified culturally when Earth has always had widely divergent cultures?"

"Ah my friend, among sheep to their fellows, they are widely divergent, but to the Sheppard they are all just sheep."

Canada and Denmark were quick off the diplomatic mark with an announcement that they would hold remote northern territory that was claimed by both in a joint special status where both countries held sovereignty and any activities could be undertaken by either country without agreement as long as there was formal diplomatic notice. The UN issued a statement calling the agreement a good start and a fine example of diplomacy. However the dispute between the countries involved nothing but a few acres of a remote snowy island and ocean drilling rights for oil in a very inhospitable environment.

As a framework for agreement this type of arrangement became popular for numerous minor disputes around the globe.

Out of the talks emerged a larger possibility. Some people in Copenhagen thought full union with Canada was an idea worth exploring. Eastern Canadians did not immediately dismiss the idea. Quebeckers mulled the idea, unwilling to quickly dismiss a large number of bilingual French speakers. Most people in Western Canada thought the idea a bit preposterous, knowing any actual decision on such a matter would take many decades to percolate through their culture.

Several other nations followed suit in resolutions to their minor border disputes and even proposals of union, especially where the issues were minor and the countries themselves culturally similar. While the talks led to better relations between nations they did not produce any breakthroughs other than agreements similar to that between Canada and Denmark.

China and India agreed to split the difference on their disputed territories, and delineate disputed territory as special joint lands which operated under both nations and neither, with each nation holding veto power over any activity within the designated territory. India and Pakistan did not come to any agreement on Kashmir but they did agree on the areas that were in disagreement, removing some of the ambiguity from their cross claims and reducing tension in the Himalayas.

In the meantime details from the alien encounters were slipped into simple NASA bulletins. There was no mention of aliens being on Earth or living among human populations. That contact was made, and that the beings were human in appearance, seemed revelation enough to start.

More details were provided to the public in a fairly regular way. As soon as media interest in questions which arose from one release of information the UN would release more to help answer the questions, but ultimately providing a place for more questions.

Once all the details were made public the revelation that the alien physiology was identical to homo sapiens was released. The dam of intellectual distance burst, and the ensuing firestorm engulfed churches, faith groups of all kinds and provided a demand for evidence.

Then it was divulged that the aliens used a form of ancient Earth language as their primary language tool, at least in its written form.

Everyone wanted to know what it was . . . that was the key to understand the aliens. The Security Council decided to withhold the information as long as possible. However pressure built rapidly, information leaks and claims were rampant. Protests increased, with antigovernment demonstrations. It was decided to release all the remaining relevant information in hopes that several pieces of controversial news would fray and protests would decentralize with the number of potential issues.

The revelation that Phoenicians were somehow tied closely to the aliens put a spotlight on the Lebanese who quickly became central figures in an new intrigue. More than one government official wondered out loud how a small and insignificant population could have survived for so many thousands of years, surrounded by hostile cultures, without some alien knowledge or help. The Lebanese themselves were not surprised as they had for millennia managed to maintain their hold on their land and culture, though they denied off-world help.

Jews in Israel were also targeted with many noting how they had survived for millennia through many ebbs and flows in their historical condition. Several commentators noted how they had referred to themselves as a chosen people, and wondered if that had been derived from extraterrestrial origins. The Israelis merely shrugged and said they didn't know any more than was revealed in their scripture. Many anti-Semites and enemies of Israel were not convinced.

Dwarfs and midgets the world over were highly scrutinized. At first they enjoyed the attention after being marginalized for so long, but then the attention became too great to bear.

The controversy predictably moved in many directions at once. In an effort to quell curiosity and show good faith, Mr. Henderson spoke to world leaders, explaining the existence of a Moon colony. Special interviews with him and other representatives of the alien worlds were conducted for public consumption.

The Moon colony was on the far side of the Moon, right where previous scans said it was. Red-faced government officials from several countries had to admit they knew it was there. Henderson explained the aliens had sought anonymity when the Moon was being explored as First Contact was premature at the time and their mining activities were peaceful.

Given the revelations regarding the Moon colony the project to visit the Moon was upgraded to a full scale expedition to the alien home planet of Eiosia. The aliens provided the gravity propulsion system which gave the voyage about a year's travel time in each direction, though much longer would pass on Earth.

Jenn Fielding, Ivan Bolrenko, and his wife Mika Oh all agreed to join the voyage which was expected to take less than three years in total thanks to the gravitational wave propulsion technology. They recruited a fourth crew member, Chinese national Yang Li. This time Bolrenko was in command.

Jimmy Ho Wang was fully ensconced in the Chinese government directing its policy on the aliens. It was his recommendation which gave Yang Li the green light. Rene Martin was similarly called upon by the French, who internally were torn between having him on Earth aggressively working on technology or in a first responder situation on the spacecraft. Mike Donohue was also engaged in his work and believed himself too old to undertake the journey. His recovery the first time around had been lengthy.

The prevailing wisdom on Earth was a wait and see approach. Once the rocket took off Mr. Henderson requested a meeting with the UN.

"Now that your exploratory team has left. I would like to explain our situation to all of you. Your exploration expedition will find out these details in time, but it is our contention that they not be pre-disposed to any judgement of what they encounter. And my contact with you will corroborate their reports."

"Look Mr. Henderson, if you have been withholding things it will not look good on our inter-terrestrial relations," said the representative from Brazil. "Especially if it has put our astronauts in any danger."

"If I may. . . this Mr. Henderson claims to be an Earthling, for want of a better name, but searching our records he appears to have surfaced about 40 years ago. We have no record of him prior to that and his government issued ID appears to be fraudulent," said the American representative. "He is not the last of a long line of people in the know about this extraterrestrial civilization."

"So Mr. Henderson, perhaps you can fill us in on the truth."

"Ah, I expected as much. I had no wish to lie to you but if I appeared as a completely off-world intelligence it would have jolted you a bit too much. So you want the truth . . . okay, I can now provide it."

"It is a long story and we have a need that you know it. I was placed here on this planet after your Moon visits produced Contact. We knew it was only a matter of time before Contact would occur again. First, some background . . . There are four other colonized planets as we have revealed. And there is a rebel group who is seeking autonomy on one of those planets. There are some violent factions among them, but they are small and do not appear to be gaining traction. Violence is not our way. However, they are belligerent in defence of their right not to be exposed to our advanced technology. Limited contact appears to be the wish of a clear majority, so those who want the technological advantages are being strongly encouraged to emigrate. However, our problem is more fundamental.

"We have been among you for thousands of years," the little man said, shifting in his seat. "We are the leprechauns, the tiny trolls of myth, the small quiet almost magical people of song and story. Most of us come and stay for some time and are replaced by others so there are few of us that were born here and stayed and thus achieved standard human stature for Earthlings."

"We have studied and watched, only rarely intervening in human affairs and generally only at a personal level. We are essentially the forward watch for our civilization. While we monitor humanity for signs that we should reveal ourselves to you, we spend our time searching for anything that might help us, especially in the world of herbs and concoctions for medical or genetic research. We are, as I said, identical and apparently seeded from some prior civilization. But you see, our population is dwindling. On our home planet the population has dwindled to only a few million, where once it was many billions. We have found no medical reason for this."

"On the other planets it is falling fast, and on Amorra, the other planet that was colonized at the same time as Earth, they have decided they do not want a close connection to us, fearful that their growth will be hampered by whatever is causing our decline. Interestingly our populations on Earth and in mining colonies, have continued to grow at a reasonable rate. Amorrans who emigrate are helping us rebuild our populations."

"What we really want is you. We would like millions of Earthlings to consider locating to our home planet and reinvigorating our population. We are genetically the same. Your explorers will verify all of this upon their return."

"Why are your people dying?"

"They are not dying, sir, well, not in any way other than simple old age. What is occurring is that they are not replenishing themselves. We are having very few children. You see, with most of our material wants automated, it appears there is little spark to life - additional efforts provide no reward to unmotivated millions, and games and competitions of skill have run their course. We are culturally exhausted."

"Imagine a civilization with 3000 more years of technological advancement than you have. We have essentially invented our way out of want and need. Games and other pastimes of skill have been completed, mastered so there is no more advancement or wonder or joy in competing. And our scans of our part of the galaxy suggest that after Earth there is nowhere else to explore that is within range of our technology. We are adrift."

"And now that our numbers on our home world are so low, we do not have the numbers to institute any sort of reform. The other worlds are fearful that they too will be seized by this ennui once they have fully developed their planets. The fourth world wants no part of us as if quarantine will keep away the plague of no or low expectations."

"And how do we know this to be true, Mr. Henderson?"

"It was necessary to invent the other scenario, which is true in itself, just not the whole story, so you would accept the situational realities with the least amount of concern. We are physiologically the same as you - we are homo sapiens, as you call us, and are merely transposed and evolved in a slightly different way. We want you to join us but understand if you want to remain apart in some endeavors. A few million of your fellow terrestrials would likely do for our needs."

"And you propose we just give people the opportunity to emigrate? What's in it for them?"

"Yes, there is a great tradition of that on Earth, and there would be many millions who would benefit from the immediate cessation of their daily wants and needs. What's in it for them? Everything. Of course we would like to carefully screen individuals who want to emigrate, much as the United States did when people came in from Europe in the 19th and 20th centuries, when they checked for disease, mental capacity and the like."

"The big advantage for Earthlings to emigrate is that all the technology is fully implemented there. On Earth it will take perhaps a decade or more, should you choose a quick introduction of all the technological advancements, before they can be provided to all or almost all of your citizens. And of course there is the possibility that you as a planet, will choose not to take it at all."

The United Nations decided to provide this new information to the public in advance of the return of the expedition to Eiosia. After some debate the details were transmitted to the spacecraft which had not yet caught the gravitational wave which would fling it out of contact.

"I knew this seemed too good to be true," said Bolrenko.

"It's not like it's something sinister. They just wanted to ease us into their situation much like we wanted to ease our populations into the alien contact," said Fielding.

"They didn't tell us everything, but at least so far, it doesn't appear that they've told us any lies," said Oh. "Of course we'll know the truth of that and many other things once we arrive. At least we are going with open eyes."

"Guess that depends on your definition of a lie," said Yang Li. "Or truth."

"Lies by omission are still lies," said the Russian. "It makes me wonder if they have come clean with us entirely or if they are working up to something else. Could we be walking into a shooting war as third party diplomats? Could there be something else we are unfamiliar with - as human as these guys are supposed to be, they are still aliens who have evolved on another world for thousands and likely hundreds of thousands of years apart from us. That Henderson guy's nose was funny. Perhaps it was just formed a bit different due to the atmosphere on Eiosia but maybe it's an indication of something more significant in his physiology."

"Now Ivan, I know you Russians don't have a lot of trust of outsiders, but at least wait for evidence of treachery."

"Mika, I have waited. We need to be wary. Waiting too long for evidence of treachery will engulf us in the treachery. This twist is evidence enough that we should at least be going into this expedition with our weapons drawn and antenna up."

She considered for a moment, her jaw dropping and then closing. "Yes, you are right. Caution is prudent. What is it the Americans say? 'Trust but verify.' I think I understand that now. Though wasn't that sentiment directed at you Russians," she said with a gleam in her eye.

Bolrenko glared at her a moment and then broke into a grin. "Da. But I remember my history of treachery at Port Arthur and on the Yellow Sea."

"And I remember Pearl Harbor," interjected Fielding.

"You don't remember it, you only read about it. That's not the same thing. And you Mika are splitting hairs," said Bolrenko. "I was referencing the situation not suggesting firsthand knowledge."

"Really, while Pearl Harbor might seem like a sneak attack to you, without the whole story of the diplomacy leading up to it, the situation in Japan and the economic issues in south east Asia, you really don't know the Japanese point of view which takes the attack as more of a warning shot across the bow of an emerging bully nation, an attempt at a bloody nose to back the US out of Asian - Pacific concerns."

"Do you really want to go there everyone. We all have historical grievances," said Fielding. "We need to be acting on behalf of our entire world rather than remain mired in our national mindsets."

"I remember when Renaud Martin realized that arguments or violence on behalf of those arguments would not change the historical reality. He laughed about it."

"Yes, he did, but the past informs us about the present and predicts the future."

"Yes, we do need to remain impartial, and act on behalf of all of Earth, but never forget that people are products of their background and upbringing. These things are in you and impossible to entirely divorce yourself from."

Chapter Fourteen

Those on ship had to reconsider their approach to the mission.

"So we are not going as ambassadors, we are going as emigration officers, land agents and the like. I would not have signed up for this had I known," said Bolrenko.

"Oh Ivan, we are still ambassadors. But think of it, we will see firsthand the alien civilization and learn how they achieved their technological prowess and ascertain if the place is habitable for humans," said Fielding. "I think it is more exciting than landing in an alien city and trying to figure out a lot of new technology while being brought up to speed on thousands of years of alien history."

"I wanted to see strange sites and wild technological advances but it sounds as if they solved human needs but couldn't solve human wants. One must wonder at their technological marvels and shake their heads at their philosophical failures," said Yang Li the only member of the crew not to make the first trip.

"Yes Yang, perhaps that is our ultimate mission, to determine if our humans can adapt to a society with no rewards and no obligations," said Mika.

"Think about it . . . any emigrants will absolutely fall in love with the place as all their needs are taken care of. It is succeeding generations that will falter. Perhaps the solution is to restore the need to strive and work toward something."

"But what? It's the old philosophical question; without the need for work to live, people will not live to work - too many people will be happy to simply exist, in effect live it up, without feeling the need to accomplish anything. It might explain why they are only a little ahead of our level of technology. They solved the big problems and then settled down to enjoy it."

"Yeah, but from what we've been told, they've written all the symphonies, completed all the plays and novels and movies and explored all the things in the human condition and they are out of gas as a civilization. It sort of goes back to the old sci-fi conundrum of the problems with immortality. In this case perhaps not the immortality of each person, which they don't seem to have con-quered, but rather the immortality of the civilization from one generation to the next. How would a culture evolve that had nowhere to go?"

"I guess we will see."

"And each successive generation is further removed from the hard truths and realities that helped to create and build the successful civilization. Think about it. It would not be possible to reject the technology - you would have a riot on your hands, and frankly there are only so many people in a society who are driven to accomplish things without being pushed. Too many would simply push for local power, gangs and crime for its sheer thrill, or just slide deeper into their couch and watch a bit of entertainment for the 100th time."

"If these people have travelled light years to ask for help, they must be in a world of trouble."

"Good analogy," said Jenn.

"Jenn, why did you come on this flight?"

"I see this as the real completion of our first mission and the curiosity it developed. I want to complete that and really find out what we are dealing with. If it had been another 12 years, I likely would have said no, but having conquered the largest cipher puzzle of my life, I wanted to finish up. Plus the idea of seeing Ancient Phoenician used as an everyday language was a bit of a pull."

"Who knows if Henderson was being straight with us on that one."

"We will find out. They seem to have mastered English well enough. Or at least Henderson has. Maybe he's legit."

Once deployed the gravitational wave propulsion rendered any communications outside the ship impossible so the astronauts settled into a simple daily routine for the year that their flight would take. The aliens had provided telemetry information to guide their ship. Having already undertaken a long space flight, keeping fit was second nature to them, though this time they concentrated more on keeping their leg muscles strong as the gravity on Eiosia was expected to be as much as three times stronger than Earth gravity.

Given the difficulties that Donohue had had there had been special provisions made for the trip, as it was unknown how Yang Li would fare or how the gravity propulsion would affect them. The Eiosians said they would be provided with anti-gravity suits upon arrival as it was expected they would need them for any lengthy outings. The suits would allow gravitational support for their legs and core muscles until they were able to adapt. Still, the stronger they were to start, the easier it would be.

They were contacted earlier than anticipated about their impending arrival. They were told they were being taken to Athelna, the first planet to be colonized.

"I thought we were going straight to Eiosia," said Oh. "I don't like the sounds of this."

"According to contact from the alien planet there was a change in the mission as Athelna is currently as close to Eiosia as it gets, a perfect time to visit. Apparently they are suggesting that a quick visit here will get us acclimatized for our lengthier visit to Eiosia, which is only a short gravity propulsion jump from here."

The astronauts were uneasy with the change - their antenna had definitely risen. Their guide offered no indication that the change in plan was unusual. After making orbit they took a landing craft to the surface and were guided in by a gravity tractor beam to a perfect landing.

"When we were able to travel through interstellar space we found beings like ourselves, an atmosphere almost identical to Eiosia and a basic writing system that closely matched our own," said an alien who greeted them and introduced himself as Marcus Ahre, who had been assigned to show the landing party around. "It seemed that our planets had been seeded by an intelligence some time before.

"We took the approach to slowly integrate with the inhabitants who were at the beginning of their technological age, with rudimentary mass production, improvements to transit, heating and communi-cations. We believed that integrating with them should be done in a way to allow them to experience the rapid increase in technology over several generations rather than making a great leap forward."

"It didn't work though, did it?" asked Fielding.

Ahre shook his head, "Once they saw what was possible, through our actions, they demanded to be treated equally. Our justice systems resisted at first but there was a rapid disintegration of that view and people who bucked the system and took matters into their own hands. Before two Athelna years had passed the Athelnans had equalled us in technology but did not have the necessary historical reference points to completely understand it or appreciate it."

"And how did that end?"

"Much as you might expect. You will see the end result. Cultural disintegration rapidly took over the population who began to look exclusively at Eiosia for direction. They had multiple civil approaches to life, much like your Earth does; but their own civilizations rapidly looked to Eiosia for direction and validation. We on the Home World had expected some of this approach but did not anticipate its rapidity nor the almost pitiable approach taken by much of the Athelnan population."

"So you are Eiosian?"

"Well yes, but it isn't really any distinction now. This happened many generations ago. For many years native Athelnans have thought of themselves as Eiosian."

"Was this assimilation approach taken with the third planet to be colonized?"

"No. People there were really a single civilization which had scattered across the planet in their early history. Again they appeared to be from the same seeded source that we were. There were some local customs but generally they worshipped the same gods, had the same attitudes and communicated the same way. We realized we would be fighting a losing battle to cap the introduction of technology to yet another similar world to ours, so we simply caved in from the start, informed the indigenous population that we were their brothers and they could join with us. They did so very enthusiastically though we had difficulty getting them to understand the technology; that it was science and not magic, as they had not really experienced a full technological age and the rapid advancements that it brings.

"Our anthropologists have now determined that the technological stage is very important for people to experience. Understanding that new technology can rapidly change culture and day to day existence does not come quickly to unprepared populations. Fortunately they were only a few generations away from finding an industrial age on their own, so, the transition had its difficulties. It took about two complete generations, as especially the young were able to grasp the changes fairly quickly, and were more easily adapted to them. We took the approach to move through technological advances quite rapidly rather than move all at once to the same level of science as we had on Eiosia."

"Gravity here is significant compared to Earth. Is there some relief for us?"

"Yes we have provided gravity control suits for you, actually just a pair of trousers that will counteract the higher gravity and allow you improved movement. We could adjust the strength of gravity for a whole area but of course that would impact our own people as well."

The landing party readied for travel around Athelna, donning the pants and moving to a self propelled platform. They saw that most people stood on the platform and held railings which could be folded down into seats when the platform moved more rapidly. There were gravity locks on each passenger but they were not foolproof, but rather a light tether for additional safety.

"Please be extra careful as we move. I suggest sitting as your gravity suits will counteract the extra gravity hold the platform places on travellers when we move."

The platforms existed in several incarnations, some were pre-set, including the first one the visitors used which took them through the arrival building to a pre-set destination, like a bus or moving sidewalk. Once there they left the building on another one which was directed to its specific destination via voice command. This more autonomous vehicle also had controls built into one of the sitting positions so an operator could operate it without voice commands, which was especially useful for precise and rapid changes to its use. Ahre took this position.

"We saw these things on Rugby," said Bolrenko. "We didn't know what they were of course, they looked like building foundations. I wonder if the actual foundations where buildings stood were also gravity platforms that could be moved in an anti-gravity way?"

"It is possible through I am not familiar with all of the minute operations of our mining operations."

"This platform material is similar to the foundation bases we saw. They must have taken the propulsion units with them when they abandoned the colony on Rugby, otherwise we would have found them," said Fielding.

"Yes, Ms. Fielding, the anti-gravity propulsion units were removed from Rugby once the operation there shut down. It is standard procedure for all completed projects. The technology is quite intricate and not very heavy. They are engineered specifically for mining operations so the units are recycled when a location is mined out. The platforms themselves are just reinforced fibre, a basic building material."

The group was flown to an agricultural area a few miles from the air and spaceport, passing a large city on their way. The platform was roughly the size of an average room, with three rows of four seats. As it moved it flew almost like a hover craft only a few centimeters above the flat ground of the airport. There was no perimeter wall or roof to the vehicle. Warned about the protective force fields, they could feel them but also knew the protection was light and would not prevent an accident if the platform crashed into something. The force field did keep riders dry and safe from flying insects or vegetation blown around in any weather events. It also prevented them from falling off, though the pressure of the tether was almost imperceptible on top of the huge gravity on the planet.

Once they moved outside the boundaries of the airport the platform rose to ensure a safe flight over the gently rolling terrain. As there were no hills in their general area that rose more than five meters above level ground, the platform rose to about seven meters in altitude and cruised over the fields towards a group of buildings.

"What you see is almost completely automated. In the past we would have used this arrangement of fields and processing with a few live operators and overseers to ensure it ran smoothly and to fix problems. However, now even that function is regulated by robot. You can see several of them in operation near the building we are approaching."

The straight sided building looked to Fielding to be the same kind of construction she had seen on the asteroid, a tin-like material which upon closer inspection was embedded with a thin wiry matrix for strength. This was no shed however, it was much bigger even than a barn on Earth. they knew it was large even from a distance but as they neared it the enormity of the building impressed them all. It was only when they were close that they could see that around the building there were purpose built robots, without any human form, built for their specific task.

"Do you use this type of construction material a lot?" she asked.

"Yes, you would have seen it on the asteroid. It is something we use for buildings where aesthetics and wonder are not required; storage buildings, industrial concerns, food processing. In fact it forms the shell of even our most beautiful constructions much as your ancients used simple bricks to build and marble to complete the look of their buildings. I might say that we have observed that building techniques themselves on Earth are fairly standard to all of our colonized planets but your view of finishing has fascinated our theorists. The carved marble, the addition of large numbers of small details has had our architects quite aghast. Construction on all the other worlds is far more basic. There is a theory that suggests Earth had a wider variety of construction materials rather than more imaginative inhabitants. That theory is being studied."

"The air here seems heavy. Not that it's difficult to breathe but it feels like I am inhaling 'chunkier' air," said Mika.

"An excellent observation. The Athelnan atmosphere is similar to Earth but it contains higher concentrations of Neon and Argon, heavier gasses, which account for your breathing. It has been slowly engineered over generations to more closely resemble the atmosphere of Eiosia."

"Those shouldn't harm us but what about long term? Is there any study of the effects of the different atmosphere on those from off world? I assume that the makeup of the atmospheres on the other planets are not identical with this one."

"Strangely they are similar. We made our changes to eliminate any issues between planets, as we expected much back and forth. That travel didn't materialize as expected but we now have atmosphere's that are aligned more consistently. Our scientists have speculated that the atmosphere was engineered by the culture that seeded the planets with identical intelligent life, and it changed naturally over many years. The big question is why it did not happen on Earth?"

"Perhaps they were interrupted in their effort. Your evidence so far suggests Earth is the last of the planets in this group, does it not?"

"Yes, but we have done a wide search of other nearby systems since we found Earth and Amorra. Where we have looked, we have found nothing more."

"Are you anticipating more planets will be found?"

"Given the fairly large concentration of habitable planets in this small area of space, yes, there was an expectation of more, however we have searched much of near space, out to about 20 light years and have found no more. Three dimensional space at those distances requires a lot of effort to search, even if we concentrate only on the stars in that vicinity. The search did lead us to discover a number of asteroids which are rich in minerals which we can use and so have established operations."

"Why would people consent to the hard life of miners, and travel to these distant outposts?"

"It hasn't been difficult to get volunteers, as there are many people who still have a drive to accomplish things. Some go because they want to get an off-world experience. Of course we make the terms of these volunteer assignments attractive with privileges, insisting on the off-world experience as a prerequisite for other privileges, such as government service, higher education and access to various finite resources."

The platform had continued to glide toward the farm buildings. Once they arrived the platform lowered and they were quickly swept inside and slowed down so they could see the processing. In some areas very rudimentary robots performed repetitive work of unloading harvest baskets. Further down the collected produce was sorted and directed along the line by means of a scanner, looking for size, degree of ripeness, and other important data points. There were janitorial robots cleaning up any excess produce or waste that reached the building's floor. There were mechanical robots ready to intervene should the processing line break down or a robot worker need servicing.

"While the collected produce is being unloaded, the scanners are taking intricate data sets on the location in the field that a particular plant grew and matching it to its nearby plants to get a reading that will help with future planting and tending of the crop."

"You may have noticed the rolling hills we travelled past to get here. That landscape was terraformed to produce the right amount of sun and shade on the plants to promote rapid and healthy growth. We haven't yet been able to engineer the light from our sun but we can change the places its rays hit with some precision."

He said there were several large towers on the perimeter of the farm fields where light was being pumped to generally cover the fields in a second and even third wash of natural light. He explained that solar arrays gathered the light, which was then condensed and directed to specific light pumps which diffused the light and directed it where it was needed.

The travel platform had cleared the activity in the barn and moved again to the outside. It rose to about 10 meters, turned slightly, waited until all the riders were secured in seats, and once level again, rapidly accelerated toward what was apparently a city in the distance.

"At this height we will be able to enter the city without any fixed obstacles. Once we are in the main part of the settled area, the platform is programmed to avoid the large buildings. In fact, due to the larger number of vehicles in the vicinity we are using a proscribed flight path grid. Once we enter the grid the platform integrates into it and we move automatically due to our destination pre-sets and commands from the operator. The grid is like your city streets but is three dimensional, with the more rapid travel on the top."

"So where is the population and what do they do?"

"The population on Athelna has dwindled since we took them into our group. The technological advances particularly in labour saving and health mean that family size has decreased as parents are quite certain of their progeny's ability to survive to adulthood. Most people live in the larger cities though a few prefer the quieter country life and even indulge in a bit of small scale agriculture."

"Can we meet some of these people?"

"Of course, we have several families who have agreed to let you into their homes."

"How about just dropping down between buildings and speaking to whoever comes along?"

"We could do that, however, while people have been informed of your visit, catching them completely unawares is unusual in our culture and might be jarring to them. You must remember that you are much larger than they are, due mostly to the gravity differences and other factors. You would have to communicate through a language interpreter as we have lost the need to know more than the single language that we have used here and on the other worlds for many hundreds of years."

"You speak perfect English."

"I do, it is my specialty. I am enjoying myself immensely, I can say, trading thoughts back and forth with a native speaker is enriching. I am having some difficulty with your colloquialisms and contractions of speech."

"What about Mr. Henderson's ability to communicate telepathically? Can't you do that with us?"

"Mr. Henderson, yes. Well, that is a learned skill. It takes time to be able to project your speech. Have any of you received communications in that way?"

They all shook their heads.

"I can try but I have never done it in English, or anything else other than our native speech, so I'm afraid that it would not be possible without much effort."

"Okay, try . . . "

"I already have tried to send you a greeting in my own language and in English. You apparently received nothing. Perhaps we can try again later?"

"Okay, I'll look forward to that. So what do people do with their time?" asked Fielding.

"People do what they want, within reasonable limits. Our overriding credo can be translated roughly as 'Do without rancour'. Yes, that is pretty close, the actual credo has several layers of meaning. So many people find their interest and explore it. Some like myself study other cultures, both existing and ancient. Others study mechanics and efficiency to make our machines and processes as perfectly efficient as possible."

"To be frank, we have promoted that our useful lives should be engaged in activities which stimulate the brain. Essentially everyone must do something and it must be tangible however we leave the individual to ascertain where their interests lie. As an incentive we mandate that any achievements must be referred to through the person who accomplished them. It is a reward system for adding to our knowledge and cultural base. The problem for those so motivated, is that their interests are never completely divorced from their everyday thinking, meaning that people essentially work all the time, it's just that they work on whatever interests them. That, however, has a limited utility to society as a whole."

"On Earth only the very talented or those independently wealthy can live that way."

"And perhaps that explains your rather slower development? Not enough minds working on improvements and efficiency."

"You seem awfully interested in efficiency," Fielding said.

"Why yes, efficiency reduces the need for additional resources and effort. It frees us up for other things."

"Like?"

"Art, cultural pursuits, athletic contests, further considering our culture and way of life. We use most of our lives to understand what we have achieved. There are some people who think that solving human needs is a mistake and has led to unfortunate incidents in some locations.

"Most of our progress is achieved by those who have spent the necessary time in learning all they need to push our understanding further. Our social scientists have speculated that our technology has slowed in its improvements because it now takes the entire human span of life just to get the proper background to delve into improvements. There are things in place to counter this effect, such as super specialization and advancements that are now coming from machines themselves but that has produced mixed results as those without a complete understanding of our society and culture are unable to direct science into useful things. Much of our study of the other linked planets was on cultural expression and what those who did not have to work, did to make themselves useful."

"And what did you find?"

"We found a whole array of things that we integrated back into our culture. Freed of the drudgery of providing for ones daily needs people will fall into a wide arrangement of living styles. Everyone pursues their interests with vigor, but not everyone has interests that require vigor or produce vigor. In other words there can be many millions of artists, say painters, but few of them will produce works that are esteemed by an large group of people."

"Once there is an acceptance of perfection in art it is too bland to be of interest. We long ago understood that art in all its forms requires the unexpected and unexplainable in order to maintain human interest. Meaning, in essence, that there is no perfect achievement in art."

"I suppose that makes sense and might be expected," said Fielding. "What about technological advancements, exploration or scientific discovery?"

"Rather slower progress I think, as we have fewer people interested in such things and we have advanced significantly for our needs. Most of the work that is done is speculative, though people have the ability to test their hypothesis fairly easily. We have advanced significantly in travel and communications but recognize that some advancements are of little human value. Our telepathy requires unimpeded pathways. In other words we cannot use it between buildings or rooms in a house.

"We can produce holograms for face to face communications, but when a live person speaks to a hologram the minor flaws in time lag and live comprehension of their counterpart as a projection render the ability to accomplish this as unsatisfactory. It was a group of amateur scientists who discovered and developed the gravitational wave open space travel system. They are still working on it and how to more easily tap into waves and use them with greater efficiency."

"There's that word again."

Their host laughed, "It is a basis for how we live."

"What about the human need for power?"

"We've long ago solved the need for large amount of energy, you have seen the technology on the aster . . . "

"No, sorry, power, political control, leadership and revolution? Has everyone just fallen into line? Are there no instances where some-one wanted to seize control of your society?"

"Yes, those things did happen in the distant past, in fact quite violently. It was the violence that ended up putting a stop to it as government forces simply turned off the agricultural production and energy units. Violent rebel groups were able to operate for some time despite those measures but eventually they were brought back into society."

By this time the platform had entered the city, adjusting to a slightly higher altitude in the outskirts of the built up areas, flying through many buildings before rapidly descending, in three bursts to ground level, which consisted of parkland and pleasure gardens between buildings.

"Have we seen the complete level of your technology?"

"I'm not sure that is even possible given the huge advances we have made in almost every area of human condition. You have seen technology in transit, communications, robotics and heard about some in medicine and power generation."

"What is the life expectancy here?"

"Our bodies grow and age just as yours do. We have had some medical advancements which reduce the loss of vigour as we age, and which completely eliminate disease and body breakdowns and which allow for repair after accidents."

"You are like Mr. Henderson in stature. Is your height and weight within standard parameters?"

"Yes. I am by your measure one metre, eight centimeters in height and I weigh about 45 of your kilograms. Due mostly to the gravity we are shorter than you from Earth and a bit more strongly built, to function efficiently in the higher gravity. In addition we have been working to engineer our people to consume fewer resources.

We do recognize that some additional size has its advantages, but the resulting gravity battle make engineering larger things and people problematic."

"What about engineering people smaller?"

"We considered that as well, but a certain size is required to manage our environment. The physical size of machinery and flora and fauna require us to be roughly the height we have naturally achieved. In fact when we make our visits today we have chosen abodes that conform to your height rather than standard sizes we use."

"So how far are you ahead technologically?"

"Simple math suggests that we were engaged in space travel more than 3000 Earth years ago, so we are correspondingly far ahead technologically. However, your lower gravity has allowed you to travel and explore outer space much earlier than we did. The high gravity on our worlds was difficult to conquer. The discovery of how to manipulate gravity on Eiosia allowed us to escape our planet and discover the other nearby inhabited planets. Of course technological advancements move rapidly up once a society reaches the information age. Though it does slow significantly once you've parsed out all the advancements that come from the rapid processing of data bits.

"The next stage is the interstellar age, though from our experience that is more of a exploratory time than one of increased technological prowess. Moving people around is moving people around. We have been able to engage in matter transference, but not with living things. We can do it with inanimate objects, moving a table from here to there, but we cannot do it with a human being or even a plant. Our abilities in this area are limited to direct lines of movement. In other words I can move a chair or pot to anywhere there is a direct line of sight, which limits the usefulness of the technology. Most of our advances are in efficiency, that word again, and it is in that efficiency that we focus much of our science."

They moved into the building where it was immediately obvious they had entered a living space. A middle aged woman greeted them.

"The living spaces in this building are all accessible by platform from the outside. There is a stairway inside for emergencies only."

The Earth group moved forward eager to speak to a native Athelnan or Eiosian. They towered over the dwarf sized human who appeared a bit subdued by the meeting. She gestured greetings but did not speak.

"My name is Jenn Fielding, and my companions are Yang Li, Ivan Bolrenko and Mika Oh," Jenn said while gesturing to each member of the group.

"I am Kiko," she said haltingly. "Our last names are lengthy descriptors of our background and lives, usually made smaller for distribution but accessible for anyone to find out about us. I have been here for only a short time. I have spent time in other cities."

Kiko's English seemed to improve rapidly. She asked them to be seated and wondered if there were any questions. She was slim, but not skinny, shorter than the Earthlings but no shorter or taller that those accompanying the party, though short by human stand-ards. She was as dressed in a loose fitting gown of a silky, gossamer like material, which appeared light and strong. It had a floral pattern above the waist but was a solid sea-green below the waist. When she walked it was almost like she was floating despite the strong gravity.

The Earth party struggled to move easily. They had been equipped with anti-gravity suits, pants really which covered their legs and attached with a belt at their waists. This device counteracted the heaviness making them feel only about 1.5 times as heavy as they were on Earth. They did not move about rapidly.

"How do you live Kiko?"

"What a strange question. Each day I suppose, doing those things that need to be done in preparation for doing those things I like."

"What is it you love?"

"I am involved with the young ones, teaching them, and then I engage in flowers, gardening, horticulture and tending my plot. I have one type of flower that is named after me as I grew it from a series of hybrids. And how do you live your life Jenn Fielding?"

"Well, I explore."

"Just like I explore plants."

"Yes, I suppose. I explore new worlds and cultures and mostly languages. Your English is very good."

"Thank you, I think that is why they chose me for our meeting."

"How long have you known English and why did you learn it?"

"I have spoken it for about three months in preparation for your visit. I had studied it before in written form."

"You were able to learn it that fast?"

"Yes, though I am still learning it as we speak to one another. I was asked by the . . . by our leaders. Cannot you do that as well?"

"No Kiko, I cannot learn languages that fast. In fact I am an expert only in written language. Most languages I know I have never heard spoken, like the type of language your culture uses - something similar to Phoenician."

"That is very strange. Tell me more," said Kiko in fluent Phoenician.

Jenn stiffened. She recognized something but found the tones and the intonations unexpected. She slowly pieced together the meaning by repeating the short sentence that Kiko had uttered. She had never heard the language spoken, though she had mentally tried to sound it out as she worked with it.

"Is that your native tongue?"

"Yes, and no Jenn. It is a form of our language from many years ago. We speak a modern form of it, one built for technological terms and situations which did not exist when this language first flourished. My people abandoned it and built their new tongue around the basics of its form."

"It is very similar to an ancient language on Earth."

"I am not surprised, our people visited your planet and likely left their language. Is that not the big breakthrough for which you are credited?"

"It is. What else do you do with your life? You mentioned things without even talking about language skills."

"Oh, Jenn, do not misunderstand me. I have been fed English and learned it only recently as it was implanted in my brain prior to my immersion in its forms. I heard synthesised versions of you and your friends speaking it to gain pronunciation. And now I am here with you. And I continue to learn."

Yang Li cocked his head. He immediately turned to Ahre. "Is Kiko a robot?"

Ahre looked shocked. He slowly looked at each member of the landing party. "Well, no, not to us, but I guess to your way of thinking she could be. She has had technology implanted in her brain to enable rapid learning. That is one of the things we have done to counter the need for an entire human life span to acquire enough background knowledge to advance our science."

Li looked directly at Marcus Ahre. "Are you a robot?"

Ahre looked confused. "No. I have never thought about it that way. I suppose I am automated in some ways. In body I am made of mostly replaceable parts. My brain and its function and thoughts are my own, I do not have any alterations to my brain function. We developed sentience transfer many hundreds of years ago, but I have not required it yet."

"This feels strange," said Kiko, as she moved to get them all tea. "I feel so light."

"It is the artificially reduced gravity Kiko. Our guests are not used to the high levels of gravity that we live with."

"Why did you travel to Earth and the other colonizing planets?" asked Li.

"For the same reasons people have done so since time immemorial. To look over the next hill, to see beyond the known. We wanted to explore and our explorations uncovered the previous seeding of planets as we are all what you would call homo sapiens. It seemed prudent to bring us all together and create colonies of people on all nearby worlds. We will expand beyond them once we under-stand the gravity propulsion system or invent something better."

"However our invention of a vastly extended life has left a void in our social imperatives. There is little or no need for additional people. But we do have a need to study culture. So we also moved to other planets to study their cultures, and how they developed independently. We have approbate anything that was good, integrating it into our own ways, and once that has been achieved invite them to join us as equals, bringing them into our sphere.

"We would like you to join with us. Bring us new vigor and gain from us the secrets of everlasting life."

"But where are the people here, this is a vast city?" asked Bolrenko.

"They are all around us, engaged in their various pursuits. The vast majority simply engage in entertainment. For some they prefer research. Some people shut themselves down for long periods of time, to re-emerge when enough change has occurred to make life interesting again."

"The fourth planet in your colony, Amorra, does not want to engage with you do they?"

"Their world council is afraid of what they may become, with some people not adapting to changed purposes. And yet, there is a sizable group that wants immortality. Who can blame them?"

"Immortality? What are you religious beliefs?"

"Our ancient ones are much like yours, as we implanted them into your ancient populations. However in more recent generations most of our people have dropped the old ways, while still paying some heed to those traditions. Our technology has rendered God useless."

"Does nobody die anymore?"

"Yes, accidents do happen, suicides occur. Once a human life has been extended technologically they are incapable of conceiving new life. People usually decide to have their children in their relative youth. But our populations have dwindled in recent centuries. Mass death is unknown since the quest for dominance was ended."

"The quest for dominance?"

"Yes, the rebel battles I mentioned earlier when some people wanted to control the direction of our social development. It occurred long ago. It was a period of stagnation for our civilization. But conquering it made people very aware of their place in the world and their desire to remain outside the bounds of those who would choose for them."

"What is the point of your lives?"

"A fundamental question, since much of the point of life for thousands and perhaps millions of years, has now been fulfilled. It isn't really any different than yours. Our people strive to new things, just not as hard as you, who haven't conquered human basic needs, still do. And you may have noticed this trend among your own populations; as life expectancy rises, the primary concern of most people becomes living the longest. The point of life becomes clinging to it. As with many of us."

The four visitors became quiet , asking muted questions about the city organization, government, and city services.

"I think we are ready to continue the tour." They thanked Kiko for her time and welcome.

And they flew to other cities and some smaller more rural communities. People all lived much the same though some preferred to have more responsibilities. They toured areas of great natural beauty and saw wonderful monuments to historical events and people. These things were explained to them with a simple background to aid their understanding of cultural touchstones.

After those travels, which took many weeks covering the entire planet, they undertook to travel to Eiosia to see the heart of the civilization.

Once securely down on Eiosia there was a different feeling in the air. It pushed Bolrenko to ask if the chemical composition of the atmosphere was very much different from Athelna. It wasn't.

What they found was profoundly disturbing. The spaceport was in the middle of a wild, natural area. Nearby there was a city, but even through the distance they could tell it was dead. Not that it had been abandoned it had been killed.

"My god, there is no activity. Nothing is moving. There is no life, just the swish of the wind in the fields of grain or tall grass. I don't even hear birds," said Mika. "How long has that city been dead?"

"Once the insects were removed the birds all died," said Ahre. "That city has been abandoned for many hundreds of years. When the cities died they were recycled and we returned the land to a natural state. Many others like it have been removed though in recent times we have little use for large amounts of construction material."

The others acknowledged the observations. "Is everybody living underground?"

"Well, yes, in a way," said Ahre. "There are many cities that are no longer required to house the existing population. The population on Eiosia has diminished significantly. The violence of the quest for dominance reduced some totals. Others left during the Quest.

Others still found no reason to continue and have passed on child-less. Most people who remain live in very concentrated cities some of which are underground. It's more efficient that way.

"Many people here have had themselves rendered dormant waiting for a time when their world had changed enough to make their wakefulness worthwhile. In some cases it is a technological change they are waiting for, or others are looking for a specific amount of time to pass. It's our form of time travel."

"So these people are essentially all robot, save for the specific memories and mental capacities and constructions of their owner?"

"Yes and no. There is a limit to the natural human life span. People make the necessary upgrades to their physical bodies as they feel the need," said Ahre. "We have conquered stasis and can keep people in a sleep state with very low function for many hundreds of years before they need to be revived and their strength built up again."

The group took an extensive tour. Seeing large modern cities, older cities chock-a-block with ancient structures and cultural centers, and vast agricultural plains complete with regional processing centers for all manner of resources, from mining and metallurgy to farming and food processing and everything in between. They also saw innumerable dead cities and environments which had been once agricultural lands which had been reclaimed by the wild.

In several instances they saw wide empty areas dotted with cultural and historical landmarks that were still maintained. Huge stone edifices and other building monuments like step pyramids and wide stone paved courtyards remained while the cities around them had been cleaned away.
The home planet was vast and had once been very developed. Almost no place had not felt the hand of development, though

much of it now was wild but were essentially spaces of managed parkland. And while there were populations sustained by automation, the Earth tourists were also shown areas of abandoned, run down, broken down cities.

"We have engaged in systematic recycling of our ancient cities which were built cheaply to house a huge population during the initial stages of our genetic engineering project. Our populations soared as inevitable death was pushed back. Eventually our population decreased here on Eiosia, where once we were home to about 50 billion people, this world is now home to less than three billion."

"What happened to everyone?"

"They moved to other planets in our group or they died, in the period where we had not mastered the skill of transferring brain capacities into purpose built neural networks. Our physical mastery over death is only fairly recent. Until then we were able to vastly extend useful human life but not indefinitely. The 50 billion figure was reached several thousand of earth years ago, and has been slowly dwindling."

"We have conquered shelter, as you have seen. We have conquered food and want, people are free to do as they please. This is the end goal of human achievement. It's a paradise."

"Isn't that the elephant in the room of religious descriptions of the afterlife," whispered Bolrenko to Fielding. "We are promised when we die that we will be free from want or need but nobody ever tells us what we will all be doing for eternity. It seems like a very long time with nothing to do."

"Angelic ennui," she whispered back with a smile. "No wonder the angels intervene to help us from time to time. You can only play

Euchre for so long."

Fielding decided to stay on Eiosia for a time to study their language and its use. Having thousands of years of continuous use of a written and spoken language was an opportunity for study that she could not miss.

They had extensively studied the evolution of their language. She was essentially able to trace the development of Ancient Phoenician into the post-industrial age, and beyond. She tried to learn the language but was stymied beyond the simple phrases used by tourists. She did better with the written form.

Yang Li took some time to study industrial processes. Mika Oh and Bolrenko took a lengthy cultural trip together trying to understand how the different cultures on Eiosia in the ancient past had moved together to create a singular way of life. It appeared that technology had much to do with it, from streamlining communications, to getting everyone on the same page in their cultural touchstones, to ending the powerful urge to take required resources from weaker societies.

They found that the cultural touchstones remained strong for many generations even after they had really ceased to exist. It was the differences that fed humanity's tribal instinct, the need to belong to a sub-group, and be happy with that membership and difference. Where such touchstones did not exist they were created by inhabitants.

They came together to share their experiences and to ensure they had seen everything necessary and conducted their research into the Eiosian culture very thoroughly, collecting as much data and firsthand accounts of everything they could to occupy them in analysis during their lengthy return to Earth.

The real issue remained with Amorra and its lack of interest in integrating into the Eiosian whole. They were unable to meet with any representatives from that world, as they refused to come to Eiosia and travel to Amorra required more time than the astronauts were willing to take.

Chapter Fifteen

They had taken their leave and returned by shuttlecraft to their ship, left in orbit. A lengthy round of goodbyes and an agenda for follow up visits between Eiosia and all its colonies were agreed to. The Eiosians did not put any pressure on the visitors nor did they insist upon a timetable, only an agreement to keep lines of communication open.

The door to the airlock had not been shut for two seconds before they all looked at each other strangely.

"Right, said Li. "I'll say it first. What a hell of a choice to make."

"Either way we have to choose," said Bolrenko. "I see where Athelna and Amorra and the other worlds have gone. It's as if the future, the glorious future that we are all working on and hoping fervently for, is a false image, a giant mistake."

"Eiosia is a planet of robots without any purpose, save to continue to exist, as if they have built a society so perfect that it cannot be destroyed."

"If that is the end of our striving for the betterment of humanity, I think we should quit now," said Mika.

"My God, what has man wrought?"

"And you know it will be impossible to stop once this reaches the masses who are still struggling with elements of life and survival, with their economies and their own limitations. It's like the Eiosians have hit a roadblock in their evolution by taking a dead end road."

"Yes, and what's worse, they don't recognize it as a dead end, rather they celebrate their efficiency. They are culturally blind."

"But what choice do we have; to condemn those who struggle on Earth to a cycle of drudgery, poverty, death and want?"

"We need to find the original civilization, those people who seeded all these planets. How did they succeed in beating this cultural ennui?"

"Maybe they didn't. Maybe seeding the planets was a choice, hoping that one of them would take a different path, would refuse to take the easy way. Maybe the Amorrans are our only hope."

The astronauts had set the controls for the auto-acceleration to light speed where they would catch the gravitational wave and be flung through space time back to Earth in what would take them about a year of travel time, including the necessary speed up and slow down from the shattering speeds they would reach. They had spent many months on the investigation segments of their trip, meaning about a three year round trip in their time and perhaps a seven to ten year segment of time had passed on Earth taking into account their light speed travels.

In the mean time, Earth had been visited by Eiosian ambassadors representing all the inhabited planets. They had tried to make sense of the huge cultural differences between the two societies. They were fascinated by the different approaches to the same issues and concerns that each dominate culture took on Earth, and equally by the arguments between clashing cultures that they found.

Various factions on Earth were very resistant to giving up any of their sovereignty in the interests of greater co-operation. Diplomatic battles for dominance increased as some people on Earth believed that co-operation would be imposed and those with the greatest cultural sovereignty would win the battle for supremacy. Others thought the time for supremacy had passed.

The three great pseudo empires on Earth pushed for dominance in their own way. The Chinese pushed hard in Africa and South America and the United States made major inroads into Chile and Argentina. The Russians pushed hard in the Caucuses and at the fringes of Europe. India emerged as a cultural powerhouse, sort of aligned with the United States and Europe but still independent of them, as their historic culture experienced a revival. Sorting out its various strands was near impossible even for the Indians. European culture and that of the sub-continent began a dance to which no-one knew the steps.

All these cultural empires clashed with each other. The push for dominance reached its non-violent limit with only India still fully independent despite European and Chinese pressure, Russian pressure and American pressure. And of course the explorers were entirely unaware of this turn of events on Earth.

The astronauts were universally appalled by what they had seen in their explorations, but only Mika thought it could be stopped. She insisted that they recommend that travel between the planets be restricted and technological innovation be shunned. She argued that any leakage into Earth culture would be viral and infect the whole planet. The others saw no way to accomplish that task and were resigned that there was no way to stop it. After much discussion they did entertain the idea of founding a colony in opposition to the forces of change - and yet deep down, they knew it was unsustainable no matter what they did.

"We'd be like the Amish," said Fielding with a mocking smile. "Our lack of acceptance of the new technology would be cult like, almost a religious adherence to the old ways. And slowly but surely we would be dragged into the newly 'modern' world as the conveniences and advantages of the technological marvels would draw us away from our drudgery."

"Yeah, as we draw closer to death, the knowledge that death did not need to occur or be final, would itself be fatal to our societies. I'm certain that any desire to maintain our old ways would be destroyed. And any group that attempted to suppress the advances would be a footnote in history, met with skepticism, wonder, disbelief and a gentle mockery that we could ever have been so naive."

"So when do we start?" asked Mika.

"I'm not even sure we should," said Fielding. "It appears that to avoid the death of our culture and society we have to allow individual death to occur. What a strange paradox. Anyway, where would we do this? How could we insure there be no encroachment from outside technology? How could we justify holding technology back from people who could benefit?"

"That's just it. We have seen the future and we know they don't really benefit."

"Yes, but is it our place to make the judgement?" asked Fielding.

"Whatever we report will go a long way to helping that decision get made."

"But you know in the end whatever the decision, people cannot help but be drawn into a lifestyle that appears to give them every-thing they want. Even if it's bad for them."

"Are you qualified to make the call? Who died and made you God?"

"The Eiosians."

"They didn't die and they aren't God."

"That's a matter of your point of view."

Yang Li took this argument in. He had a different idea. Instead of creating an old order society on Earth, why not create an Earth society on Eiosia, which appeared to be the planet most in need of people.

"What about letting everyone who wants to avoid the technology emigrate to Amorra?" he asked.

Chapter Sixteen

That was it really.

John Overholt was awaiting the return of the natives to Earth and the resultant wave of change they would bring. He had had some communication with Bill Henderson and had gleaned from him the nature of life on Eiosia. It wasn't hard to draw the same conclusions as those who had seen it firsthand. The Eiosians had introduced some of their body replacement technology, which immediately improved the lives of those with lost limbs, failing joints and poor eyesight. They had also introduced their improved power cells and provided anti-gravity technology to Earth companies.

As these wonders were introduced, Overholt was thinking his way through the gravitational wave phenomenon to try to understand it. It was different than the technology of controlling gravity, as it was more of a discovery of what existed rather than a development of invention.

In the quiet of the array he tried to puzzle out the nature of gravity and its properties. The array itself helped to open his eyes a little wider.

He thought, we live in a three dimensional world but exist in a galaxy of six spatial dimensions, three of which are related to movement and are virtually invisible to us in our daily lives. Do they have anything to do with the gravity propulsion? he wondered.

Overholt kept running over the physics he knew, thinking first that everyday living takes place in three dimensions of space; height, width and depth. He added the fourth dimensional consideration, time, but that is not a spatial dimension. In a flash Overholt saw the reality. There are three other dimensions of motion. And there are three unaligned dimensions; light, gravity and time. What about acceleration? That appears to be a dimension if it can slow the passage of time, he thought. Maybe acceleration is time? Maybe acceleration is tied to the three spatial dimensions of interstellar space.

And he saw that motion is actually the addition of three dimensions on top of those that are usually observed. While things that exist in space have three dimensions of mass, they also travel in three dimensions of motion. So a human standing on Earth has height, width and depth in the space his mass fills. He is also travelling around the world as it spins, around the sun as it orbits and around the spiral arms of the galaxy as it turns - essentially moving in three different ways at the same time. However his mass moves though the three local dimensions of space as well. Overholt thought a fourth could be considered and that is the speed that the entire galaxy is moving away from the presumptive Big Bang. Given that observations suggest the universe is expanding, then presumably the galaxy itself is moving in some direction relative to other galaxies. All of this motion is occurring in three dimensional space. Or is it?

He wondered, if there were four dimensions of stellar movement and a corresponding four dimensions of unaligned dimension, non-spatial ones, light, gravity, time and acceleration, then could it be that there are four spatial dimensions on Earth and not just three?

But the ultimate issue with the universe, appeared to be the acceleration of the galaxies away from each other, Overholt thought. Why do all the stars and galaxies appear to be moving away from Earth? If they are moving in space, relative to their motion initiated in the Big Bang, wouldn't they be moving at roughly the same pace in an outward direction from the location of the Big Bang as some of the stars and star clusters nearby. Shouldn't at least some stars and galaxies have been blown in the same direction?

This six or eight, or potentially 12 dimensional space that Overholt now considered was actually noticeable on Earth in terms of days as the Earth spun around its axis and in terms of seasons as the Earth travelled around the Sun. In some way of thinking, that spin and the orbit of the Earth around the Sun is what produced time. It gave an amplitude to the motion. That amplitude is time.

He tried hard to focus his mind on why such obvious dimensions in space did not register the same as height, width and depth do as spatial dimensions on the surface of the Earth. He also tried to explore the effect such dimensions might have on us, and where the potentially hidden forth spatial dimension might be, but he drew a blank. The mental strain of juggling all these esoteric ideas in an attempt to provide order to them was difficult. His head started to hurt.

And if he allowed the extra dimensions such as time their due in his thoughts, he was inexorably drawn to motion and gravity as additional dimensions, but apart from the ideas of spatial dimensions that were usually considered. And then there was light, light which appeared to exist as both a wave and as a particle. It sure seemed to be the basic unit of creation.

He concentrated. What is the whole package? What ties it together?

He was forced to conclude the unifying force is gravity. Gravity is mass. Without an outside force, gravitational mass causes movement. Time provides gravity the ability to create motion which in turn attracts enough mass to create light. And light illuminates time which allows the cycle to repeat.

It sort of held together as a theory but only loosely as there were several iterations where various non-spatial dimensions seemed to work in different ways on each other. But it was enough that Overholt thought he was on to something.

The gravitational waves that the space travellers were using to shorten their journey would provide some insight, if he could figure out how they worked.

He drifted back to the six dimensions of space. Or was it eight? And in doing so closed his eyes to help visualize it.
"You are on to it Mr. Overholt," said a familiar voice. Was he day dreaming? Was he inventing an alter-ego to help guide his thoughts?

"The travellers are using gravity to circumvent the three dimensions of motion. Think about the speed the Earth is travelling in space, in all three dimensions, around its axis, around the sun and around the Milky Way. What is the aggregate of all the acceleration?"

Overholt had already done the math. About 610,000 miles per hour, actually quite slow in the scheme of physics where light travels 186,000 miles per second.

He realized the difficulty of someone who had lived all their lives with three dimensions plus time considerations trying to grasp additional dimensions of space. It was a daunting task as every experience a person lives reinforces the three plus one dimensional field. Anything that might creep in from another dimension is explained away or ignored as impossible, or unattached to the consideration of dimensional existence.

Ever hear strange noises? Could that be some interaction between extra dimensions and your own reality?

"So how would 610,000 mph of unnoticed acceleration affect standard dimensions?" Overholt asked himself aloud.

"There would be a very faint effect in relativity," he heard the voice say. "Negligible but measurable. "What about all the speed with gravity?"

"I can't see any connection. Certainly there is an effect, but how big an effect and how does it manifest itself and why does it matter?"

"The bodies in our galaxy are travelling with us, at the same speed through an expanding universe," the voice said. "It is other galaxies which appear to be all moving away."

"So the gravitational force between stars in the Milky Way is relatively constant, but gravity between galactic systems must be weakening," Overholt surmised. "And how the gravity operates should reflect changes in motion and light."

As soon as the light bulb went off in his head, it went out. Thinking beyond three dimensions was a difficult mental construct as there was a need, but not a requirement to maintain contact with all the variables, an almost impossible task for a human mind, shaped as

279

it was by its limited environment.

Overholt opened his eyes and saw Mr. Henderson standing in front of him.

"Was it you I was speaking with? It felt like my own inner voice."

"Yes, I was trying to guide your thought process. I'm glad you could hear me. That's unusual in a big person. You have talents you have not yet mastered Mr. Overholt. Multi-dimensions are difficult enough when we are only dealing with three. The six you are thinking of are actually something other than pure dimensions. And the other dimensions: time, acceleration, motion, light and gravity are something else entirely. You were on it when you saw them as variations of the same thing. Gravity affects motion and acceleration. Motion is a function of time. Light is the wild card. It is produced by gravity and it is retained by high gravity, as in a black hole. And yet, black holes are gravity wells which do not produce light - why not? Gravity is the key to the universe. Gravity is mass. Why does some gravity ignite into stars while other gravity wells are dead, black holes? The answer is the difference in the nature of the matter each has attracted. Is the transit system uncovered by the Eiosians really a harness on gravity waves?

"The very strong gravity on Eiosia was the scientific impetus to uncover the secrets of gravity. Without knowing how to harness gravity the Eiosians could not escape the gravity of their planet and move into their interstellar age."

"Are the physics of higher dimensions well known to all insurance adjusters on Eiosia? Why are you helping me?" Overholt asked.

"I feel a kinship with you John. I have lived on Earth, in a somewhat solitary existence due to my special background, much like you who have toyed with concepts virtually nobody on Earth can fathom.

Trying to express these things comes across as awkward and is socially constricting. I know about that."

"How do you manage to live in both worlds?"

Henderson straightened up to his full height of just over one meter. He took a deep breath.

"I really only live in this one, John. I have knowledge of Eiosia but I have never been there. In fact without some manipulation of the gravity there I doubt I would survive. Three times the gravity of Earth would be fairly debilitating for me."

"But didn't you admit to being an off-worlder?"

"No, not at all. The government claimed they had no paperwork on me. I think they were trying to rattle me. I have a birth certificate and a Social Security card. I was born in Modesto and have lived in California my whole life. I have been visited by citizens of Eiosia and Amorra for several years. They provided me with ample evidence of their suppositions. I have no reason to doubt them. Certainly the information brought back from the first interstellar trip to the mining asteroid proved what I had been told was true. And that was supported by what we knew of the mining operation of the dark side of the moon. And yet, I am still human, a Californian, and I want everything to work out for us. Given the animosity between peoples on Earth, that appears to be a tall order.

"As for the aliens bringing us an age of peace and contentment, I have my doubts that such things can be peaceably achieved. There are some who want to take advantage of the coming golden age to make sure they themselves are golden," Henderson said.

"So what is the secret of the gravity wave propulsion? Will it bring peace on Earth? Our astronauts are using it. We must know."

"Alas the Eiosians have not yet provided the secret, they merely provided the specs for the drive and had it built for the craft. I'm sure Earth scientists are working it out."

"I hadn't heard that and I am supposed to be a project consultant. I guess that accounts for why the propulsion was never considered."

"Perhaps you need to ask some questions about why that is? Why is there an apparent concerted effort to fake the research while conducting other research in secret? John, this contact with the Eiosia will change Earth forever. I believe that it is positive change. There are also a set of people who refuse any change at all. They would want Earth to experience its civilizational cycle without interference."

"Civilizational cycle? Doesn't advanced contact presume an end to it?"

"Indeed. That is what we have found in two systems we found. Life had proceeded to about where Earth is now, and then it had ended, we are not entirely sure why."
"Ended? Does it have anything to do with my consideration of additional dimensions?"

"Probably not. Not unless these people are hiding in higher dimensions," he laughed. "The dimensional problem is mostly one of human construction, an attempt to find the key to the unexplainable. I meant 'ended' in the sense that the historical path we are currently on is so irrevocably changed that we enter a new age."

"So you have no additional insight?"

"Not really. I have heard hints that this change has not always gone smoothly on other worlds. Some people want it to be mostly an intellectual exercise without practical application. Others battle so much that the battle is the practical application."

"I was really on about the gravity waves. What about them?"

"Not the same issue. Okay, I suppose the gravity waves are in there somewhere, but so is length, height and depth. Eiosia did not discover gravity wave propulsion due to an improved understanding of dimensional space, or because they had a rough or smooth transition to a new era of peace and stability."

"That doesn't sound convincing. So why are you here again?"

Henderson shrugged and slouched down in his chair. "Like I said John, I kind of feel for you. Working hard, grappling with all sorts of difficult things, not really caring where they lead, as long as they lead somewhere. And, it appears that that somewhere behind the curtain, there is a dimension of space where most people are not allowed. And that will be overshadowed by Eiosian bio-technology."

"Well that sounds very cloak and dagger. It is all that bad? I care where they lead. I am hopeful in understanding this stuff for the betterment of mankind."

Henderson laughed, "Now I've heard everything. You only want to know because it's something you don't know. And on the side if might help your career and give you a measure of immortality."

"No, that's more like Ethan. Well, I suppose, but I expect whatever I find will be beneficial."

"Sort of like Oppenheimer," said Henderson. "What did he say? 'I have become death. Destroyer of worlds.' What would you do if you found something destructive? How would you know?"

"I think I'd know. We were required to study Oppenheimer and the idea of making evil discoveries; scientific ethics, and stuff. What always struck me was that while Oppenheimer said that, 'destroyer of worlds' he was just quoting the Bhagavad Gita. What was it on about?"

"It's essentially about the battle between good and evil, between the ethical and moral struggles of human life. How can you foresee the ethical conundrums or social impact when you cannot foresee the science? I have to go John, remember the dimensional continuum is merely a construct and the other elements are not really germane to the issue - they are interesting outcomes of the force of mass, but forces just the same."

"So how do I find the gravity propulsion secret?"

"Perhaps it has already been found. In the end, is finding it going to change our reality? The aliens have searched for other inhabited planets and found none. The gravity propulsion brings our five worlds together but our own research suggests that for now this little group of civilization, being that we are all very similar, is the only intelligence in the universe. And it isn't all that intelligent, as it hasn't conquered its own paradox."

Overholt began to object. "Not that we don't expect to find someone else out there, but so far we have not, and we've been looking for a long time," said Henderson. "Just sheer numbers suggest additional intelligence is out there. And the propulsion system is also suggested by the same infinite continuum but how does it work in three spatial dimensions? How does it apply? What's the order of growth in the infinite? What kind of infinity do we exist in?"

Henderson had moved to leave and closed the door behind him as he finished speaking. Overholt knew there would be no evidence of him if he checked. He puzzled his brow, pursed his lips and thought hard.

Overholt couldn't help but continue to mull the problem, but now there were additional addendums, thanks to Henderson. And he couldn't penetrate them with the words of Henderson in his ears. Suddenly it was much more complicated than before Henderson had tried to narrow his focus. Ok, he thought, growth in the infinite? He remembered something from a long ago math class. Infinity had several dimensions. Is that what Henderson was referring to? Did each dimension have its own kind of infinity? Or set of physical laws? Is that how they could be separated and understood?

He ran it over in his mind, recalling that long ago math class. There is simple infinity: 1, 2, 3, 4 and so on forever. And there is an inside infinity: a descending one like 1, 1.1, 1.01, 1.001 and on forever, and an infinity of similar infinities of decimals. There are infinities inside of infinities: an ascending one like 1, 3, 5, 7 on one side and 2, 4, 6, 8 on the other, linked together. And there is an infinite set of these types of subset infinities: 1, 4, 7, 10 and 2, 5, 8, 11 and any other number sequence you can think of on and on. But how did this pertain to the gravitational propulsion? What secret did they find, and apparently uncover by accident? An accident so remarkable that they hadn't even really understood what they found.

He scribbled a few things down in a note pad about nothing and everything, knowing that deciphering his musings hours or days later would be almost impossible, and that his current heightened mental state was impossible to reproduce. Even if he tried he would almost certainly end up in a different mental place than the one he occupied at the time when he wrote his notes.

He wrote down Henderson's last words and made a few other notes. He put the paper away in a drawer and clicked on a cross-word. He needed to clear his head. It was hard on the brain to be swimming in different dimensions of unknown space and time, all clouded by multiple infinities.

Henderson was an interesting case. He was human in origin but appeared to be alien in stature and attitude.

Overholt thought about his erstwhile friend for a time. He had never explained the apparent holes in his story, merely demonstrated alien technology and brought a number of apparently off world beings with him. And now, Henderson was admitting that he had never been to Eiosia and that presumably his life on Earth was exactly what he said it was.

Superfluous to the issue at hand? Who knew?

Heaven on Earth

It has always been there. Those with power tried to preserve their legacy, their names and their glory. They built pyramids as mausoleums, statues and temples, they spent their gains on maintaining their place in the pantheon of human memory.

While kings built in monumental ways, everyday folk often tried the same thing with a scratched inscription here or their mark there. Into the modern era graveyards contained a small monument to just about everyone who had passed this world - a memory of a name, times lived, a photograph, close relatives and even an aphorism or something to speak into the future. But even that stone, seemingly impervious to time, faded and crumbled.

In the vastness of space, we have always been alone. For millennia mankind had little time to contemplate what might be beyond the sky as the flat land, the scrub, the trees, the rivers and mountains seemed to go on forever. And watching the stars and planets it never really occurred to him that there might be others out there, as out there was as remote and unreachable to the ancients who had no knowledge of distance than it is to us who understand the vastness of that distance.

And then man thought about the sky. Could there be other worlds, other people?

As his knowledge grew the cosmos appeared to have a pattern but it was limitless and to most, it was not a matter if we were alone but when we would find another intelligent tribe. Much like the Bronze Age Hittites or Egyptians or ancient Chinese who eventually came to know that there were other peoples out beyond their furthest hill, or beyond the horizon of their highest place.

It was supposed by some that we were first, but most didn't

believe it. Yet, in our part of the galaxy we found only organic slime, the ooze of life from which civilizations grow.

And then we found another, the remnant, the signature of intelligence, and we were not alone. Like the Babylonians seeing a trace of smoke from a fire far off on the horizon, they knew there were others, but knew them not. For us we had smoke only and that intelligence may well have been gone for millennia by the time we saw their ruins. And what a shock it must have been for the nascent Babylonians to see the ruins of world more ancient than their own, whose rumors must have travelled, much as mathematics tells us a story of another likely intelligence.

And one day we saw the artifacts of other worlds, the tangible evidence that they existed, their works, the ruins of their efforts of what remained.

And it led us to the ultimate; it led us to them, to seeing and hearing them, to having them in front of us as salient, tangible, intelligent beings from another world.

Of course, having them in front of us meant we must learn to communicate - to share ideas and more. For sharing a place, sharing safety and sharing an origin story and even a divine inspiration of existence meant a cultural shift had occurred. And people were now more than what they had grown on Earth to be.

And for all of that - they were the same. Just like pre-industrial tribes being exposed to modernity in the wake of exploration. Just like the creation of the cargo-cults in the wake of world-wide technological exposure, and the ending of the same cults as their adherents understood the truth of their world.

And now that there was someone new. We had to create a new tribe, new safe places, new approaches to the same concerns. The

Chinese saw it first. The Russians saw the Chinese and took up their approach. And the Americans, ever looking forward, blundered along, until they realized that they had been handed a wild hegemony that only their spirit could harness and maybe tame.

Chapter Seventeen

She had not seen her parents in person for almost 16 years, though there had been regular communication. During much of her time away, she was in flight at the speed of light, meaning that more time had passed for those remaining on Earth than it had for her.

She was attached to her parents but had long ago cut the tether. Given her distant job in Florida and her significant travels and top secret activities once she returned, she had not been back to California.

Her parents had moved to California once they retired to be near her brother and sister and their six grandchildren. Without children, and married to her job at the university as well as her lengthy travels, she had only the shards of a life in Florida. Her parents had built a very full life in California.

There had been many changes at the university since she began there on faculty and while she had few connections with people she was an academic star, at least in the eyes of the administration. Many people on campus knew of her as her activities as an astronaut were well known. Few people really knew her well and as much of her research was classified, she was unable to build even academic bonds with many. A trip to California would allow her to be Jenny again, rather than Jenn the astronaut.

Her father Gordon still liked to fly and did so in two small planes he owned. One, a small Cessna, he flew to travel around the western United States. The other was a small hobby plane he had built himself. With it he flew in and around the local canyons and rivers. He didn't like to get too high in it as he knew only too well that home built planes had their flaws, one of which was the thoroughness of the maintenance crew, which usually consisted of the owner and pilot.

Still, California was a beautiful state from 3000 feet and an even more amazing one from 300. He had had his hobby plane up as high as 10,000 feet but a few bouts of extreme turbulence at that altitude had convinced him to remain much closer to the ground. The plane could be transformed into a glider at any time and only difficult flying conditions where he could not jettison the engine, would make that transition a problem.

Gordon Fielding loved nothing more than floating above the mountains and zooming through the canyons of the Sierra Nevada Mountains. The peace and tranquillity were perfectly balanced by the watchfulness and heightened sensitivities required to fly a homemade plane.

Jenn had made arrangements to see her parents and siblings. She hadn't seen any of them in person since before she flew on the mission to the asteroid. Since then her life had been lived quickly with few opportunities to slow down. She had seen them and talked to them sporadically and knew that their meeting would be a bit jarring since it was the first time they'd seen each other in the after effects of relativity.

She had had those jarring experiences with friends and colleagues at FSU. Even though she shared a generation with most of them and even some memories, they all appeared to her as much older relations, uncles, aunts and cousins - people she knew but hadn't seen in so long that there was a shock at a reunion. She was afraid of any future school reunions.

She landed at Meadows Field Airport just northeast of Bakersfield. It had changed, grown and was busier than she remembered. There was a feeling of unfamiliarity which she put off to the length of time she had been away. She was surprised at first by the line of anti-gravity shuttles ready to whisk her into town. Of course this technology had been provided by the Eiosians while she was visiting their planets.

She took an anti-gravity platform shuttle from the airport to the main station in McFarland, the small town where her parents lived, a short distance north of the airport. Last time she was in McFarland she need a car as waiting for the bus was too slow. The Eiosians had been busy.

She smiled as she saw older people have a bit of trouble with the idea of sitting on the platform while the children took to it like it had always been there. Evidently the platforms were in general use but not everywhere yet.

Once at the station in McFarland she was at a loss for how she should proceed. She didn't know if there were cabs, or platforms for hire so she stood back and watched the arrivals do their thing. It was obvious fairly quickly that people simply took whatever platform presented itself, as nobody appeared to be waiting for anything specific but simply took the next available bit of moving floor.

She bit her tongue and asked. She was right, and now realized what the little fob they gave her upon her arrival was really for. It simply took note of your purchases, such as the purchase of travel, and eventually presented you with a bill, or more likely, accessed your accounts and provided you with a file noting all charges.

Quite unconfidently she stepped on a platform, despite all her off-world exposure to the technology, she was unsure how to let it know where to go.

"Just speak your destination, lady. Haven't you ever been moved before?"

Here was perhaps the most seasoned interstellar traveller battling local technology and taking abuse from a local, like she had just arrived in town by camel.

She turned to say something but realized the explanation of her retort would suck the joy out of making it.

She spoke the neighbourhood of her destination and the platform smoothly moved away. Once aloft she spoke more specifically the address. Gliding above the trees, using the old street grid as a path the platform wound its way from freeway to arterial road to local street, in some places it varied from the streets in a more direct path to its destination, through parks or along stream beds. There were still cars using the roads but the traffic was noticeably thinner than it would normally have been. Platforms moved along the major routes and a few, like hers, appeared to be on solitary journeys.

She passed the local high school with its lush lawns and spacious playing fields. She noted that much of the parking lot had been given over to a new building, attached by a breezeway to the older structure.

In fact she noted that many of the areas that were once parking had been shrunken and changed to parkland or given to new construction, especially in areas that were heavily built up.

"So how do they store the platforms once they have arrived?" she thought out loud.

"I can be held for use for 90 minutes or provided an instruction to return at a set time. Or you can arrange with Transportation Central for a platform to pick you up, either on a public network for one price or individually ordered at a specific time for a higher price. In urban areas platforms have taken over public transportation for no cost to the rider, though they are only available on heavily travelled routes, with times, routes and destinations clearly marked," the platform answered. "Platforms also come in different sizes depending on your need."

She twisted her head, this stuff didn't exist in Florida yet. She turned onto her parent's street. Sidewalks still remained, either because people were encouraged to walk for exercise or because it was too expensive to remove them. Many driveways had been shorn from their lots and replaced with grass or in some cases building extensions. There were still cars about but not as many as she expected in an upscale suburb in the middle of the day. She wondered what new construction looked like - what architects thought was essential and esthetically pleasing now that the car was on its way out? She wracked her memories of the styles of construction on Athelna and Eiosia remembering the platform connections with the upper storeys of high rise buildings.

The platform glided to a stop and emitted a gentle tone. She stepped off unsure how to dismiss it. It hovered in the air a few inches above the ground. Once she stepped off it settled back to Earth. A timer appeared on the floor which began counting off seconds from a two-minute standing start.

"I guess I have two minutes to engage it with instructions or it will leave," she said out loud, looking for an answer. She got one.

"Yes, I can stay for 90 minutes, I can come back at a specific time, or you can order another platform when necessary, all at applicable rates."

"And what are those?" she said feeling slightly ridiculous speaking to a floor. Below the time display a chart of rates was displayed in lighted numbers and letters on the floor.

"I am done for today, thank you for the ride .. ur ah, thank you."

"You are most welcome. Please travel with us again," it said as it rose slightly and glided off.

Fielding watched after it for a moment, before adjusting her grip on her suitcases and turning to walk slowly up a narrow walkway which had originally formed part of the lengthy drive. Six cars could have parked here comfortably, at least before the hot house was built. A glass hot house now took up the space of the former driveway. She noted some herb plants, some flowers and a few standard home garden types like tomatoes.

Everything was perfectly in place. And then she saw the reason why. A youngish man was fussing with a large flowing bush just to the side of the brick built house. He waved at her and she waved back a little unsure of herself.

"Jenn, the Astronaut," he called out across the yard, making no effort to put down his clippers. "Your mother is waiting for you inside."

"Um, thank you." She was expected so maybe he was looking out for her.

She pulled at the door and entered the house, knocking loudly as she did. Immediately she became aware of how strong the sun had been. It was cool under the roof, but not the kind of cool one feels upon entering an air conditioned building coming out of a hot, humid afternoon. All the familiar smells were there, cookies in the oven, a pie cooling on the stove. They were just muted. She called out and heard an answer from the front room. Turning the corner she saw her mother, a bit older looking than she remembered, sitting in the high back chair with a magazine on her lap.

"Jennifer, honey, how wonderful to see you. I am so glad you are home. Come here, I'm not fully mobile yet as I am still recovering from my latest surgery."

Her mother stiffly rose out of the chair and stood very shakily with one hand on the back of the chair to steady herself.

Jenn dropped her things and moved into the room. It had not changed from the last time she was here, about 17 years before, not long after her parents had retired. Though to her, she had been there shortly before she left for the asteroid, which was only seven years before.

She had not expected this. She thought there would be some change, especially with her parents who had aged many years in the relativity of her own travels. Her mother was nearly 20 years older than the last time she had seen her and was now close to 85 years old, but she appeared to be only a bit over 60 and looked younger than Jenn expected her to look.

Jenn herself was now chronologically 55 years old but due to the affects of relativity she was physiologically about 46 or so. Doctors had studied the travellers extensively to try to determine the affect of their light speed travel and their faster than light travel with the gravity wave. They had determined that the 14 years of travelling at or near the speed of light had caused them to age only about three years. They had actually aged a little more as not all their time was spent at speed.

"You are looking very well mother."

"I am feeling well too except for these knees which were operated on."

"You had both your knees replaced at the same time?"

"Oh yes, I should be up and around even now for a bit each day. I have already done my walking for the morning and I'll do some more in a little bit. Your father recovered from his replacement surgery very quickly. He was almost hale in a few days. You must have seen him on your way in."

"That was Dad?"

"I don't know who you saw, he was out trimming the bushes and doing some work in the hot house."

"That was him, he looked younger than I would have expected. In fact so do you, Mom."

"Such a thing to say. You look fine too!"

"No Mom, it's just that I have been subject to the effects of relativity and I'm told I have only aged about three to five years due to my travels at light speed. I saw the affects as some of my colleagues at the University had aged significantly while I was gone. It was quite the topic of conversation."

"Well, I thought you would know, since you were involved, medical science has advanced leaps and bounds since you've been away. But then that is part of why you were gone, wasn't it?"

"I suppose it was mother, among other things. I simply cannot get over how well you look."

"Oh it's much more than just looks. I've taken tennis up again, and even played a little golf. Bridge with the club seems so sedate now. I even skied a couple of years ago but found that it was a bit tough on my back and neck. Maybe I'll give it a go again now that my knees should be better than ever."

Jenn cocked her head. "Mother, what with my travels and relativity and that, how old are you now?"

"I'm almost 86, why do you ask?"

"Well with relativity I have lived about 55 years but I have only aged to about 46 years. I'm not sure I'd be up for skiing myself. Though I must admit the gravity on Eiosia, Athelna and Amorra put a tremendous strain on my body which I can still feel. Mostly in my large joints, my knees, spine and shoulders. Thank God for the anti-gravity suits. We had to wear them all the time. The gravity there was just too much. Without them it felt like you were being pressed into your chair from acceleration all the time. Quite an odd feeling when you are not moving at all."

"And so Jenn that's about how you look, in your later 40s with a bit more than the usual wear and tear on your body."

"Such a thing to say," mocked Jenn gently. "But you mother, look like you are still in your 60s and you have recently played some active sports, but you are 86. Doesn't that strike you as strange?"

"Not anymore honey. The medical advances help us to age more slowly, in fact almost not at all, and though our minds are still active, and sharp thanks to new treatments, our bodies are like new."

"So much more than just your knee joints was replaced?"

"Yes, yes of course, like everyone else. The Eiosians brought us this technology and almost everyone has used it. Older people more so I guess, as it is needed more and new to us here. We replace parts that are no longer working, younger people replace parts damaged beyond repair."

"So this technology was being given to us by the aliens during the time we went to explore their worlds?"

"Yes, it was introduced here not long after you left. Mostly just improvements to existing surgeries like knee replacements and hips but also more advanced like elbows, wrists and necks. It just became natural to expect available fixes to common problems after accidents and the infirmities of age. It's only fairly recently that we've been introduced to more organ and soft tissue replacements that are far less traumatic than our old way of doing things. We were positively medieval."

"So you've had some of that surgery yourself?"

"Why yes, everyone I know has. Well at least the older ones. We are all getting to that age, you know?"

Jenn was afraid to ask. She steered the conversation away from the obvious question to talk about her siblings and father. It turned out that they too had been involved with these new medical advances. But she was drawn back.

"Mother, how much of you has been replaced?"

"Well, let me think a bit," she cast her eyes to the ceiling. "Pretty much all of my joints. Though it's taken a number of years. First I did the feet, my ankles were hurting a lot and my arches had fallen badly. That went so well that I then I did my lower legs because the circulation was poor. By that time the procedures were fairly common. It worked so well I had no hesitation to do my hands and then arms and shoulders. The joints were wracked by rheumatism and I couldn't get the muscle tone I wanted. Then things started to go wrong in my abdomen, so bits were replaced."

"I see," said Jenn. "What about Dad, and the rest of the family."

"Your father actually took to it before I did. A friend of his was an early adopter and recommended it. You know how active your father used to be. The surgeries gave him a chance to go back and play ball again, which he does now on two teams. Your brother and sisters have done a few things as parts break down. But they are younger so don't have the need like your father and I. The surgeries are actually easy, and the recoveries fairly quick, a week at most. They have a way of 3D printing inside you. At least that's how it's been described. They don't even break the skin, and there are no stitches except in a couple of procedures where they are attaching new soft tissue to existing tissue. For bones and joints they use a matter transference of the material that's being implanted. It's all done to measure.

"So what is left of the real person, the original Audrey Fielding?"

"I'm still me, if that's what you are asking. Think of Nelson's flagship the Victory."

"Nelson?"

"Yes, the British Admiral and victor at the Battle of Trafalgar. His flag ship had been shot at, battered and beaten, worn out and torn at in battle and through heavy use. Each time it sailed to its harbor some of the damaged parts were replaced. A new mast here, new decking to replace broken and damaged planks. New cannon hole covers, new wood on the hull, improved kitchen facilities and upgrades where ever needed. After a time it had been virtually completely rebuilt, one board at a time over many decades. Was it still the same ship? Was it still the Victory?"

"Of course it was," Jenn said without conviction, and then she cocked her head. "It still looked the same, carried the same name and had the same history, didn't it?"

"Exactly, I too am the same Audrey Fielding, just a bit polished up."

"But mother, what about your soul?"

"Such a thing. How dramatic of you! We don't worry about such things much anymore, though I still attend services, mostly cause I'm used to it, and the companionship of my friends and neighbours gives me comfort.

"I doubt my soul left me when I did my knees. I'm going to guess your soul is not in your knees. Nor did it leave when I had my hands or feet done. So what would make it leave? If it's still there then I'm still intact."

"My friend Mike Donohue has conducted some experiments to find the soul. He thinks he knows what it is."

"Okay, what did he find?"

"The human brain is interconnected, with millions, perhaps billions of synapses, or connections. In each person the number of these connections varies, while the actual wiring, the specific connections are different. They are different in where they lead, in what quantity and in what order of hierarchy are they called upon in various situations. Given the many billions of potential connections and options and order of their use, it is reasonable to suggest that this is the soul, the essence of the person, which cannot be copied by any known technology.

"So," she continued, "if you have your brain replaced, even if it is programmed with all the synapses and memories, it is impossible for a computer to replicate the specifics of your brain, the preferred connections and timing and layering of all this information that makes you, you.

"Perhaps it's like saying that the blood of the fallen sailors who died in combat on the Victory is no longer present when boards and decking and masts have been replaced, so it may be essentially the same vessel, but it doesn't have the soul of the original. The contributions of many people have not been included in the replication."

"I never thought of inanimate objects having a soul. Nevertheless I might say that if there are a finite number of neural connections, no matter how large the number or what their degree of intercon-nectivity is, they can be reproduced. You would say that without my brain I am just a robot built to replicate Audrey Fielding?"

"Yes. You would not be Audrey Fielding, you would be a replica. A very detailed, virtually unchanged replica. But you are not the real thing."

"So I should think twice about having the brain function replaced by a digital Artificial Intelligence when that time comes? My brain will break down eventually," said Audrey, sitting down with a wince.

"Have you ever seen a machine that did not break down at some point? Yes, it is a significant existential question. You should think seriously about the reality of you without your own brain. I am simply not convinced that a digital version of your brain is the same thing as the original. We do continue to produce new brain cells throughout our lives. They are integrated into our synapses. On Eiosia and the other planets connected to it, many people had elected to forego the complete transition to machine. They stopped at the brain function and allowed themselves to die once the brain ceased to work properly."

"And the others?"

Jenn dropped her head forward to her chest. "Yes, there are many more who are afraid of death and so allow the brain replacement procedure. Scientists there say there is a subtle difference in people once they've had the procedure but their science has not been able to pinpoint the effect or the cause. But they do not doubt that it is there.

"It appears that the Eiosians have hit the end of the cultural quest. They have conquered want and need, and they have virtually conquered death. But their civilization is dying. There is nothing to reach for as everything appears to be in their grasp."

"Maybe there really isn't an end it's just a new start, they have evolved," said Audrey. "The difference might be simply the change in those who fear death but who have been provided with a new lease on life."

"That, mother, is perhaps the most apt description. A lease on life. Those who have completed the procedure have extended their being but in a way, much like using an asset they no longer really own."

"I have considered the eventuality of needing the replacement. Death is no longer inevitable. The continuation of life is a powerful urge. What would you think if I succumbed to a digital replacement?"

"My immediate thought is that I believe I would be an orphan. At least an orphan in the adult sense, once our parents have passed on. What I would have is a walking talking book of memories, and one that appears to be able to add new pages. It is impossible to determine what I would think until actually faced with that eventuality."

"So you would prefer me to die and pass away?"

Jenn sighed deeply. "I don't know. I didn't say that. But it is the natural order. On the surface of the issue, no of course not, I want you always there, here. I would not want to lose you or dad, or anybody close. Who would? But deeper down, knowing that everyone passes on, at least until now they have, there was a sad expectation of a life completed, a book closed. Brain replacement and the indefinite extension of some kind of life, changes almost everything about human relationships. Perhaps even about what it means to be human."

The clipping outside had stopped. The front door opened and the gardener entered. Jenn could see it was her father, but instead of being old, he had replicated himself as a younger man, about 35ish, so his age did not deflate his physical powers.

"You are what remains of my father?" she said.

He smiled. "Is that anyway to say hello after so many years. How was your flight?"

"Dad, I am struggling with this. I have had some time to consider it as we travelled, but seeing it so starkly in my own family, is very disconcerting. I haven't had time to really consider it."

"I have, and I heard your description of us. Faced with death, you will do it too. Faced with pain, wracked with disease, with each day getting a bit more grim, you will succumb to the restoration surgery. It is virtually painless, save some recovery time. And you live again. Not without your baggage of a long life, but that is put aside and you no longer wear every weakness, every wrinkle, every evolutionary bad break, bad digestion from a life of poor eating habits, or a clicking joint, or a balding head. You are restored."

"Restored? More like rebuilt to new specifications. Perhaps when the time comes Dad, I shall. Do not mistake me, I do not judge. I am merely speaking out loud many of the thoughts and conclusions that were reached by the astronauts who visited the faraway worlds and saw what hundreds of years of these practices did to their societies.

"Have you considered the future? How many times would you replicate? Do you want to be immortal? Should you be?"

"I have had several of my joints replaced more than once," said her father. "In fact I have been encouraging your mother to get some of her aging replacements redone."

"Is life all about longevity?"

"No, it is about quality. If I kill myself in an accident I would be okay with that. I still fly my hobby plane."

"Really," said Jenn. "You have traded your soul for longevity. I understand the desire to do so, and I've seen what happens when this is continued over many generations. It is not what anyone really considers life. When your society is really a large number of robot shells, what is it really?"

"It works for me," said Audrey Fielding.

"And me, said Gordon Fielding. "And for everyone I know."

Audrey pushed on the arms of her chair. She lifted herself to a standing position and stretched her torso, pitting muscles against muscles. She gasped at the exertion.

"I'm feeling different. My legs are strong. My knees are not even there - there is no pain."

She stiffly took a step and then another, almost expecting a touch of pain. And then she took two quick, deep lunges and spun her body on the ball of her right foot. She landed squarely on her left foot in an athletic ready position.

"I can hardly wait to play tennis again."

"It should be quite the match, dear. Old Doug Naismith said that his Colleen has much the same procedure as you and she is back to playing twice a week."

Jenn stood in the room trying to take it all in. Her own parents had already succumbed to the wonders of the medical advances without knowing or even considering the end game. Or if they had they were willing to take that consequence as a trade for today and some unknown number of tomorrows.

"How long do you plan to stay here, honey?"

"I'm due back at the university in two weeks. I thought I would stay here for a while and maybe travel to New York for a few days and take in a few Broadway shows."

"We will have no trouble keeping you busy here, dear. All my friends want to see you. You are a bit famous now. We'd like to show you off. In fact I thought a small reception at the golf club might work or a small party here. Which is best for you?"

Jenn Fielding sighed again, this time at the foibles of parents. She knew she owed them at least that. After all they had supported her desire to fly, to be an astronaut and to project herself into the future without knowing for sure if she would be afforded the opportunity.

"Whatever you'd like Mom. The golf club would be less work for you. If needed I can put New York aside for now. So tell me what other advances have the Eiosians brought with them?"

Her mother smiled. "That will be fine honey. Would you like something to drink? I'd like to hear all about your travels - especially the stuff they didn't report on the news. Your brother is coming later today and bringing his kids. You haven't seen them since they were small."

Chapter Eighteen

"We've noticed a strange phenomenon, sir. It appears the Eiosians are happy to take our transplants on as immigrants and those people are settling in well to their lifestyle."

"That's what they wanted. So what's the issue?"

"Not an issue sir, at least nothing yet, but it appears that the Eiosians are flocking to Earth to live in areas not yet changed drastically by their own technological changes - they want to be primitives."

"How many are we talking about?"

"Maybe a million, which might not sound like a lot of people given huge migrations on Earth over the centuries, but it's a significant part of the Eiosian population, though it's an estimate. There are some from the other known worlds as well, even from Amorra. We don't really know how many there are. And those migrants have been amply replaced by Earth people travelling in the other direction, to the tune of perhaps five million, and more than half of those Chinese."

"If you lived in the bowls of Shanghai you might be anxious to find a bit more living space on a technologically superior planet."

"Yes, sir. But I cannot help but think that this is a demographic switch that the Chinese are well aware of, and might even be encouraging. It started with the Chinese predominately but it seems the Russians have also tried, belatedly, to encourage Russian nationals to make the trip. Though they are more partial to Athelna."

"And the Eiosians here on Earth?"

"They are flocking to Central America, India, Central Africa and parts of South America. Essentially they are going to the poorest areas to live as we did prior to the introduction of their technology."

"So let me get this straight. We have been exchanging populations with the Eiosians. Mostly Chinese and some Russians but their arrivals are moving to primitive places? Aren't the Chinese buying up many of those areas around the world. They have two satellite nations now in each of Africa and South America. They have carved out significant presences on several large Pacific and Indian Ocean islands including Madagascar, Borneo and New Guinea. The Indians have co-operated with them in developing some of the Kashmir regions near the Tibet border with mountain agriculture and mining."

"Are you suggesting that this spread into Eiosia is part of a comprehensive plan to spread their culture around our world and onto others?"

"Have they been emigrating to other known worlds?

"Yes, but in much smaller numbers. Those worlds, like Athelna are still fairly populated whereas Eiosia is almost empty. The Amorrans have been granting landing status to Earthlings who are interested in living there, though there have been few takers."

"Demographics is destiny. At least when the Chinese decided to remain insular they defied that dictum. I wonder what the world would have been like had they decided to continue their explorations in the 13th century?"

"Much different than it turned out to be. But maybe no different than it will eventually become."

"The Eiosians seem to welcome them, and anyone who wants to help them replenish their society."

"Well the lack of a surging population sort of explains the lack of scientific growth in the last millennium or so, for them."

"I'm not sure it is a problem sir, but there is almost no way to stop the emigration. It's like people moving to North America in pre-colonial days, the movement is large and difficult to detect and not causing too much strife among the indigenous populations."

"Don't tell the Native Americans that, they may not have objected too much at first, but they sure objected later and quite violently."

"There is no issue so far with any of this immigration. The Eiosians welcome it, remember, that's what they hoped for to reinvigorate their society."

"Continue to monitor it and report every six months; more often if you deem it necessary."

"Now that there are regular commercial transports going between

Earth and Eiosia, I expect the numbers to continue to grow until some kind of balance is struck. At the same time, the introduction of Eiosian technology is perhaps reducing the desire to emigrate, assuming people are going for the technological advances."

"The inflow of Eiosians to Earth seems to have stopped much of the conflict in central Africa and in western Brazil. The Chinese have used Eiosians to augment their populations in those places and the introduction of technology has essentially ended the conflicts. Even those countries that lost territory do not seem to be too put out by it, as if the high technology they received in return has placated them."

"It appears as if Earth has unofficially joined the Eiosian alliance, and ignored the warnings of the Amorrans."

"Yes, sir, that appears to have occurred. I wonder how long it will take until the Security Council catches up to reality?"

"Perhaps never, sir. The Security Council sometimes appears to be quite happy living in its own reality. That way they don't have to react, or take sides or do anything very dramatic."

"Threat levels have been reduced in every sector. It appears that the Eiosians have at least brought with them a lasting peace."

"And for that I guess we should be grateful. But it is peace at what cost? What I see is a whole civilization that has lost its life force, in fact significant numbers of them are coming to Earth exactly because they have no vitality left. They seek it. How long will it be before they suck the vitality out of us? How long before someone rebels?"

"They have thousands of years of existence on us. It might take us a while before we reach their level of accomplishment or ennui."

"We would do well to study the Chinese in great detail. They refused to grow outward for many hundreds of years and remained weak and easily dominated. They threw off the yoke of colonizers and economic domination and then tried to control their population and keep it subservient to the greater whole. Once they accomplished that, they started to build outward, in fact they started to build little Chinas in several places in the world, and once given the opportunity they appear to be transporting that culture off-world."

"And the Eiosians are doing the same thing."

"Yes, I suppose they are but they are a dying civilization while the Chinese are ascendant. I wonder what the relative size of their populations are?"

"Best guess sir, is the Eiosians proper, meaning those living on Eiosia number about two billion. And there are many more billions on the other colonized planets. And the Chinese on Earth, at least those with a direct connection to China, rather than people who have lived for generations outside of China, but who are ethnic Chinese, probably number about 1.5 billion."

"We live in interesting times, Lieutenant."

"It will take many lifetimes to play out sir, and who knows how closed the system is? Who knows how much additional vitality Earth can bring to the greater civilization. Who knows how the changes wrought by the Eiosians will affect our own inbred desires and needs?"

"Don't forget lieutenant, we are them. We come from the same stock. They are homo sapiens just like us. What you see in them, you can expect us to match and follow. It's really just a question of how long it will take."

"The rapid acceptance of their technology makes me think it will not be very long. Ultimately how long will it take before we have the vitality tapped out of us?"

Mike Donohue continued his work in bringing the technology to Earth and mixing with the Eiosian culture.

Mika Oh decided to write a book and host a video series on her travels and experiences.

She was concerned with what she saw. The new paternal power of government was stifling society as it inevitably pushed people into a lifelong childhood by removing need and even much of want but replacing the later with nothing.

She wondered again of the Amish and their desire to remain outside of the mainstream of technological development. Our entire society is crisscrossed with a network of small, complicated, minute, and uniform technological rules, which most don't even see and all deem beneficial and unwilling to move beyond.

"This new society never forces action," she thought, "yet it constantly blocks and opposes any choices other than those approved. It does not destroy but it opposes birth, avoids death ; it is not a tyranny, but it hinders, it represses, it extinguishes, it stupefies, and finally it reduces us all to nothing more than a flock of timid sheep, of which the culture is the shepherd."

She was determined to find a solution, but it kept eluding her thought and planning.

Her husband Ivan Bolrenko was involved with the Russian determination not to be left behind by the Chinese advancements and population growth. For him the future was Russian and he was part of a team that decided to encourage Russian citizens to emigrate to Amorra and join the group who wanted to slow the advance of technology in the hope of also slowing the ennui of inhabitants.

And while this seemed at first good to Mika, she saw clearly the endgame, that instead of opposing cultures on Earth, the move to export their ways would eventually push the Chinese on Eiosia and the Russians on Amorra into opposition. However, on this she kept quiet, knowing that possibility lay many centuries into the future.

Jenn Fielding studied the advanced avionics possessed by the Eiosians made possible largely through their mastery of gravity. She also continued her systematic study of the Eiosian language and how it had evolved on different planets in the group.

Renaud Martin's company led the way on the propulsion technology, licensing it on Earth and building quite a fortune until legal wrangling opened it to all potential users. While Martin and his investors became rich from their venture, the introduction of Eiosian technology rendered much of their fortune pointless as money was of limited utility.

Realizing what was happening the consortium started buying property and built a significant portfolio of real estate, from high end, top locations, to vast swathes of ranch land and rural areas. As the agricultural revolution swept Earth, they were hard pressed to keep control of some of their lands as most productive land was nationalized for the robot operated farms.

Jimmy Ho Yang was the mastermind of the outward bound Chinese experiment. Not seeking power himself, he was content to remain a strong, powerful figure in the Chinese hierarchy, never a threat to the leadership but in full support of their global and eventually galactic desires.

Yang Li became an ambassador between Earth and the Eiosian system, dedicated to mutual understanding and cultural exchange. And Chinese nationals continued to emigrate to Eiosia even as the search for other habitable planets continued.

And while the new realities sorted themselves out, peace seemed assured and conflicts on Earth melted away as wants and needs were met. Amorra became the refuge of those unwilling to accept the wealth of technological advances available. It's inhabitants understood the danger and were actually happy to see anyone who disagreed with them leave their domain.

The reordering of civilization would take generations. And yet the probable future remained a niggle on the minds of those who considered such things. And then the future reached out one day and made its presence known.

A youngish man in uniform, hunched over a display saw something unusual.

"Sir, the signal from the asteroid Omagon 39 has stopped, or at least we are not receiving it anymore."

"That's our mining beacon way out past Amorra? Lieutenant, we all knew this day would come, you know exactly what to do."

"Yes, sir." He made a note of the time in the station logs, passed the log entry to his supervisor and turned back to the readouts.

The clock on the wall continued its metronomic advance, one numeral at a time: tick, tick, tick, tick . . .

END

"A Picture of Distance" an excerpt

Chapter Thirty - Nine - 1984

Chas looked at himself in the mirror on his way out the door. Not quite the same 21-year old he had been 40 years before. As he continued his gaze he realized that exactly 40 years before he had been struggling trying to salvage the engine of a Spitfire that had been hit by anti-aircraft fire during the D-Day invasion.

Walking the beaches now 40 years later lost in his thoughts for the last few days, Chas had enjoyed the time with old mates and his brother Bill. He kept straying to thoughts of Ver Sur Mer and his friend, the pilot Gordon McAuley.

He had written many months ago to The Caen War Memorial to get information on the museum for his trip and inquiring after the final resting place of Bill's friend Frank Edwards and his own wartime acquaintance Simon MacDonald. The museum put him in touch with a Jacques Gaspareau, a member of the French resistance during the war and a local historian.

Mon. Gaspareau wrote back saying that he did indeed know the spot where Lieutenant MacDonald was buried as he had been on a patrol that day in 1944 with his Resistance fighters when he came upon the body of MacDonald. He said the resistance often came across Allied soldiers and secretly buried their bodies to keep them out of the hands of the Nazis who were known to take out their frustrations on the corpses or otherwise denigrate their service.

Mon. Gaspareau said he would be happy to escort Chas to the site and show him around the area.

Chas remembered the events that led to Simon MacDonald's death. He had known Simon as a fellow mechanic. They had become friends as Simon was from the small town of Streetsville, just west of Toronto.

Only a few days after the D-Day landings, with the mechanics busy keeping the landing forces mobile, there had been a late afternoon call from Division for a mechanic to go to the recently seized bridge head outside of Reviers.

Chas was head deep in an engine just as the message arrived. Simon was just making the last few turns with his wrench to finish up the job on his vehicle. He volunteered.

Chas only heard of the events of that day from some of the other boys he had contact with. Simon never returned. When Simon arrived the Germans were apparently in retreat and many Allied tanks and personal were across the river. So Simon ran across the bridge without too much concern to reach a tank that had stalled and partly blocked the bridge egress.

According to those who witnessed it, a squadron of German fighters swooped down on the bridge at that moment and strafed the column trying to squeeze around the stalled tank.

Simon was hit multiple times and knocked off the bridge and into the river. In the chaos of the battle, and not really knowing that Simon was officially there, he was overlooked until several days later when he did not return to the motor pool.

Inquiries provided the story and likely end of Simon MacDonald. His body was not officially found until the burial spot was disclosed after the war. French partisans, including Mon. Gaspareau, found him down river and buried him in a quiet place without much ceremony.

After the war they provided his dog tags to officials who were able to match him up with their records and officially record his burial place. Normandy is dotted with these types of graves, usually unobtrusive, peaceful and enough out of the normal ebb and flow of daily life to be almost forgotten.

Chas was pleased that his inquiries were able to produce MacDonald's final resting place and a guide to help him find it.

Chas called Mon. Gaspareau. Thanks to the Frenchman's very European ability to speak more than one language they were able to quickly agree to a time and place to meet. Chas gave his full name to Gaspareau and began to spell it but Gaspareau stopped him.

"No, no Charles. Stuart is a well-known name around here," said Gaspareau.

Chas expressed surprise. "Oh, well, then I needn't spell it for you. I'll be with my wife. How will I know you on the platform?"

"Do not worry monsieur I will know you – what tourists we get in Ver Sur Mer usually come by car. You will be well known to me on the train platform. I can spot a tourist anywhere," he laughed.

As he hung up Chas smiled at the thought that Mon Gaspareau could see through his attempt to be more restrained than the average tourist.

"It's the running shoes, dear," said Anne, who had been eyeing him eyeing himself. "They give you away, that and the Toronto

Maple Leaf jacket you've been wearing. Honestly, even with a few more cameras around your neck, a tour book in your hand and a map in the other you couldn't possibly look more like a tourist."

"At least they don't mistake us for Americans," he said.

"But they do. And if they don't it's because of the jacket dear, not because you don't look the part."

They ambled out of their hotel room in Caen and made their way to the train station where they boarded the train for Ver Sur Mer. Securing their tickets they settled in for a 30 minute ride. Stopping at a number of village cross roads the train never worked up much speed. Soon it was slowing again as they reached their destination. A few of the passengers began to gather their things to disembark. Most appeared to be going on to Bayeux or Cherbourg. Chas and Anne would return to Caen that evening.

The train pulled into the station and it was immediately obvious there was a major ruckus occurring on the platform. It was raucous and crowded. And what first appeared to be some sort of trouble, soon looked more like a huge crowd awaiting a movie star or something.

"There must be a movie star or singer or some celebrity on this train. Listen there's even a band out there."

"Perhaps if we moved up the train we'll get clear of all the commotion. I don't even know what Mon. Gaspareau looks like. I bet he was counting on a quiet day on which to find us."

So the two Canadians moved through a few cars trying to clear the crowds. Chas saw a young man trying to manoeuvre a large box through the now open door. He was carrying a television camera.

"Here, I'll give you a hand with that," said Chas picking up the equipment box and moving through the door onto the platform, saying over his shoulder, "You'll miss the big moment if you don't hurry."

As Chas emerged, the platform erupted in a big cheer. He looked down the length of the train trying to catch a glimpse of whoever the big star was that everyone was waiting for. Anne stepped off behind the camera man who struggled with his rig.

Chas looked at all the people to see what they were focussed on but they were all seemed to be looking at him or the cameraman. The band struck up O' Canada.

Everyone seemed to have a Canadian flag, and a banner was unfurled from the facing of the station wall, which said "Bienvenue, Charles Stuart, Hero of Ver-Sur-Mer.

"What? There must be some mistake," he said to everyone and no one in particular.

A man appeared at his side.

"Monsieur Stuart, welcome to Ver-Sur-Mer, or welcome back for the first time in 40 years. When Mon. Gaspareau told me you were coming, well, I was overcome with joy. Your efforts to save our town and your extraordinary bravery to alert Mon. McAuley to our need will never be forgotten. This station is named Gare McAuley and the street on which it lies is Rue de Charles Stuart."

And so Mayor Jacques Martin of Ver-Sur-Mer directed Chas and Anne down the platform and through the cheering crowds of people. It appeared as if the whole town had turned out for the event. Every child was in their Sunday best, the boys with ties and the girls with flowers in their hair.

Down Rue de Charles Stuart they marched with a band keeping the beat alternating between Le Marseilles and O' Canada. People hung out their upper windows of the small central section of town, straining over the flower boxes to see the parade. In the midst of it all was a still bewildered Chas who wanted nothing more than a quiet afternoon in a small French town. He had come prepared to mourn his comrades.

At the end of the street was an open square with a dais to which Chas and Anne were led. Beside the square was a neatly kept cemetery with rows of white tombstones and a number of larger stone monuments. A small group of war graves were clearly visible from the platform decorated with national flags.

Several dignitaries were seated on the platform and all, save one older man, rose as Chas and Anne ascended the steps.

"Bonjour Madames et Monsieurs," Mayor Martin boomed before switching to English. "I have often longed for this day – to finally have the chance to thank our liberators for their bravery – face to face."

"On that fateful day I was a young boy living on Rue Esmerelda," he waved off to his left and explained for Chas his story as many in town were already familiar with it. "Just over there about a block from the bridge over La Provence. The Canadians saved my life, my family, my town and our beloved France."

Mayor Martin paused remembering a few fateful moments that made up most of his wartime remembrance. A tear gathered in the corner of his eye.

He remembered the day . . . .

"A Picture of Distance" is the story of three generations of the fictional Stuart Family of Toronto beginning with their matriarch and ending with her death at nearly 100 years of age—it is the story of the 20th century as see from Canadian eyes.

All Fall Down - an excerpt

Chapter Two - Two years later

"Tourists and scavengers. That's what's there."

"What about San Fran?"

"'That's altogether different - different disaster, different future," he said. "They're rebuilding. They figure they've got 100 years until the next one," he laughed. "And all those LA refugees are looking for a place to live."

"I'd like to go to New York, but I wonder what you can actually see. I'm guessing anything that could be moved has been moved - and the rest is derelict. I mean how many Planet of the Apes reactions can you have?" he grinned ruefully.

"I was there. About six months ago. It is interesting . . .for about six hours . . .then its creepy. It's not what you can see that's interesting, it's what you can't, and the little bits of life that have sprung up. Take a tour. First you go by boat and then they take you through Central Park to the Battery. The city actually still functions, well, some of it anyway. Midtown and South Manhattan are giant reclamation projects. The Bronx is largely intact and Brooklyn suffered significant damage, about half is damaged beyond use."

"Is it even worth reclaiming or rebuilding?"

"Oh yes, the city is huge and much of it is intact. It's just got a giant hole in the center now. Remember it is one of the most desirable geographic locations in the world - and now the slate is clean. Hiroshima was rebuilt."

"Ok, New York is solved. What are we going to do about Texas?"

"Solved, not really. The President has some ideas but there are a number of hurdles to jump. Regarding Texas, there is nothing we can do. They've always had the right to succeed. Now they are going to exercise it. I'm pretty sure we'll be on good terms though. The real question is, does Oklahoma try to join Texas?"

"If that happens the battles could turn violent. The Red River makes for a natural boundary and frankly, there aren't a lot of natural boundaries around there. If Oklahoma is allowed to go, then what about Arkansas, Louisiana, or at least parts of them? And at least half of New Mexico is already functionally Texas territory."

"The Sabine is our best chance to keep the borders intact. Northern Louisiana has more than a bit of Dixie in it. As for the west, there is little demand for border definition as the area is pretty empty. 'There be dragons', and all that."

The two men, clad in suits, each held a paper coffee cup. They stood in the atrium of a moderately sized, modern glass office building in Washington, capital of the United States of America, once the most powerful country on Earth, now, two years after the destruction of its largest city, truly an E Pluribus Unum - one out of many. Still a nasty opponent in a fight, it had been crippled. It's enemies were taking a longer view.

The last few years had been awash in change. The two men, Pennsylvania Senator Tom Findlay, tall, strongly built, with short dark hair punctuated with a hint of a wave above his brow; and a shorter man, a bit older and impeccably dressed, down to the watch chain crossing into his left jacket pocket was Massachusetts Governor Jim Grange. Both had been Representatives in Congress and had become acquainted then. they still spoke often.

Senator Findley, a confident of the President, was trying to manage the horrendous change to the advantage of the United States, as he intended to run for President in the next election cycle. Governor Grange was interested in the United States but only insofar as Massachusetts was part of it, or what remained of it.

Rome had been similarly attacked before New York so much of both men's efforts were to prepare for future attacks and clean up from the ones that had already occurred.

Poor map drawing after World War One and a failure to recognize festering cultural, religious and historical issues had been major causes of the upheavals that left the world shattered. They had fuelled a movement to a new order of government in North America and ultimately around the world. There remained a sizable number of variables that contributed to the catastrophic change, forcing people like Findlay and Grange to deal with the aftermath and leave the history books to be written decades in the future, when time might provide some perspective.

"And in New York of course there are two types of scavengers. Those on contract with the insurance companies and the 'independent operators' who are looking for metal, and other easily removed valuables," said Findlay.

The world had been changing slowly even as far back as the 1970's and there had been warnings in the scattered violence of embassy attacks, explosions of military personnel and equipment and assassinations. The first seismic shift had occurred on September 11, 2001 with the destruction of the twin towers of the World Trade Center, the two tallest buildings in New York. Despite the shock of that event, the shift continued its movement toward change with grinding slowness, and even though many people could feel that change was happening, a clear vision and understanding of it did not emerge. Murky connections, murky motives and the obvious conclusion of a clash of civilizations continued to be resisted.

Only after the tip of Manhattan had been destroyed by a rudimentary nuclear device on May 29, along with simultaneous attacks on Los Angeles and other US targets, did the world move fully into a new era. It was an era that still had not been completely defined as the endgame for all participants had not been identified much less achieved. A political, cultural and economic equilibrium was still some time in the future. The moving parts of society and civilization had slowed but they were still moving.

It took the United States government only 72 hours to respond. There had been much handwringing and debate on the proper response to the destruction of Rome with little actually happening as a result. The United States had been on hair trigger alert since the nuclear attack on Rome a year before New York, and had issued warnings of dire consequences should an attack on a US target occur. In some circles there had been optimism that the eventual attempt on another western city could be stopped, after all the British had thwarted an attempt on London a few months after Rome.

That optimism was misplaced as ships delivered simultaneous nuclear hits to New York, the US Naval Base at Norfolk Virginia, and Los Angeles within one hour of each other. Within an hour of the attack on New York, defence forces had managed to sink a ship headed to Boston, another headed to San Diego and another in the Gulf of Mexico whose target was believed to be Tampa or New Orleans. In their frenzied defence they sank several ships just to be sure, finding out after the fact that they'd been right about three of them. Intelligence gathering found chatter that San Fran had apparently been spared only because a large earthquake had caused significant damage in that city a few months earlier. The ship bound for Frisco had been diverted to San Diego to target the large naval base in that city but was sunk as it lagged behind the appointed hour of attack.

Islamic State had taken credit for the bombings. So had Hezbollah, Al Qaeda and a dozen other shadowy groups of Muslim fundamentalists.

The bombs were crude. Not that it mattered, but they were flung up in the air several hundred feet essentially by large catapults and then detonated. South and central LA was destroyed in a ring centered on the blast at Long Beach's port facility. It produced a wasteland for several miles inland. Destruction did not quite reach the de facto downtown section of LA located in the north west of the heavily populated Los Angeles basin. Sheer distance and the ring of mountains served to compress the blast effects.

San Diego narrowly avoided the same fate and more importantly was able to retain defense assets of the Pacific Fleet. The damage in Norfolk was not as bad as may have occurred as the ship was challenged as it approached the Naval Station. It detonated on the Atlantic side of the harbour managing to take out thousands of inhabitants and badly damaging two aircraft carriers the USS Forrestal and the USS John F. Kennedy. Several heavy cruisers were also damaged. The major damage was to the station which was no longer in any shape to house and refit the Fleet as was required.

Three detonations. Millions killed. Millions more maimed and many more yet to die from radiation. Economies, food, transportation, jobs, livelihoods all destroyed. Truth was, two years on, most of those who would die were already dead. Many thousands were still in temporary housing and were left to their own devices as to what to do with their future. A trickle left each day to start a new life, usually hundreds of miles from where their lives had been put on hold.

With two major cities existing now with holes blown out of their centers and a third urban area also largely destroyed, the United States had undergone convulsions, both in the immediate wake of the attacks and in the months that followed. Two years later the recriminations and finger pointing still had not stopped.

The once mighty United States Dollar had been hammered as the rest of the world began to use other payment methods in the wake of the attacks. The process of countries moving away from the US dollar had already been underway prior to the attacks. Knowing the US treasury would simply print more greenbacks to help the rebuilding process, the once strong dollar had taken a beating.

Within a few months, significant military retaliation had restored some of the faith in the US dollar as the currency of last resort. While the US economy had taken a huge hit there still remained a giant country and 300 million people to feed, house, and employ. In most of the country it was only the ripple effects from the attacks that had impacted the populace.

In the uncertainty, the financial world shifted its focus to a new unofficial gold standard, with several major currencies pegged to gold and minor currencies floating against the Chinese Yuan and the Swiss Franc. British Pounds, US Dollars and the Euro were forced to peg themselves to something tangible in order to retain their perceived value - they chose silver.

The currency issue was flip flopping about in turmoil almost every week. Though with every wide swing up and down the next swing was smaller until the churning valuations had flattened out.

Washington still controlled much of its former national territory; the Northeast, the Mid-western rust belt, the northern plains and much of the central west. However, Texas chafed under Washington's yoke and invoked their right to succeed as Washington refused to clean up or abandon the Federal Reserve system and could not spare the resources to stop illegal immigration.

Without a whimper Washington acceded to the demands of Texans by giving up federal jurisdiction to the Texas legislature but making it easy for Texans to use US currency and other manifestations and institutions of the old US.

Oklahoma was so tied to Texas it wavered on joining with Texas. Northern Texans welcomed them. Southern and western Texans were ambivalent. Similarly southern Oklahomans were very interested in maintaining ties to Texas while other people north of Oklahoma City did not have strong feelings.

Dixie and the Old South had also risen up and effectively succeeded as US senators and other elected officials took to sitting in a Dixie-only legislature concurrent with their US obligations. Succession was being achieved without any grandiose announcement, and was becoming more accepted and permanent with each day the Dixie legislature went unchallenged.

Washington had no ability to attend to the needs of the southern states. Those States had met initially as a southern caucus to get southern Congressmen to put pressure on Washington for help. It soon became evident that Washington couldn't help and the caucus was more of a regional government. It began to take on more and more senior level authority, but it walked a careful line as no independence had been announced. Southern leaders knew the further along they marched the more natural their new regional government would become until it was the de facto national government that it was rapidly becoming.

Florida and western Louisiana were wavering. Dixie could not function fully independently as it simply melted into the United States at various places in Virginia. North and eastern Virginia remained with Washington, as federal money was pouring into coastal Norfolk to rebuild. The hoards of federal bureaucrats who populated the southern hinterlands of Washington, extending deep into northern Virginia cemented the US federal government's hold on the region.

The question of Kentucky wasn't settled. Many in the state thought themselves as southerners because they weren't hillbillies and they weren't Yankees. There were significant groups in favour of joining the New South.

Tennessee's two US senators had joined the New South caucus early on. Florida had so many northerners in residence that the State Legislature could not muster enough support to join the New South caucus. Northern Florida agitated for closer ties with Atlanta. Southern Florida grew closer to Cuba and Mexico thanks to large expatriate populations from both those countries. A significant northern US presence in the south of Florida, from New York retirees to the federal military, kept that part of the state close to Washington.

The central part of the state was very sympathetic with the old US, as many residents had ties to the Northeast, the rust belt and the Upper Mid-west. While there was tension, the federal presence in Florida and a lack of desire for huge change kept official Florida from taking any action at all.

Louisiana was half of a mind to join Texas, and eastern Texans would have taken them. Western Texans were not so sure. The rest of the state liked the idea of a defensible Sabine River border that already existed for most of the distance between the two. The same issue occurred with Oklahoma - a well defined river border already existed but the Oklahomans were functionally more than half Texans anyway. Some Oklahomans were content with Washington while others simply wanted to play Washington and Austin off against each other. Northern Texans cared, others did not and Washington was prepared to do what it took to keep Oklahoma on side.

California was increasingly given over to Mexican influence. The earthquake in San Francisco and the bombings had cowed the Southern California population, many of whom were moving north to the Bay Area or leaving the state. The Latinos had nowhere else they wanted to be and so remained, gathering more and more influence every year. Southern California was becoming functionally a province of Mexico even if it was still part of the crumbling US.

Survivors from southern California were moving up to the San Francisco area despite the earthquake which had spawned fires rendering large areas of the city uninhabitable. The quake, a mas-sive 8.4 on the Richter Scale, left much damage to San Francisco and other cities surrounding the Bay though outside of San Francisco damage was limited to smaller areas and older buildings.

The biggest consequence of the quake, was a huge change in the local topography isolating the City of San Francisco. The fault had opened up a fissure between San Andres Lake and the Bay just north of San Mateo. The fissure continued northwest until it con-nected the southern bay to the Pacific Ocean just north of Pacifica. Effectively San Francisco was an island. As in 1906, San Francisco had been greatly damaged by fire. This time though fire damage was contained more effectively leaving a huge clean up, and many damaged and destroyed buildings. However, much of the city was repairable given enough time and resources.

The business center of the US had shifted to Chicago in the wake of the destruction of Manhattan. Certain economic activity still occurred in New York but it was small scale and mostly local - dealing with the needs of the surviving locals and with the clean up and rebuild of the city.

"All Fall Down" is the story of the aftermath of a co-ordinated terrorist attack on the United States. It traces the political, economic and social fallout across the United States and around the world.

Casting Giant Shadows - an excerpt

Chapter Eleven

The troop ship sailed triumphantly into New York harbour, sounding its horns, with the deck full of happy soon-to-be ex-soldiers. Fire boats launched a celebratory spray into the air. An unflappable Lady Liberty watched the joyful proceedings.

The ship docked and disgorged its passengers to a general liberty. A formal leave taking would begin the next day and the ship would remain in New York as a floating hotel for three days while all the men made arrangements to travel from New York to their home towns across the country. Eisenrick invited the platoon to his family bakery early the next day before they all began to get shipped out the following morning.

"I won't pass that up, Frankie," said Jocko Rollins. "I'm guessing your mom makes better stuff than you. I'd like a little bit of heaven before I head home to Missouri."

Momma Eisenrick faced quite a sight at precisely 0-800. She had just completed the rush of morning orders and was standing behind the counter with her head down, thinking of her next task, when a noise caused her to look up from her ledgers as she was reorganizing her mind for the morning.

The boys worked it perfectly. The entire platoon entered the bakery by the front customer entrance, filling the small sit down area where croissants, bread and pastries were sold to walk-in customers each morning. There was a huge hubbub of noise and confusion as they all piled in, much to Mrs. Eisenrick's amusement and consternation. She knew a troop ship had landed the previous evening, in fact it was a regular occurrence.

She put her index fingers to the sides of her mouth and whistled loudly, instantly quieting the hubbub. "What can I get you boys this morning?"

Clancy chimed up, speaking his lines, "We're looking for Frankie. He promised us a bun, like he used to make us in France."

"Oh, you know him? I'm afraid my Frankie hasn't arrived home yet," she said with a sad shake of her head.

Then the door to the ovens behind the counter burst open.

"Momma, momma, I see you've met my friends," said Frankie, who had quickly snuck in the back way through the delivery doors and donned an apron. "I promised them an Eisenrick apple pastry for bringing me home safely." He smiled a huge smile.

His mother began to shake. Her eyes welled up with tears which rolled down her face as her feet were rooted to the floor. The room was silent. Her legs felt like over cooked spaghetti.

"Oh Frankie, you're home, you're safe and you're whole. And you promised pastries to these boys for brining you home. That's all?" She threw her arms around him and hugged him tight, but only for a moment to make sure he was real. She caught herself, wiped the tears from her eyes and cheeks and mastered herself to take a stern look at her son.

"That's all? She grabbed trays of pastries and put them up on the counter. Please, eat. Everyone of you, eat with my thanks for bringing my boy home safely."

A huge cheer went up and Mrs. Eisenrick hugged Frankie again, all the harder.

"Fire up the ovens we are going to need another round of morning pastries," she yelled into the back part of the shop, always the pragmatist. The pastries disappeared in moments so more croissants found their way from the ovens and were offered and then bread was cut, slathered thick with butter. The late morning orders would be a bit behind that day.

"What's all the commotion?" asked a greying man, coming through the oven entrance to the sales area. He was wearing a heavy coat, fresh back from deliveries.

He spied Frankie still being clung to by his mother.

"Father, I am home."

The elder Eisenrick took a step back, blinked a few times and then flung his arms around his son's head. "Safe, as I always knew you would be." He recovered himself quickly. "When can you start delivering for me?"

Everyone laughed.

The Eisenrick's afternoon customers received their orders a bit late that day, but not one was upset once they were informed of Frankie's return. He was well known to their customers.

The next day as they left the ship, the Eisenrick's had made sure that every member of Frankie's platoon took with them a fresh loaf of bread and a bag of pastries for their journey.

One by one the platoon members took their leave, most bidding farewell and reminding each other of their promise to their Captain to meet again in 10 years.

Jocko was one of the last to go. It had fallen to Eisenrick and Martin Wilson to lead the goodbyes as they were New York City boys and would remain.

"Frankie, where do you think we'll meet? Where's the Cap going to get us together?"

"Don't know his plans Jocko, but knowing the Cap he has something in mind already. Could be Philly as that's pretty central. I think that's near to where his family lives. Could be California if a bunch of us end up out there. Take care of yourself Jocko. Stay in touch. Look me up if you're back in the City."

The men shook hands and Jocko turned for the platform.

As he walked away slowly Wilson turned to Eisenrick, "You know, I think it really is over now Frankie."

"Yeah Marty, I know what you mean. Everyone has gone except you and me and we're supposed to be here. Our platoon didn't really see a lot of action, more inaction from the hurry up and wait army command. Except for those offensive pushes near Arras we didn't we much action. I guess that's good. We almost all came through without a scratch."

"Oh, there were scratches, though not much that remains for most of us, except Jimmy and Larry. And don't forget that shelling we took in the village just after the battles. I think that was the last time I was actually shot at."

"Stay in touch Marty. Get back to your property deals. I've got a bakery to run. My dad said he wants to expand our operation and open a second retail location near the Battery. His brother wants to run it and his sister is talking about a third bakery in Brooklyn if the second one is a success. Hopefully the start of good times."

Frankie Eisenrick fell back into the bakery business. His uncle took a stab at running the downtown location but it was quickly apparent that he couldn't handle the early morning hours the bakery business required. The store was thriving but the logistics of running two locations was threatening to kill the second outlet.

Frankie began to run the second shop. He spent his mornings baking and supervising new employees and his afternoons drumming up business alongside his uncle in the hotels and restaurants in the twenty blocks at the tip of Manhattan.

"Yeah, I've heard of Eisenrick's. It's in the theatre district up around 50th Street, right?"

"Yes, that's our original location. We now have an operation down here on the corner of Fulton and William Streets, retail on the bottom, our commercial bakery in the back and a whole lot of customers living all around us. Fresh, is our trademark. It's fresher baked here than baked uptown and delivered downtown."

"You are right. And it's good to know your take your product seriously and are now down here. Eisenrick's has a good reputation," he thought a minute. "Look, we are doing a special New Year's Eve dinner at three locations within two miles of your bakery. If you can supply us with our needs for the night, and the product is good, we can talk about our future needs."

Frankie took the order and details. He knew from experience that getting in the door of these hotels and restaurants was all he needed. Product quality was necessary but Eisenrick's had that in spades. It was punctuality and customer service that was perhaps more important. Pastries with minor imperfections were much less of an issue than no pastries. As long as they were fresh. And Frankie paid close attention to both.

Getting the restaurants was even more important than the hotels as most catered to the evening crowd which allowed his ovens to be busy most of the day, rather than having a huge rush in the morning, and nothing later. Business was good, so good in fact that he was settling into a pattern, baking for the morning rush at hotels and a few morning breakfast places, getting those deliveries to the customers by 7 am and then doing a lunch and dinner run to ensure the freshest product possible. He had several customers who paid extra if they got the first delivery when the bread and pastries were still warm from the oven.

Frankie enjoyed the business and the constant changing of orders, delivery times and needs of his customers. He worked seven days a week, with reduced hours on Saturdays and only a half day in the morning on Sundays. People in hotels still ate their breakfast, no matter what day of the week it was.

He took great pleasure in hearing some of his customers tell him that there was another Eisenrick's bakery up on 50th street, but it wasn't as good as his. He didn't have the heart to mention the left handed compliments to his parents, but he did keep them apprised of his delivery arrangements which helped the quality of his product.

After a year, and a third Eisenrick's opening in Brooklyn, Frankie had a long talk with his father.

"Dad, I'm getting more and more orders from big retailers and these new grocery stores. They want to stock bread as their customers want to buy it there for convenience. Problem is I cannot guarantee quality and that's the backbone of our business."

The two jawed about their problem for some time. Then Frank hit upon a solution. They decided to bake bread and rolls in their stores at the end of each day and deliver them to the grocery stores in the evening, so they would be available for sale. This bread would have a bit more salt as a preservative to keep the bread fresher and edible for longer. The most important point was to call it something else because it really was a different product from the very fresh bread they had built their reputation on.

"What should we call it? How about Frankenrich Bread? It sounds German, it has 'rich' in the name to sound expensive and the whole thing is your idea," said the elder Eisenrick who was still not sold on the plan.

Within five years the demand for bread in grocery stores was 50 times that of the local bakeries which still thrived on the hotel and restaurant business.

Frank had opened a commercial bakery with no retail component and made sure the bread was delivered late in the evening or early in the morning. Frankenrich Bread was on practically every table in New York. Eisenrick Bakery still held an envied spot on the tables of hotels and restaurants in lower Manhattan and in Brooklyn.

"Casting Giant Shadows" is the story of a fictional unit in the American Expeditionary Force (AEF) in France in World War One—and the lives of the men after the war.

F. Bradley Reaume

Brad has written his entire career, first as a newspaper reporter and columnist, and then in the political and government realm before pursuing fiction.

"Past Immortal As We" is his fourth novel.

Brad lives with his wife and children in Ontario, Canada.

Also by F. Bradley Reaume

Novels

A Picture of Distance (2014)
All Fall Down (2016)
Casting Giant Shadows (2017)

Other Books

The Wonderful World of Wogs (2014) - for pre-schoolers
        As Brad Reaume / Illustrated by Nicole Flax
Other Skylines (2015) - short stories
The Rhyme of History (2014) - current affairs

97583671R00189

Made in the USA
Columbia, SC
16 June 2018